JUST ONE MORE CHANCE

BAYTOWN BOYS

MARYANN JORDAN

Just One More Chance (Baytown Boys)

Cover Design by: Graphics by Stacy

Background/Model photography: Eric McKinney

ISBN ebook: 978-0-9984832-4-5

IBSN print: 978-0-9984832-5-2

I was so glad my parents were able to make the trip to the Eastern Shore of Virginia before my mother passed away last summer. They were travelers who managed to fall in love with most places they visited, their quest for new adventures taking them far from their humble beginnings. So, to Charles and Camilla, I dedicate this book to two people who so loved the beach.

American Legion Auxiliary Information

Mission Statement

In the spirit of Service, Not Self, the mission of the American Legion Auxiliary is to support The American Legion and to honor the sacrifice of those who serve by enhancing the lives of our veterans, military, and their families, both at home and abroad. For God and Country, we advocate for veterans, educate our citizens, mentor youth, and promote patriotism, good citizenship, peace and security.

Vision Statement

The vision of the American Legion Auxiliary is to support The American Legion while becoming the premier service organization and foundation of every community providing support for our veterans, our military, and their families by shaping a positive future in an atmosphere of fellowship, patriotism, peace and security.

.

AUTHOR INFORMATION

I am an avid reader of romance novels, often joking that I cut my teeth on the historical romances. I have been reading and reviewing for years. In 2013, I finally gave into the characters in my head, screaming for their story to be told. From these musings, my first novel, Emma's Home, The Fairfield Series was born.

I was a high school counselor having worked in education for thirty years. I live in Virginia, having also lived in four states and two foreign countries. I have been married to a wonderfully patient man for over forty years. When writing, my dog or one of my two cats can generally be found in the same room if not on my lap.

Please take the time to leave a review of this book. Feel free to contact me, especially if you enjoyed my book. I love to hear from readers!

Facebook

Email

Website

Author's Note

Please remember that this is a work of fiction. I have lived in numerous states as well as overseas, but for the last thirty years have called Virginia my home. I often choose to use fictional city names with some geographical accuracies.

These fictionally named cities allow me to use my creativity and not feel constricted by attempting to accurately portray the areas.

It is my hope that my readers will allow me this creative license and understand my fictional world.

I also do quite a bit of research on my books and try to write on subjects with accuracy. There will always be points where creative license will be used in order to create scenes or plots.

All books have errors, no matter how many author, editors, proofers, and readers have looked at the manuscript. If the errors are minor and do not affect the story, please forgive and ignore. But, if you find errors that you deem necessary to report, please send me an email with your notations and do not try to report to Amazon.

Be kind to authors... we are human!

authormaryannjordan@gmail.com

1

Headache? Hell, more like hangover.

Blinking rapidly, Grant Wilder was grateful for the lack of early morning stirrings in the sleepy town. With one hand on the steering wheel of the police department SUV, he rubbed his forehead, trying to still the pain stabbing behind his eyes.

He drove slowly down the beach road, his gaze focused straight ahead. The town's public beach on the Chesapeake Bay, just over the slight dunes, was ready for a day of tourists. On the other side, stately homes stood as sentinels guarding the bay. Turning onto one of the side roads, he proceeded with caution along the tree-lined residential homes. Some in a state of repair, some used as beach rentals, and many with the loving upkeep of residents who knew they were lucky to own a tiny piece of heaven, known as the Eastern Shore.

Wincing, he hated to admit he drank too much the previous evening, but the engagement celebration of his best friend, Mitch Evans, the town's police chief, to the woman he had cared for since they were children was cause for Grant to forget his early morning patrol.

Movement on one of the side streets had him jerking his head to the left, only to groan at both the shooting pain in his head and the realization it was only the garbage truck stopping in front of a house, the banging of trash cans interrupting the peaceful morning. Thankfully, the old town's streets had been laid out in a square grid making it easy for him to view the area at each intersection.

The men dragging the garbage cans over to the truck threw their hands up in a wave and Grant returned the greeting, grimacing slightly at the movement. Continuing down the road, he forced his eyes to focus, while making sure not to jerk his head around, in an attempt to quell the dull ache.

Straining to see along the street as he heard a small motor humming, his gaze landed on the hot pink scooter puttering by, a long, blonde braid flying behind the shapely figure of the woman driving. The wild-patterned, tie-dyed shirt in brilliant colors paired with purple capris was familiar to him, and the desire to honk and wave warred with the desire to slump down in the seat and hide. *God, I was an ass last night.*

The sounds of dogs barking interrupted his self-loathing, and he looked up just in time to see an elderly woman straining against the leash of her dog while another man held on to his. *Oh, great...just great.* Pulling to a stop, he radioed his location to the station and alighted from the vehicle.

"Officer Wilder!" they both exclaimed at the same time before glaring at each other.

"Mrs. Malton...Mr. Royer...can you not control the dogs this morning?"

"That dog of his keeps wanting to...to...you know... with my dog and he isn't doing anything to stop it!" the elderly woman said, her arms stretched outwards as her dachshund strained at her leash toward the large basset hound. "Petunia is terrified!" Mrs. Malton's jowls waggled as her bosom heaved in outrage.

"My dog?" Mr. Royer huffed. "My Harold just wants to get past you and your little hussy won't leave him alone." Turning toward Grant, he narrowed his eyes as he ordered, "Do something!"

Grant watched as the two elderly residents continued their narrow-eyed glaring. Dropping his gaze to the two dogs, their noses eagerly straining forward, it seemed obvious they just wanted to greet each other. *Why can't the owners get along the way the dogs want to?*

"From what I can see, the dogs just want to sniff around a bit and then they'll be happy to move on—"

"Sniff? Sniff?" Mrs. Malton chirped, narrowing her eyes toward him. "I know what that dog of his wants and it's not just a sniff."

The two dogs, now kept apart while still straining at their leashes began baying and barking, adding to Grant's pounding head. Mr. Royer's thin arms were never going to be strong enough to control his pet, so Grant stepped over to take the leash from him. "Let's rein him in and then we can let the ladies pass."

"Us? Why us?" Mr. Royer spouted. "I live on this side of the street. She's the one who comes over here."

Grant quickly reeled in the basset and nodded toward Mrs. Malton. "Move on by now, and may I suggest in the future that if you have to walk your dogs at the same time, you stay on opposite sides of the street."

Moving to scoop her smaller dog into her arms, Mrs. Malton glared at the two men as she walked past them. "I would think that a true gentleman would allow a lady to walk where she pleased." Before either of the men could respond, she cast a disparaging glance down to Harold, his tongue lolling to the side as he panted. His soulful eyes followed Petunia as she was carried off.

As Mrs. Malton waddled down the sidewalk, Grant turned his gaze back to the small man standing next to him. Relaxing his hold on the hound, he asked, "You got it now?"

Lowering his bushy eyebrows as his lips turned down in a frown, Mr. Royer pouted. "Don't know what her problem is. She thinks the sidewalks are her personal property, and her dog is the queen!"

Stifling a tired grin, Grant nodded his agreement as he walked back toward the SUV. "Next time, just walk in a different direction before Harold gets a sniff of her."

"Who? Petunia or Mrs. Busybody?"

"Either one, Mr. Royer. Either one," he chuckled.

Climbing back into the vehicle, he once more called in his location and began to drive slowly down the street. Head still pounding, he hoped he encountered nothing more than the dog walkers before he had a chance to make it into the station.

The oldest part of Baytown was surrounded with Main Street on one side, closer to the small harbor, the Chesapeake Bay on another, where the public beach enticed townspeople and visitors, and a park situated in the middle of town. About fifteen years prior, a developer built a golf course community on a large farm, and it was annexed into the city as well. On the other side, another developer built large vacation rental homes as well as a marina and a seafood restaurant.

Turning the corner, he noted a group of children riding their bikes toward the beach. Waving at the youngsters, he grinned—both at their early morning enthusiasm and the memories it brought back. Growing up in Baytown on the Chesapeake Bay, he had spent many hours running the streets, riding his bike, and hanging out with his friends. The group of boys had been given the nickname Baytown Boys because where you saw one...you saw them all. Even their high school team's adopted the name. The group had dispersed after high school, most joining the military, before eventually coming back to Baytown to live.

He and Mitch joined the Army, while the two MacFarlane brothers, Aiden and Brogan, served in the Marines before coming back to take over the family pub. Zac Hamilton had joined the Navy before becoming the fire chief, and their friend, Callan Ward, was still with the Coast Guard, now stationed locally at Baytown.

Driving past the building housing the newly established American Legion, he remembered they had a meeting this evening. *I hope we get started on the youth teams. I need to talk to Mitch about helping when I get to the station.*

Grant rubbed his chin, realizing his morning shave had missed a few spots. His hand moved up to his forehead in an attempt to once more still the headache threatening. *Drinking too much last night was a stupid thing to do!*

The engagement party for Mitch and Tori Bradford had started at The Dunes Restaurant's but ended up at Finn's Pub. The dinner included family, friends, and some of the town's important residents. The mayor and his wife made their appearance, and of course gave a lengthy toast, which was more of a political speech than an engagement toast. By the time the dinner was over, the group of friends migrated into town to the pub owned by Aiden and Brogan.

I need to finish this pass by Main Street and head into the station. I hope Mildred has some aspirin...and coffee. The thought of freshly-ground coffee enticed him as he passed Jillian's Coffee Shop and Galleria, but he knew he could not go in and risk the ire...or the condemnation of the beautiful shop owner. *Not after last night's performance.* Fighting the urge to drop his chin to his chest, he heaved a sigh. *Yeah, I deserve this headache,* he thought, his mind drifting to the previous evening.

·   ·   ·

Even when I kept my distance from her, I always noticed when Jillian walked into a room...and I noticed her last night. Lime green dress, tight in the right places, showing her tanned legs, nipped in at the waist— but wait! Who the hell had their hand on her waist?

Moving through the room quickly, I made a bee-line to the other side to gain a better view. Hmph! Some young, hot-shot asshole was standing next to her like he owned her. Fucking hell!

Turning on my heel, I saw one of the local waitresses standing alone near the bar, eying me. Stalking over, I was determined to hit the bar and if I managed to snag the waitress at the same time? All the better.

Yeah...that plan blew up because I kept my eye on Jillian and finally found a time to approach her. And berate her for her date. Not my best plan. I should have stayed away from her.

Sighing once again, Grant parked the SUV in the police station lot before climbing from the vehicle and making his way through the front door. The sight of Mildred Score, the indomitable receptionist and operator, greeted him. The fact that she was holding a cup of coffee and two aspirins in her outstretched hand only made him grin wider despite the glare of the fluorescent lights overhead.

"Oh, my God, Mildred, you're a lifesaver!"

With narrowed eyes, she shook her blue-grey curls at him and said, "I had a feeling you were tying one on last night. What on earth were you thinking, Grant

Wilder? Drinking last night when you had patrol this morning!"

"He wasn't thinking with his head, that's for sure," Ginny Spencer quipped. The town's only female officer dropped her usually serious demeanor to taunt Grant. Her dark-brown hair was pulled back in a sleek, tight bun, her sharp, hazel eyes rarely missing a thing.

Shooting her a painful glare, he took the proffered drink and pills, downing them both quickly. Just then, the two other officers walked in. Looking over at Grant they both grinned. Sam Stubbis, the oldest member of the police force, moved past Mildred to the coffee maker while Burt Tobber clapped Grant on the shoulder as he passed him.

"You hanging in there this morning?" Burt asked. "You were still going strong when I left last night."

"Yeah, well, you and your wife had to get back to relieve your babysitter, so you hardly stayed very long," Grant grumbled. "It's not like I was that much later than you."

"I remember the days of closing down a bar," Sam reminisced, patting his slightly protruding stomach as he helped himself to a pastry brought in by Mildred. "But those days are over for me." Lifting his gaze to Grant, he added, "And never before patrol."

Grant slumped into a chair at the table in the work-room, hoping Mitch would make his appearance soon so they could get to business.

On cue, Mitch walked in. The tall, handsome Police Chief was still wearing the same smile that had graced his face last night every time he had caught a glimpse of his fiancé, Tori. "Morning, everyone," he greeted.

"God, you are entirely too happy, Mitch," Grant grumbled, hanging his head.

Mitch's steely gaze dropped to his officer and friend, and his smile widened. "Looks like you drowned your sorrows a little too much last night."

At that, Grant's head jerked up, his frown meeting Mitch's grin. "Drowned my sorrows? Hell, I was celebrating my freedom!"

"Whatever," Ginny said, rolling her eyes.

Grumbling under his breath, Grant sipped his coffee, grateful when Mitch took pity on him and began the meeting.

The first items on the morning's agenda dealt with town business and Grant struggled to focus on the notes. Suddenly Mitch's tone changed, and Grant sat up, watching his Chief's jaw tighten with anger.

"Heard from the State Police that drug runners are beginning to use the Eastern Shore instead of Highway 95 that runs from Florida to Maine. It takes longer to move drugs through here, but they think they have less of a chance of getting caught." Mitch pinned his group with a hard stare before adding, "I don't want anything passing through our town."

"Are they just running?" Ginny asked.

"Not sure right now. The State Police are stepping up their patrols out on the main road going through. They just want us to be vigilant, especially when pulling over speeders with out-of-state tags."

"If they stop here, there's enough of a youth population to be of interest to drug runners," Burt said. "So far, we've done a fair job keeping it out."

"Speaking of youth," Grant looked up, "will the next American Legion meeting get the youth baseball league going?"

This subject captured the attention of the entire squad since they were all members of the new American Legion. Mitch, as the newly elected President, nodded. "Yes, make sure you're at the meeting tonight. We'll get the youth league started."

"Been wanting to work with the boys that had their basketball hoops taken down. They might like playing baseball," Sam commented. "It's a way to keep the town manager and mayor off our backs." Earlier in the summer, Sam had come under pressure to keep the teens from hanging around an old school. They had not been a problem, but according to the manager, Silas Mills, they presented a "blight on the town".

"Just boys?" Ginny asked, her eyebrow rising in question.

"No, no, not just boys," Mitch assured. "The leagues have girls in them as well."

The squad continued to discuss the ongoing cases and work schedule for another half hour. Once dismissed, Sam and Burt pushed their chairs back, nodding at the others as they headed out to begin their patrols. Ginny moved into the other room to sit at her desk as she worked on a few open cases.

Grant, grateful to be able to go home since he only had to pull early morning patrol, was about to leave, when Mitch called him back.

"Let's talk in my office, shall we?" Mitch asked.

Grant knew that even though he and Mitch were friends from childhood, at work, Mitch was the boss. And he could tell that Mitch's professional invitation brooked no refusal. Following him down the short hall and into the office, he plopped down heavily in the utilitarian, metal chair across from Mitch, who settled in the creaky wooden chair behind his desk.

Glancing at the files scattered on the desk, Grant did not envy his friend's responsibility. Even though the small force pulled their weight, it fell on Mitch's shoulders to make sure the department was well-run. Gazing into Mitch's face, he knew that meant not showing up for patrol with a hangover, no matter how mild.

"I know, I know," Grant said, his chest tight. Seeing Mitch's raised eyebrow, Grant continued, "I drank too much last night, even though I knew I had early morning patrol. I swear Mitch, it wasn't that bad. I've got a headache and confess to not feeling my best, but I'd never show up for patrol unable to perform my duties."

He eyed Mitch while rubbing his slight scruff, wishing once more he had done a better job shaving. Seeing Mitch's mouth curve into a slight smile jolted him back in his seat. "What? What are you grinnin' about?"

Mitch laughed out loud and said, "Jesus, Grant, you're acting so guilty, if I let you keep talking, you'd confess to God knows what!" Mitch sobered as he shook his head. "I know you're sporting a slight hangover, but I also know you'd never put yourself or this town at risk by going out on patrol if you couldn't do the job."

Slumping down further, Grant scowled at his friend. "Then what the hell did you want to talk about?"

"How about the reason you left the engagement party early and headed to the pub in the first place?"

Grant's scowl deepened and he considered denying there had been a reason. One look at Mitch and he knew he could not get away with that. Sighing, he said, "It was just weird seeing her there with a date." *Jillian. Shit, why is it even hard to say her name?*

"Look, you and my cousin have danced around each other since you were kids...kind of like me and Tori."

Grant pinned Mitch with a stare. "I beg to differ. You fell for Tori when you were eight years old. I, on the other hand, was not in love with Jillian back then."

"Oh, no? You didn't tie her shoelaces together when she took a nap on the floor of the playhouse? You didn't chase her with bugs and frogs in elementary school? You didn't beat up Roger in middle school because he was picking on her? You didn't—"

Throwing his hands up in defense, Grant groaned, "Okay, okay. Jesus, I had no idea you were keeping fuckin' score!"

"You're one of my best friends, and she's my cousin. Of course I was keeping an eye on you two."

The silence in the room settled over the pair, each lost to their own thoughts for a few minutes. Finally, Mitch said, "I know you care for her. What I don't know is why you keep her at arm's length? When I moved back to town and discovered Tori had moved here also, I couldn't wait to make her mine."

Grant struggled for a moment, trying to find a voice to his thoughts. "Jillian and I aren't like you and Tori." Heaving another sigh, he confessed, "I don't know, Mitch. I...I'm just not the right man for her."

"Okay," Mitch acknowledged, gaining a quick, wide-eyed look from Grant. "Hey," he shrugged, "I didn't say I agreed with your assessment, but if that's how you really feel, then why the drunk-fest when she showed up to a party with someone else?" Leaning forward, his elbows resting on the desk, Mitch continued. "You need to either let her go completely or decide you want to go for her. Either way, sitting on the fence is only hurting both of you."

Grant's gaze jumped to Mitch's pensive face. "She's hurting?"

Shaking his head, Mitch said, "That's for you two to figure out. But for now, go home. Sleep and go for a run. Get the rest of the alcohol out of your system and be back here, clear eyed and ready to go tomorrow. And I'll see you tonight at the meeting."

Standing, Grant knew Mitch had gone easier on him than he deserved. Walking to the door, he looked over his shoulder and nodded. "Thanks, Chief," he called out with a wave before heading out to his jeep, the idea of a hot shower and a nap calling to him. Passing by the coffee shop once more he tried to put thoughts of the beautiful Jillian out of his mind.

2

Her dark mood in contrast with her bright, tie-dyed shirt, Jillian slammed the coffee pot down harder than she meant to, causing a few patrons in her shop to look up in surprise. Forcing a smile onto her face, she called out, "Sorry, folks! Don't know my own strength!" Hoping they bought her excuse, she inwardly cursed.

"Do we dare ask what has you in such a snit?"

Jillian tossed her long, blonde braid over her shoulder, recognizing the voice before turning around. Cutting her eyes to the side, she watched as her two best friends walked over to the counter.

Katelyn MacFarlane, with her long, black hair, stood in contrast next to Tori Bradford whose reddish-blonde tresses hung down her back. For a second, Jillian was reminded of the Barbie dolls that the three used to play with when they were children. Each had one that looked like them and their dolls would mimic their friendship and adventures.

. . .

The Baytown Boys found us playing one day and made fun of our lookalike dolls. I tossed my Barbie down onto the sand near the beach and ran off, not wanting to cry in front of the boys. Later, Grant Wilder came to my house, the discarded Barbie in his hand. As he held it out to me, he said, "I like it... it looks like you." He scuffled his feet on my porch as I took the doll from his hand.

"Why did you bring it back?" I asked, staring at him. Of all the Baytown Boys, he was the one with the cutest smile.

"Like I said, it looks like you. And something that pretty shouldn't be thrown away."

With that, he turned and leaped off my front porch, running down the street, leaving me standing alone with the Barbie in my hand. As I looked down at it, I wondered, "Did he just call me pretty?"

"Earth to Jillian," Katelyn called out, waving her hand in front of Jillian's face. With a concerned look, she continued, "Are you all right?"

Blinking rapidly, Jillian shook her head to clear the cobwebs. Thoughts of the little boy mixed with the man who held her heart and managed to crush it over and over again. "Yeah, just walking down memory lane, that's all." She re-plastered the smile on her face and said, "Y'all want something?"

"Coffee, please," Tori replied, eying the pastries in the showcase. "And how about a blueberry muffin." Grinning, she added, "If you're not still too angry at the coffee pot!"

Katelyn laughed as Jillian rolled her eyes. Jillian's Coffee Shop and Galleria was bustling with the early morning crowd as the scents of freshly-ground coffee beans tantalized the patrons. The murmur of conversations was muffled with coffee orders called out, the hiss from the expresso machine, and soft jazz music playing in the background.

Within a minute, the three women headed up the polished, wooden stairs to the gallery on the second floor. Settling into chairs at a small table overlooking Main Street, they dove into the goodies and sipped the steaming coffee. The morning sun streamed through the tall windows, illuminating the pieces of artwork on the walls.

Tori leaned back in her chair, her muffin decimated, and said, "No matter how many times I'm here, I still can't believe how you turned this unused upstairs into such a unique space."

The three women cast appreciative gazes around. The old building had originally been a store in the late 1800's and fell into disrepair over the years. The store passed through multiple owners and eventually ended up bought by Jillian's parents. Determined to return the store to its former glory, they kept the solid wood paneling, carved wooden support poles, and the glass display cases on the sides of the long room downstairs. They turned the rest into a coffee shop and Jillian's mother began baking pastries to sell along with the coffee.

Antique tables and amber sconces on the walls softened the sunlight that came through the front and gave the quaint shop its ambience. Jillian had worked in the shop as a teenager and when she came back after college her parents turned most of the business over to her. She loved running the little coffee shop and during the tourist season she was busy since they added a light lunch to the menu.

But it was the unused upstairs that had become her joy. She restored the second floor to the same glory as the coffee shop downstairs and showcased local artists' paintings on the dark-paneled walls. She moved a few of the glass cases up as well, to exhibit pottery and other artists' work. Coffee shop patrons could take their food upstairs and sit at the tables surrounding the area to enjoy the arts while enjoying the treats.

At this time of day, the area was empty except for the trio of friends, leaning back in their chairs sipping their morning brew. Katelyn eyed Jillian speculatively before asking, "So, are you going to talk about last night?"

Jillian shot Katelyn a glare before turning an apologetic gaze toward Tori. "I'm sorry. Last night was your engagement party and we should be celebrating, not talking about my pissy mood."

Tori leaned forward, placing her hand on Jillian's arm. "Oh, sweetie, don't apologize. We've celebrated my engagement enough and, goodness knows, we'll all be wedding planning soon anyway. But Katelyn and I are worried about you."

Appreciating their concern, Jillian gifted them with

a small smile. "Guys, there's nothing new to tell. Same old, same old."

"Well, if it makes you feel any better, Brogan wanted to kick Grant's ass last night!" Katelyn said. Her brothers, Aiden and Brogan, were best friends with the other Baytown Boys, but were also protective of the girls they grew up with.

The three women sat in silence for a few minutes, each lost in thoughts of the past.

"I wish I could let him go completely," Jillian finally said. "It would be so much easier. But no matter how I try, something always happens."

"What happened last night?" Tori asked. "I know you came with one of the new teachers from the high school as your date...who, by the way, was a real cutie!" The trio laughed before Tori continued, "But the next thing I knew, Grant had you over in a corner and then stormed out with some...uh..."

Spearing her friend with a pointed look, Jillian finished Tori's sentence. "He stormed out with some bleached-blonde hookup. That was what you were going to say, right?"

Both Katelyn and Tori grimaced at the same time, their expressions noticed by Jillian, who let out a huff of breath loudly before staring out the window for a long minute. Finally, she said, "Girls, you know the story. I've been in love with Grant for as long as I can remember. We were practically raised together...well, us and the other Baytown babies."

Tori said, "I remember when I was six years old and

first came to visit my grandmother here and you all adopted me right away. Of course, we thought the boys had serious cooties back then!"

"Yeah, well, not much has changed," Jillian quipped, rolling her eyes before settling them back on Tori. "And you got your handsome prince."

Nodding, Tori agreed. "It took a long time, from falling for Mitch when I was six years old to over twenty years later when we finally ended up back in Baytown. But you're right...I did get very lucky."

Jillian smiled at her friend, glad for her happiness. Tori had not grown up in Baytown like the others but came every vacation and summer to spend with her grandmother who owned the Sea Glass Inn. After high school, Tori and Mitch did not see each other for almost ten years but both moved to Baytown as adults —Tori, when her grandmother passed away and left the Inn to her, and Mitch, after returning from military service and a career with the FBI to become the town's Police Chief. They had recently gotten together, and last night's engagement party had been a chance for the friends to celebrate their happiness. Many of the other Baytown Boys who left high school to join the military had also moved back to town, discovering the small hometown they longed to escape from was now calling them home. Grant was one of them.

"So," Katelyn broke into Jillian's thoughts, her fingers drumming on the table. "What happened last night?"

Jillian, gaze focused on the patterns her fingers were

tracing on the tablecloth, gave a small shrug, attempting nonchalance, but knew in her heart she felt anything but indifference, as a long sigh escaped. "When Grant came back to Baytown last year after ten years of being gone, I thought we might have our chance, but as you know, he has firmly placed me in the friend-zone. The cold, frigid friend zone. And my attempts to move back into a warmer place near his heart have been met with nothing but rebuffs. Chance after chance I gave him, but he's pushed me away for the last time. I finally decided it was time to focus on me. My shop," she waved her arm around toward the art covered walls, "my galleria, and just me. So, instead of going alone to the party last night, I asked Ben, the new PE teacher at the high school."

Pinning her friends with a determined stare, she continued. "I knew I'd be staring at Grant flirting with others all night, so I figured it was time for me to show everyone that I had moved on. The few men I've gone out with in the past few years weren't real contenders for my heart. But now, I think it's time for me to actually go on a date with someone who might be interested in me. Hell, I'm not getting any younger, and it's time to face up to the fact that Grant will never be to me what Mitch is to you, Tori."

"I'm so sorry, sweetie—" Tori began, but was interrupted by Katelyn.

"That's such bullshit! I know Grant cares for you. He's just so stubborn and pigheaded and...and...augh! He's wasting his chance to be happy!" Slamming her coffee cup down on the table, some of the liquid splashed over the rim. "Sorry," Katelyn mumbled, grabbing a napkin to wipe the spill.

Jillian could not help but laugh at Katelyn's outburst. Her friend, normally practical to a fault, had hoped that Grant and Jillian would one day get together. She sobered as she thought of Katelyn's own broken heart. As kids, Katelyn had won the affections of one of the Baytown Boys—Philip Bayles. The two had been inseparable, even withstanding the teasing by the other boys. But Philip, like the others, had joined the military after high school, and was unable to keep his promise to come back to Katelyn to marry. Killed in action, he was now buried in the Baytown cemetery. It had been almost six years, but Katelyn had dated rarely since then, despite the insistence of her friends that Philip would not want her to be alone.

Shrugging once more, Jillian said, "It was time to move on, Katelyn. Maybe for both of us."

"I take it Grant wasn't happy to see you with someone else?" Tori prodded.

"Well, it's not like I haven't had to watch him with others ever since he came back! He's flirted with just about everyone, and while I have no idea how many he has actually slept with, he's certainly earned a reputation!" Jillian replied, her chin trembling before she shook her head slightly, steeling her resolve. "But I show up with someone else and proceed to watch Grant drink too much and get angrier as he does. Ben went to talk to some of his friends and Grant took the opportunity to get me alone. He ragged on me about going out with some young jock, which pissed me off. Then accused *me* of being a tease."

At that statement, both Katelyn and Tori's eyes bugged wide. "What the hell?" Katelyn sputtered.

"Oh, he was letting the alcohol talk," Jillian said, her heart squeezing at the memory.

"Maybe the alcohol was letting him speak the truth, in a way," Tori surmised. "Maybe it was his convoluted way of letting you know he's still interested in you and not as just a friend."

"Well, it was a dumbass way to do it," Katelyn huffed.

Nodding, Jillian agreed, "Yep, that's what I thought. Anyway, Ben came back over, Grant shoved into his shoulder on his way past us, and then grabbed one of the young, new teachers that came to the party. Jesus, she must have only been about twenty-one years old and had a god-awful giggle that set my teeth on edge. I think she works at the high school with Ben. He seemed to know her."

Katelyn raised her eyebrow in surprise. "With that high-pitched giggle and that rack, she'll have the teenage boys' attention!"

"Yeah, well, she had Grant's attention last night," Jillian admitted, her voice now low as her shoulders drooped with the familiar ache in her heart.

Katelyn and Tori shared a glance over Jillian's bowed head, both sighing in unison. "Maybe he didn't—"

"Doesn't really matter if he took her home and banged her silly or not, does it?" Jillian interrupted, eyes glaring out the window, staring at nothing. "The fact is, he could have either told me that he liked me and wanted to be with me, or he could have left me alone to be with my date. But instead, he confused me, then stalked out with a pickup right in front of me. If that's not a royal kiss-off, I don't know what is!" Her voice took on the sadness in her heart as she added, "I just don't think I have any more chances left in me to give." Sitting up straighter, her face pinched for a few seconds, she blew out a breath, puffing her wispy bangs upward. "But, ladies, I'll tell you what I've decided."

Capturing the attention of the other two, she said with conviction, "I'm done. Done with holding out hope that one day Grant will suddenly decide he does want me. Done with sitting around waiting for him. Done with allowing him to ruin my fun. And done with us talking about him!" Her voice now steady, she hoped she would be able to follow through with her declaration. "Instead, I want to tell you what I've got going on up here!"

Katelyn and Tori's gazes jumped to the direction Jillian was pointing. Before they could ask, Jillian jumped up from her chair and moved to a small desk in the corner. Grabbing a file from the top, she brought it back to the table and opened it up for the others to see.

"I love the coffee shop downstairs and since mom and dad travel more now, it really has become my own. But it's the galleria up here that I'd like to focus on next. I've been in contact with some more artists in the area and offered them a spot to showcase their works here. Since the coffee shop closes after lunch, I'd like to host some wine and cheese nights up here. I'm even hoping to bring in some art dealers from around the area, not just the tourists that wander up here to look."

"I love that idea!" Tori gushed, catching Jillian's excitement.

Katelyn's wide smile matched Tori's appreciation. "Girl, you just might have something here! I think it's wonderful!"

Jillian said, "Well, I don't want to dream too big. And I know it's crazy, because I'm not artistic myself. But I've always loved the painters who come here and capture the beauty of the Eastern Shore. I'd love to be able to be the middleman between their work and marketing it beyond this area."

"Do you have any other artists you're going to be talking to?" Tori inquired.

"Actually, I've lined up several. Mitch's friend from the Army who moved here is one of them."

"Lance?" Katelyn asked, her eyebrows raised in surprise.

"I know, right?" Jillian answered. "He's about as antisocial as they come, but he does beautiful work with the sea glass. I don't know if he'll be interested, but I've got an appointment to talk to him tomorrow. And then there are two painters that live in Accawmacke County, just north of here, that I'm in discussions with. And there's a potter who has a studio about fifteen miles north who has expressed an interest in my endeavor. He said he would come down later this week to meet with me."

"Wow, I'm so impressed," Katelyn admitted, a wide

smile on her face. As the three women stood to take their coffee cups back downstairs, they embraced. "And proud of you, girl."

Jillian fought back the bite of tears that stung her eyes as she felt her friends' arms around her. "Well, it's time. Time to take back my life and move forward." *Now, if only it didn't hurt so much giving up on Grant.*

3

A long nap, followed by a run on the beach worked wonders for Grant's disposition. The breeze coming off the bay as he ran had cooled the sweat running down his face as his feet pounded the sand. Now, back in his small rental house, standing in the shower, the water washed the sweat from his body, invigorating him. After pulling on a pair of boxers and well-worn jeans, he walked into his kitchen, grabbed a water bottle and chugged the cold liquid. Fixing a sandwich, he threw some chips on the plate before finally settling into one of his Adirondack chairs on his porch.

His house did not have a beach view, but it backed up to a wooded lot, and he could hear the surf a few blocks away. He kept the grass mowed, but old flower beds sat untended, weeds overtaking the few flowers that attempted to blossom. A vision of his parents' neatly tended backyard flashed through his mind as he closed his eyes at the high school memory of Jillian planting flowers with his mom while he mowed the yard. *Hell, will there ever be a time when she doesn't pop into my head?*

Sighing, he took the first huge bite of his sandwich as Brogan walked into his backyard and sat down in the other chair. His normally stoic friend was no different now, as he leaned back in the chair, closing his eyes appearing to simply enjoy the afternoon sun. His long, dark hair was pulled back in a low ponytail and his muscles stretched the black Finn's Pub T-shirt.

Grant cast a sideways glance at his friend while chewing the bite of ham and cheese. Swallowing, he asked, "You gonna talk or you just come over to hang out while I eat my lunch?"

The silence continued for a few minutes as Grant finished his sandwich, washing it down with chilled bottled water. Finally, without opening his eyes, Brogan asked, "You want to talk about last night?"

"Jesus, who talked to you? Mitch?"

"Nope."

"Well, I've already talked to Mitch this morning and there's nothing to tell. Hell, it's not like we're a bunch of women who need to sit around and analyze everything."

Brogan rolled his head sideways against the tall back of the chair, his eyes pinning Grant to his seat. "I know, Grant. I see it."

Furrowing his brow, Grant stared back, no words coming. He waited for Brogan to explain, wondering where his thoughts were heading.

"You came back, but not the same." A long minute

passed once more. "And don't think I don't recognize it," Brogan admitted.

Minutes passed where the far away sounds of children playing, birds chirping, and the occasional car driving down the road were the only interruptions in the silence. Grant knew Brogan came home from Afghanistan battling inner demons, as they all did, but had never heard him speak of them.

"I don't talk about that shit, so I don't expect you to," Brogan said. "But you had someone to come home to."

Grant sucked in an audible breath before letting it out slowly. *Jillian. So, we're back to Jillian.* "Nothing to talk about, man."

"Yeah, that's what I figured." Brogan slowly leaned forward, placing his hands on the wide, wooden chair arms before heaving himself up. "Don't forget, we've got a meeting tonight," he said, referring to the American Legion.

Glad for the change in subject, Grant nodded. "I'll be there. I think the new resident, that buddy of Mitch's, will be there. Lance...that was his name."

"Good, we need more new blood in this town." With that, Brogan headed back around the house, disappearing from Grant's sight.

Still sitting in the chair, the warm sun beating down on his face, he wondered about Brogan's unexpected visit. *I know the answer...after last night's stellar, drunken performance, they're all wondering what the hell is going on with me.* Closing his eyes as the sun streamed down, warming his face, he wondered the same thing, as a long-ago memory came back.

.   .   .

We boys sat in the rickety shed in the back of Callan's yard. Callan's dad had bought a new shed to keep his lawn and garden equipment, and we convinced him not to tear down the ancient one still leaning against the back fence. Dirt floor, wood slats for walls with spaces between the lumber, an old tin roof. We'd created the clubhouse as kids, and it served as a place to gather.

Callan stepped inside, a bag of frozen peas clutched in his hands. He held them out to me, and I took them, holding the icy bag on my knuckles, wincing at the sting. I kept my eyes on my hand, not wanting to see the expressions on my friends' faces...much less hear their taunts.

No one spoke and I was no longer able to stand the silence. Without looking up, I said, "What?"

"Nothin'," Brogan's reply came to me from the side, causing me to quickly glance at him. His face held no recrimination...just admiration.

I looked around the small, wooden room at the other Baytown Boys, seeing their smiles as well.

"You hit him good," Mitch claimed, ducking his head to hide his smile. "If that kid complains, I'll tell my dad it was in self-defense!" His dad was the police chief, and I was grateful for his support.

I was thirteen years old and had just gotten in my first real fight...and over a girl. Some teenage tourist was bothering Jillian, and while she was Mitch's cousin, before he could defend her, I jumped up and punched the guy in the face. As much as my hand hurt, I figured his nose felt worse.

"I wasn't gonna let him make fun of her!" I protested, knowing I had thrown the first punch.

Brogan nudged my shoulder from the side and with a nod of his head, gave his silent approval of my actions.

"The girls may be a pain in the butt sometimes, but no one mistreats them," Zac pronounced, stating what we all felt.

"Do you think I scared her?" I wondered aloud, remembering the horrified look on Jillian's face as the kid ran away holding his nose.

"Naw," Aiden said. "Girls like having their honor defended."

Brogan smacked the back of Aiden's head and asked, "Where the hell did you learn something like that?"

With a smirk, Aiden puffed out his chest. "I heard Rachel Myers say that in class the other day. She read it in some book and was going on and on about how she'd only fall for a man who defended her honor."

"So now you're getting your girl advice from Rachel Myers?" Brogan laughed.

"Hey, she's got boobs, so she ought to know something, right?"

Brogan popped Aiden in the back of the head again as he said, "Boobs aren't the same as brains!"

Just as his brother was slumping back, Mitch agreed. "I think that's right," he said. "I think girls know when someone's trying to stand up for them."

Mitch was the most upstanding kid I knew, so his words gave me hope. Taking the frozen peas off of my hand, I flexed my fingers, glad they all worked properly. Grinning at the *others, my heart lighter, I said, "Come on, let's get back to the beach."*

Within a few minutes, we were back on the town beach, and Jillian walked straight up to me and grabbed my sore hand. Her blue eyes, the color of the water on a summer day, sparkled as she lifted my slightly swollen fingers to her lips. Placing a kiss on them, she whispered, "Thank you," before running off with the other girls.

Standing on the white sand, I gave a loud "whoop" before running after the others.

And now I'm the one deserving the punch. Opening his eyes, Grant stood and took his empty plate to the kitchen, the warmth of the sun—and the memory—fresh on his mind.

———

Jillian looked up as she heard footsteps on the staircase leading to the galleria. Standing, she walked over to greet her visitor. Tall, incredibly handsome, intelligent eyes that quickly scanned over the open space. Sticking out her hand, she smiled up at him. "Mr. Greene?"

Her hand was engulfed in his much larger one as he replied, "Nice to meet you, Ms. Evans."

"Please, call me Jillian."

"Lance," he replied. "I understand you're Mitch's cousin."

"Yes, I am, but please don't hold that against me," she joked. He nodded curtly, but did not smile. *Hmm, okay, I guess we better get right down to business.* "If you'll join me, I'll explain what I have here and what I hope to accomplish."

She turned and walked over to one of the tables, coffee and pastries already in place. "I took the liberty of preparing a small snack , so please, help yourself."

He sat but made no attempt to either drink the coffee or avail himself of a muffin. Instead, he focused his gaze on the artwork around the walls. Jillian watched him, her nerves now in full force. Since Mitch, the Baytown Boys, and some of the older veterans in the town had re-established the American Legion, her cousin had been instrumental in inviting some of the other military veterans, who did not have a hometown, to consider moving to Baytown. Lance Greene was one of the early transplants...and one of the most enigmatic.

Sucking in a deep breath, she smiled once more as she began. "I have a few local artists that showcase their work here, and I'd like to expand. Mitch told me that you create art using the sea glass that you find in the area. I'd like to see some of your work and would love to have you display some of it here. My goal is to begin hosting evening events where buyers would come to see the art. Perhaps it would give you more marketability."

His gaze met hers as he said, "I'm not looking to expand further than I have. I create...just to create. I need to make a living like everyone else, but I don't want it to be more than that."

Thinking fast, she responded, "Then you would

have a place to share your creations. Even if you weren't interested in selling any of your pieces, you would be showcasing some of the talent...and raw materials from the Eastern Shore."

"If I don't sell, what do you get out of it?" he asked, his gaze dropping to his hands resting on the table.

"Mr. Gree—I mean, Lance. I'm not in this to make a lot of money." She noted his gaze jumped back to hers at that confession. Taking a fortifying breath, she explained. "I've lived in Baytown my whole life, except for college. I'm a small-town girl at heart." Giving a little shrug, she continued, "I love the people and the culture. I make a decent living with the coffee shop downstairs, so this is not a money-making venture for me. If something sells and I get a commission, great. But for me, I just want to show others what beauty can come from the Eastern Shore. As you can see, I have painters, wood-carvers, and someone that does metalwork. I even have someone who makes herons from PVC pipes! I'm going to be talking to someone later this week about his pottery. So, I'd love to have you exhibit your work here... whether for sale or just to share the beauty of your craft."

Her speech complete, she wiped her palms on her jeans, wondering what he was thinking. His unemotional face gave nothing away.

He shifted his eyes, contemplating the warm, paneled space, stopping to observe the natural light coming in from the tall front windows. Looking back at her, he nodded curtly as he stood. "If I had any doubts about your endeavors, Jillian...you've just put them to rest. I'll offer some pieces for you to display. And if you want to sell them, fine. But donate the money or something—I don't want it."

She tilted her head to the side, pondering aloud. "How about we consider the donations to go to the American Legion or some other veteran organization?" For a second, she thought she saw a flash of life in his eyes before the mask slid back down in place, and he simply nodded.

Beaming, she jumped up to shake his hand. "Thank you so much," she gushed, knowing she did not sound professional, but could not hold back her enthusiasm. Seeing the corners of his mouth curve up slightly, she smiled even broader. Following him as he descended the stairs, she wondered what was hidden behind his handsome, but steel, exterior. And noted that while she was excited to have his artwork with her, he held no romantic interest.

Following him outside, they stopped on the sidewalk, and he turned to face her. Shaking hands once more, he said, "I'll be in touch."

Grasping his hand with both of hers, she squeezed in excitement. "Thank you so much, Lance. I can't wait to hear from you. I think this will be wonderful for both of us."

With a curt nod, he walked to his vehicle. Her genuine smile still firmly in place, her gaze followed him until it landed on a man standing outside his SUV parked across the street. The man, leaning back with his muscular arms crossed over his chest and one thick leg crossed over the other, stared back. Glaring. *Grant? What the hell is he doing?*

She stared for a moment at his face, observing a mixture of surprise and what appeared to be anger directed at her. His gaze slid to the side where Lance was driving away, and for a second she entertained the notion that he was jealous. *Well, after last night, you don't get to go there, buddy!* She watched as he lifted his hand to wave, and she stood straighter. Spinning on her heel, her braid whipping around, she stomped back into the coffee shop, placing the CLOSED sign in the window before slamming and locking the door.

Dropping his chin to his chest, Grant placed his hands on his hips, standing at the edge of the street for a moment. Chest heaving with a huge sigh, he wondered what he was doing. *Hell, I was just driving down the street when I saw Lance come out of Jillian's shop with her. And then she grabbed his hands, smiled up at him like...like... fuck...like I want her to smile at me.*

Looking at his watch, he decided to make a stop before going to the American Legion meeting. Getting back into his vehicle, he drove a few miles out of town and parked outside a modest home whose backyard backed up to the dunes overlooking the bay. Walking to the front door, he knocked once but knew it would be unlocked. Opening, he shouted, "Mom? Dad? You around?"

"Grant?" he heard his mom call from the kitchen. Marcia Wilder walked out, wiping her hands on a dishtowel. Her dark brown hair was now streaked with a bit of grey she proudly proclaimed all the Baytown Boys gave her with their antics growing up. She barely came to his chin as she threw her arms around his waist. Giving her son a hug, she said, "Come on back. Your dad's parked in front of the ball game before going to the meeting, and I'm baking a few pies for the church sale."

Following her petite frame as they turned the corner, he saw his dad reclined back watching football. Grant inherited his athletic build from his father, who had played football for the local high school many years before Grant graced the same field.

"Don't get up, dad," Grant rushed to say, seeing his father reaching for the handle on the side of the old recliner. When his mom bought new furniture years ago, his dad insisted on keeping the worn, brown recliner, saying it was broken in to fit his body. His mom had argued and while his dad normally gave in to her, he stood, or rather sat, firm. And so, the ratty chair was now occupied and Grant had to admit that his dad appeared relaxed.

Sitting on the sofa facing the TV, Grant leaned back, the comfortable aura of the family room settling over him. A patterned rug was centered on the wooden floor underneath the maple coffee table. The sofa, a rocking chair, and recliner surrounded the flat-screen TV mounted on the wall over the fireplace, family pictures crowding the mantle. After a few minutes of his father's grunts at the late hits and a few curses at the official's calls, Toby Wilder turned the volume down and looked over.

"Got something on your mind, son?"

Grant, visibly startled before asking, "What makes you think that?"

"'Cause you haven't made one comment about this game in the past ten minutes. Our team's losing, and I'm not sure you've even noticed. That, my boy, tells me your mind is elsewhere." Pinning Grant with a steely look, he said, "Everything okay at work?"

"Yeah, yeah" Grant assured. "Job's good. No regrets there."

"Baytown's not as exciting as your job with the Virginia Beach Police force."

"No, thank God. Everyone thinks of Virginia Beach as just a large beach city, but no one thinks about the gangs, drugs, hell, dad, even the Russian mafia has a presence there."

Just then Marcia walked in with a tray holding three pieces of pie, along with two beers and a cup of tea."

Jumping up to take the tray from his mom's hands he set it on the coffee table. Looking at the beer, he said, "Uh...I think I'll get some water." By the time he got back to the family room, his parents were eating their pie, saying nothing, but he could hear the unasked questions hanging in the air.

Plopping down on the sofa at the opposite end from his mom, he wondered what to say. *Oh hell, they know me better than anyone.* "Gotta confess, I drank too damn much at the party last night, so I'm just taking it easy today."

Hoping his explanation would suffice, he took a bite of pie, moaning in ecstasy. "Mom, your pies are the best." With his mouth full, he looked over to see his mom staring in concern.

"It's not like you to drink too much," she commented. "Especially at the engagement party of one of your best friends. Anything happen last night?"

He continued to focus on his pie, hoping his voice sounded nonchalant. "Just had a rough night, that's all."

"It didn't have anything to do with Jillian Evans showing up with a date, did it?" his mom asked quietly.

Choking on the last bite, he gulped a drink of water to wash it down. Looking up guiltily, he said, "Does everyone in town know about last night?"

His dad tried to hide his grin as he finished off his piece. "I guess your mom and I just figured you two would finally get together one day. It doesn't take a lot to see that she's carried a torch for you since y'all were kids. I gotta say, when you came back from the Army and moved to Virginia Beach, well, I thought you might meet someone there and settle down. But you came home a lot to visit, and it seemed like you and Jillian were good friends. When you decided to move back... well, I hoped you two would make it official."

Grant leaned back, heaving a big sigh. His dad was more verbal while his mom tended to sit back and observe. He looked over at her, noticing her watching him carefully. Saying nothing, she simply cocked her head to the side. He recognized the gesture—it was her silent invitation to talk or not, but she always left it up to him.

"Jillian's a great woman," he said, stating the obvious. "But people change. Grow up. Not everyone's as lucky as Mitch and Tori," he added.

"You and Jillian want different things out of life?" his mom asked quietly.

Furrowing his brow, Grant shook his head.

"You've found someone else?" his dad prompted.

"No, that's not it," Grant denied truthfully.

"You just don't love her," his mom stated. "And that's fine, son."

Huffing in frustration, he shook his head again. "I'm...just not right for her. She deserves the best."

At that, his parents shared a glance before looking at him, concern in their eyes. "And you don't think you're the man for her?" Marcia prodded.

"Not anymore," he said, his voice low. The three sat in silence for a moment before he looked at his watch. "Oh, man, Dad, we've got to go. The meeting's in thirty minutes."

Remembering the American Legion meeting, Toby jumped up from his seat and leaned over to place a sweet kiss on his wife's lips. Grant followed, buffing his mom's cheek before the two men headed out to their vehicles.

"See you there, son," Toby called.

Grant waved at his dad before heading down the driveway. His chest was tight as he thought of the conversation they just had. Glad for the interruption, he drove back into town, determined to focus on something besides the cause of his unworthiness that he had almost divulged. Reasons best left back in the mountains of Afghanistan.

4

Mitch, the newly elected Commander of the local chapter of the American Legion, rapped the gavel on the podium. Grant's gaze roamed over the assembly, pride swelling inside his chest. *We've got a good crowd tonight.* He knew Mitch had been worried. It was not hard to get people to come to the first meeting where everything was new, but to continue to sustain that number of attendees once the real work began was a concern.

Wearing his navy blazer with the American flag pin in one lapel and the American Legion pin on the other, he observed the group as they sat down. Brogan, the Sergeant-at-Arms, closed the doors of the meeting room in the small Baytown American Legion building. With another three raps of the gavel, the members stood.

"The Color Bearer will advance the Colors." As the assembly stood, Grant watched as an elderly man from the back marched forward, the American flagpole in his hands, and set it in the floor stand.

"The Chaplain will offer prayer." A minister from one of the local churches who served as Chaplain, stood and prayed as the group bowed their heads in unison.

The POW/MIA Empty Chair Ceremony followed as the members recited the procedures. A chair was designated as a symbol of the thousands of American POW/MIAs still unaccounted for from all wars and conflicts involving the United States of America. The POW/MIA flag was placed on the Empty Chair. The assembly appeared eclectic to the untrained eye. Men... a few women...ages running from about twenty-five to almost ninety. At that moment, in a stance of solidarity, they all turned their faces toward the Empty Chair.

Grant, as First Vice Commander, stared at the chair for a long moment. A memory of long ago pushed to the forefront of his mind. Grimacing, he closed his eyes tightly, shoving both the image of the chair and the image of a fallen soldier he had held in his arms from his thoughts. Sucking in a ragged breath, he straightened his shoulders as he opened his eyes, training them on Mitch at the podium.

After the Pledge of Allegiance and the Preamble to the American Legion Constitution, the gavel was rapped once more to indicate that everyone could take a seat. Aiden, as Post Adjunct, read the minutes from the last meeting. Normally joking and irreverent, he adopted the seriousness of the occasion and Grant had to grin at his solemnness. Aiden stepped down from the podium and took his place next to Grant, then looked up in surprise when he was shoulder bumped from the side.

"Who knew you could handle such an auspicious duty?" Grant whispered, his smile lighting his eyes.

Narrowing his eyes in mock censure, Aiden lost the serious expression as a grin curved his lips, before grunting as Ginny elbowed him from his other side.

"Shhhh," she whispered, her lips pursed in reproval.

Zac Hamilton, as Finance Officer, stepped up next and gave the report of the finances. Ginny followed Zac and, as the Post Service Officer, gave a brief description of her duties.

"I'm responsible for bringing to the attention of all veterans and their dependents in the organization the rights and benefits granted them by law. There are a lot of wonderful services available through legion channels, as well as those of other agencies in this community. I will also be serving as Chairman of the Veterans Affairs and Rehabilitation Committee and will work closely with the Children and Youth Committee. I know that we will be spending some time tonight getting those committees staffed for the coming year."

After finishing the standard portion of her report, she looked over the crowd and added, "As one of my duties, I will be enlisting the aid of the Eastern Shore Mental Health Group, which consists of several counselors and psychologists, as well as medical doctors, to be available to our members who are struggling with mental health issues from having served."

Grant's gaze darted quickly to the Empty Chair before lifting back to the front of the room. Hoping to be unnoticed, he realized both Mitch and Ginny's eyes were on him.

"I realize this topic might be very uncomfortable for many of you. While the military recognizes the importance of the mental health of its members and veterans, it's often not talked about in ways that encourage us to seek it out. So, to make it easier, I'll be contacting each of you individually to share the information that the ESMH group can provide."

Forcing his face to relax, Grant watched as she made her way back to her seat, his mind on what she said. He knew Brogan rarely talked about his time overseas and Aiden tried to joke his way through any lingering emotions. And *Mitch?* Mitch seemed all right, and even if he was not, Grant bet that his relationship with Tori would help. Zac, the most open of all of them, talked about his time in the Navy, but never divulged any problems. Lance, closed off, sat to the side while newcomers, Jason Boswell and Gareth Harrison, sat at the end of the row, their eyes riveted to the podium.

Glancing over, now that Ginny was back at her seat, he wondered about her. *Hell, I work on the police force with her every day, but don't really know her.* It hit him that perhaps she needed counseling as much as any of them.

Mitch had taken the podium once more, but before he could speak, one of the older men in the Legion asked to speak about what Ginny had just announced.

Mitch nodded and assisted the man, walking with a cane, to the front.

He stood, slightly stooped, as Mitch lowered the microphone. One gnarled hand gripped the top of his cane as the other held on to the podium. Mitch stepped back but remained just to the left of the man in case he needed more assistance.

"My name's Chester. Chester Barnes. Served in World War II. Didn't go to Europe…I was in the Pacific." He shook his head for a moment and said, "Back then… when we came home, we didn't talk. People just accepted that we fought, and we didn't have to put up with any of that nasty stuff that our Nam brothers had to deal with." He eyed a few of the men in the room who had served in that era. "But still, we were expected to come home, get jobs, get married, and start families." His rheumy eyes gazed out over the crowd and Grant was mesmerized along with everyone else.

"So, that's what I did. I had some nightmares… things I saw…things I had to do. But no one talked about counseling back then. Hell, we didn't even know the words *mental health*. 'Bout fifteen years ago, when I was seventy-five years old, we had a preacher here in the Methodist Church in town that started meeting with some of us who had served back then. His father had served and, once back, became an alcoholic. Some of you might remember that preacher…he was a good man. Anyhow, he talked to us and, more importantly, got us to talk."

Chester shook his head a little sadly as he continued, "Wish I'd known seventy years ago about the kind

of relief that comes from unburdening your soul."
Standing up to his full height, which only came to
about Mitch's mid-chest, he added, "So, I'm glad Ms.
Spencer is taking up this cause and I want everyone to
think long and hard about using the services. Especially you younger ones." He pinned the front row with
his stare, saying, "You're gonna need it."

With that, Chester turned away, allowing Mitch and
Zac to assist him back to his seat. Grant's heart
pounded and hoped no one else could hear it, but also
wondered if there were others whose hearts were
pounding just as fiercely.

Before he could ponder more, Mitch turned the
program over to the committees' reports and then they
discussed the new youth teams. Finally, with decisions
made and new meeting dates established, they were
ready to finish.

The chaplain led them in a prayer once more and
then, with three raps of the gavel, the saying of the
Commander's Charge, and the retiring of the colors,
the meeting came to a close. The group hung around
for a few minutes talking and Grant observed the easy
camaraderie between the older members and the
younger ones.

The group of friends finally headed to Finn's Pub,
having already decided to end their meetings with a
drink. The pub's entrance held a dartboard to the right
and an old fireplace and sofa on the left. The original
building had been a bank, one of the early brick struc-
tures in the town. While renovated, it retained much of
the original brickwork walls and floor from years gone

by. The bar ran the length of the right side with tall, mismatched bar chairs up against the counter. The left contained tables already full of patrons and the kitchens were in the back.

Grant observed the eclectic group. Callan, one of the original Baytown Boys, was still in the Coast Guard but luckily served at the small station in the Baytown harbor. He brought along a few of his CG buddies, all who had joined the American Legion. Aiden and Brogan ran the bar as usual with lighthearted, familial banter between them. The two large men, both with long, dark hair and similar builds, were often mistaken as twins.

Jason, a heavily tatted biker, had opened a garage in town and was working on opening an adjoining tattoo parlor as well. Long hair in a ponytail, shaggy beard, and bulky muscles, he appeared incongruous next to Ginny's petite, button-down persona. Gareth sat in a booth with them as well. Tall, with dark hair and dark eyes, the private investigator's easy-going manner belied his sharp observations of everyone around. Lance was in the corner talking to Mitch quietly and Grant knew that crowds were not his scene. The conversation from the group behind him rolled to the youth league and plans were made to meet up at the town's baseball field on the next Saturday.

Lost in thought, Grant did not see Ginny coming until she slid onto the bar stool next to him. He eyed her suspiciously, not saying anything as he took a swig of the one beer he was allowing himself. She sat silently until he finally broke down and asked, "Got something on your mind?"

Ginny pulled out a card from her pocket and slid it toward him on the polished surface of the bar. "Don't worry, you're not the only person I'm giving this to tonight, but you're the first one I thought of."

Dropping his gaze to the print of the card, he recognized the ESMH contact information. Jerking his head around, his eyes wide with confusion, he bit out, "Me? Jesus, Ginny, we work together every day. We're police officers, going out every fuckin' day. Are you telling me you don't think I've got my head screwed on right?"

Her brown hair was sleeked back in a tight pony-tail and Grant realized he had never seen her when she was not completely professional. Her hazel eyes assessing his, they stared at each other for a long moment.

"I never said I thought you didn't have your head screwed on right," she stated firmly. "If I wasn't one-hundred percent sure of your commitment to the police force, we wouldn't be sharing duties." Her gaze dropped to the card lying on the bar between them. "But there's not one of us who couldn't use someone to talk to about what we saw and did over there. You included."

Shaking his head in frustration, he growled, "I swear if one more person brings up the party the other night, I'm gonna—"

"What Grant?" she bit out, interrupting. Heaving a sigh, she said, "Hey, I don't know your history with anyone in this town. I've only been here for two years. But it doesn't take a brain surgeon to see that underneath your cavalier exterior lies someone who's hiding things."

"Oh, yeah? And just what are you hiding, Ms. Spencer?" His frown met hers and his eyes pinned her to the seat.

Pushing the card over toward him slightly, she replied, "We all have something to hide, Grant. Even me. And that's why I'm talking to the ESMH group this week." With that pronouncement, she slid from the barstool and moved over to some of the others.

A shadow passed in front of him, and he lifted his gaze to see Katelyn helping her brothers behind the bar. Her dark hair and blue eyes resembled her brothers' Irish looks, and her temper could match theirs any day. He expected to be on the receiving end of more shit since she was Jillian's best friend, so he made a move to leave.

"You need another beer or you good?" she asked, her voice and expression neutral.

Eying her speculatively, he said, "Naw, I'm good." As an afterthought, he added, "Thanks." Still bracing, he was pleasantly surprised when her gaze moved to the group behind him, listening as they talked about the youth sports' league.

Nodding toward the patrons behind him, she said, "It's a good thing y'all are doing here. I hope we can start a Legion Auxiliary soon. There're plenty of family members who'd be good for it."

Swinging his head around again, Grant smiled at the thought of the good they wanted to accomplish. "You're right, Katelyn. This is a good group. It was, way back in the days of the Baytown Boys, and still is now."

He watched as a small, faraway smile settled on her face as she said, "I just wish...well, never mind. Life's too short for wishes. Gotta make the most of what we've been given." With that she turned and walked into the back, leaving him dumbstruck. *Philip. Fuckin' hell, Philip.* He knew Katelyn had been hit hard when her boyfriend did not come back from Afghanistan—they all had. He had considered Philip to be one of his best friends back then, but the sadness still in Katelyn's eyes struck him right in the chest.

Turning back to the group, he noticed Gareth's gaze following Katelyn as she made her way to the back of the bar. The idea of the two of them together seemed right and for an instant he wondered if he could help that along. *What am I thinking? I'm no matchmaker! Hell, I can't even take care of my own relationships, much less think of someone else's!*

As the group of friends began heading out of the bar, he slid off the stool, tossing some money onto the polished counter and stared at the ESMH card for a second before sticking it into his pocket. Walking out into the fresh ocean air, he threw his hand up in a wave goodbye. With Katelyn's words ringing in his ears, he thought about Jillian as the card burned a hole in his pocket. *Life's too short for wishes...gotta make the most of what we've been given.*

Jillian nervously peeked out the front window as she stood in the galleria. Smoothing her hands down her red skirt before making sure her hair was tucked neatly, she checked her makeup in a small mirror. *The last thing Mr. Dobson needs to see is some country-bumpkin hoping to showcase his pottery.*

With three painters, a local sculptor, woodcarver, a jewelry designer, plus a few others on board, and now with Lance agreeing to display his sea glass artwork in her shop, she was hoping to snag the potter.

Oliver Dobson's name had been given to her by an acquaintance and she had contacted him a few weeks ago. She tried to see if he had a website but found nothing. Nor did he have a studio until recently. It appeared that he was commissioned to do work for clients but did not mass-produce. He had now purchased an old garage in the northern part of the county and was setting up an apprentice program for a few potters-to-be. When he talked to Jillian, he said that he now had the opportunity to produce more work, plus the work of his students, and was interested in her galleria.

Hearing a male voice entering the coffee shop and speaking to one of her workers, she made her way to the top of the stairs, giving her the perfect opportunity to observe him as he ascended.

Tall, dark hair neatly trimmed. Clean shaven. Immaculate, navy, pin-striped suit with a pale lavender tie. As he neared the top, he looked up, and she worked to keep from gasping. Hollywood was the only word that flew through her mind. Latching onto his gaze, she realized his eyes were assessing her as much as she was noting him.

Sucking in a quick breath, she stuck her hand out, greeting, "Mr. Dobson. Welcome to my galleria."

Stepping onto the second floor, he took her hand in his and held it firmly. "Ms. Evans. It's a pleasure, I assure you."

As she led him to the same table where she had met with Lance, she waved her arm around the space keeping a running monologue of the artwork displayed. "As you can see, the original wooden panels still grace the walls and provide the perfect setting for the artwork. All artists are local and, where possible, use local raw materials or muses."

Reaching the table, she gestured for him to sit down and then sat across from him. His dark eyes continued to stare until she blushed and looked down nervously.

"I'm very sorry, Ms. Evans," he apologized, blushing slightly himself. "I don't know why I assumed you would be older, but I'm pleasantly surprised to find that a very attractive woman is running this business. And so very successfully."

"Oh, my parents started the coffee shop downstairs years ago, and I took it over from them, having worked in it most of my life, except for college. And, please, call me Jillian."

"And you may certainly call me Oliver. Where did you go to college?"

"Old Dominion." Laughing, she added, "It's not very far, so I've been a hometown girl all of my life."

Smiling, he shook his head and said, "Don't apologize for that. I've had the opportunity to travel the world, but you see where I've landed? The very rural and quaint Eastern Shore."

They continued chatting for a few more minutes as Jillian explained her concept to him and how she felt she would be able to assist him with sales. At the end of her little speech, she took a deep breath and added, "Oliver, I know that you already create pieces for individual clients, and while I very much want to showcase your pottery here, I'm not sure my galleria will gain you very much."

Nodding, he said, "For myself, I've decided that I would like to spend more time teaching the techniques to some specialized students that have agreed to work here with me. But they are unknowns, and their work will need to be showcased. This is a great opportunity for them, as well as for me. Beyond that, I'll also be actively marketing them, but don't want to bog myself down with the details of shipping. If it is something you would consider, I'd be more than willing to pay you to ship out our pieces for a commission. You will hopefully sell some here, but we'll probably sell a lot more directly. If you handled all our shipping, you'd be helping me out a lot while also earning a bit more yourself."

Tilting her head, she smiled. "That's very generous, Oliver. I'm sure the shipping wouldn't be too much for me to handle—"

Chuckling, he said, "What you see here is the cleaned-up version of myself. I much prefer the plain clothes of the potter and working in my shop. I'd package the pieces, since I know how to ship pottery, but then they would be sent by your galleria to my clients. That'd take one burden off of me and give you more of a chance to promote your business. And since you'd also be displaying some of my work and the work of my students, I'd be over to drop off boxes anyway, so it's a win-win for both of us."

Letting out a sigh of relief, Jillian leaned back in her chair feeling the warm sun streaming in through the window. Her dream was coming true right before her eyes.

"You appear happy, Jillian," he observed, returning her smile.

"I am, very much. I can't thank you enough for your faith in my business, that you would also allow me to market and ship your artwork."

Standing, they shook hands, and she noticed he held on to hers longer than necessary. *He's handsome, no doubt about it.* She glanced down at their connected hands, a flash of disappointment coursing through her at the lack of heat she felt from their contact. *Not like Grant—nope, stop! He's passed up his last chance with me!* Smiling up at Oliver, she slipped her hand from his and said, "I'll walk you out and you can let me know when to expect your first delivery."

Grant stomped up the stairs of the coffee shop, ignoring the concerned expressions on the faces of Jillian's employees as they eyed the angry officer. Rounding the top of the steps, he came face to face with the woman he had just witnessed standing outside her shop, her hand once more being held by another man. *Damn, first Lance and now this guy. And who is he anyway?*

"Grant? What are you doing here?" she asked, her voice strident as she warily observed the red-faced, tight-lipped man staring at her. Legs planted wide, his hands were on his hips as he glared, causing her to move back a step.

"Who the fuck was that guy out front? The one you were hanging onto?"

Not answering, she blinked several times. Suddenly, jerking out of her stunned silence as fury poured though her, she spouted, "It's none of your business! You don't have to know everyone, and certainly not everyone I'm talking to!"

"I protect the town, so I sure as hell should know everyone...especially if some stranger is lurking about!"

Jillian's breath rushed out, her chest heaving.

"You've got to be kidding me," she said, her voice suspiciously low and controlled.

"I've never seen him around here," Grant contended, his words less sure now that he saw her gaze snapping at him.

Just then, one of her servers from the coffee shop called up, "Jillian, I hate to interrupt your...uh...discussion, but I need you to sign for the morning delivery."

Narrowing her eyes as she drew a shaky breath, she said, "Excuse me," shoving past him as she jogged down the stairs.

Grant clenched his jaw as frustration coursed through his body. Swinging his eyes around, he spied a business card lying on the table in front of the large front window and he hurried over. **Oliver Dobson, Dobson's Pottery, Eastern Shore, Virginia**. Committing the name to memory, he turned quickly as he heard Jillian's feet pounding up the stairs.

Before giving him a chance to speak, she stepped forward and poked him in the chest, her voice now rising. "You know what, Grant. I'm glad you came here. I'm glad to finally have the chance to tell you exactly what's going on! You want it, well here it is, buddy!"

She stepped forward one more time and he stepped back in surprise. Looking down at the delicate finger poking him, he did not have a chance to placate her before she blasted.

"You asked me to be your girlfriend in high school, and I gave you my heart. That was your first chance. Then you asked me to wait on you when you joined the Army, and I did. I. DID. I waited. I didn't go out on a single date my senior year of high school. Didn't date when I first went to college. Why? Because you asked me to wait for you. That was your next chance to have me."

Chest still heaving, she glared at the face that had haunted her for years. "I gave you a chance to come home to me like you promised, but you didn't. You came home, told me that you had changed your mind and left to go live and work in Virginia Beach. But like a fool, I still clung to the hope that one day you'd return to Baytown, and that was another chance I was willing to give you. And you did. You moved back over a year ago. But not home to me. Nope, I've had to watch you with other women, but never me."

Turning, she stalked over to the large window overlooking Main Street, crossing her arms protectively in front of her, her breath ragged as she blinked to hold the tears back.

His gaze held the beautiful woman standing with the sunbeams catching the light in her hair and the stiff set of her shoulders. Her body, encased in a light blue blouse tucked into a red skirt that cupped her ass in a way that screamed class and sexy all at the same time. Sucking in a breath, he hated himself for once more alienating her. *This is exactly why I should just stay away.* "Jillian, I never—"

"No," she interrupted, sucking in a shuddering breath, still staring down at the street, her voice now spiked with sadness. "No more, Grant. You used up your chances with me. You want friendship only...that's what you'll get. No matter how much it might tear me up, that's all you'll get." Turning back to stare at him, she added, "And that friendship does not include you coming in here questioning me about who I'm seeing."

"Please..." he said, unable to keep the pleading out of his voice, his hands lifting at his side.

She stared at the face as familiar to her as her own. His brown hair, short with just enough length at the front to stand on end when he ran his hand through it. She loved seeing him in the old police uniforms but had to admit the new navy polos with the BPD logo and khakis looked just as good. She knew if she walked forward, she would be able to stand with the top of her head nestled just underneath his chin. Closing her eyes for a second, she shook her head slowly, letting out a long sigh.

Cocking her head to the side, she asked, "Please what, Grant? Are you asking for one more chance to break my heart?"

He stood there, the battle waging within. The truth he had tried to bury for so long was that Jillian had stolen his heart when they were children playing on the Baytown beach, and dreaming of a life with her fueled his adolescent dreams. But the man that came back from the war was not the same man she fell in love with, and he did not know how to reconcile the two.

"I don't want to break your heart," he said, the words slipping out on a sigh. Running his hand through his hair, he said, "I...I'm sorry." Turning on his heel, he jogged down the stairs and slammed out of the coffee shop leaving Jillian rooted to the floor.

Fat, silent tears slid down her face as she realized her heart just broke one more time.

Grant parked the Police SUV and called in his location. Acres of shoulder-high crops lined the fields of the farm. Looking over at Burt, they stepped from the vehicle and walked along the path toward the barn. The officers noted two children at the edge of the fields before the kids ducked down to stay out of sight. Grant grimaced while Burt cursed. The local school had given them a list of the children who had not shown up for the first two weeks of the school year and were unaccounted for, hoping the town's police could aid in the truancy.

"School day and these kids are out here working the fields instead of being in school."

Grant, following the dirt, tractor path around the weather-beaten barn, came to the wide-open door. An old farmer, his stomach pulling at the fabric of his stained coveralls was tinkering on a tractor. He looked up as Grant rounded the corner.

Wiping the sweat from his brow with a faded bandana, he stood up and called out his greeting. "Officer...what can I do for you?"

Grant pulled off his reflector sunglasses and jerked his head toward the field where the corn stalks were tall and green. "Those your kids out there in the field, Mister...?"

The old farmer laughed, "Hell naw. My kids done

grown up and left years ago. My name's Jeffrey Todd. Them's some neighbor kids that help me out. Their dad works for me, and he brings his kids." He narrowed his eyes, making the crow's feet at the corners even deeper. "What's the problem? They in trouble? I ain't gonna have no trouble on my place."

"Mr. Todd, the trouble is that school's started, and those kids aren't in school."

"Humph, that ain't my problem. I ain't their parent."

Just then, a small man appeared from the back, busy wiping the grease from his hands. He stopped suddenly at the sight of Grant and his eyes dropped to the Baytown Police Department logo on Grant's shirt. Eyes wide, he backed up a step, flight written on his face.

"You the father of those kids?" Grant asked, watching the nervous man wring his hands.

"Yes," came the soft reply. "I'm Keith Montwood. They're good kids...they're not in trouble," he hastened to say.

Burt walked into the barn with the two boys in tow. One looked to be about ten and the other one close to twelve, but Grant had to admit it was hard to tell from their size. Their eyes were as wide as their dad's and the youngest one's chin trembled as he battled back tears.

Grant knew since Burt was a father himself, he had dealt easily with the boys, but still understood their fear. Turning his head back to the adults, he softened his voice as he spoke to the father. "They're not in trouble, but they need to be in school. It started two weeks ago, and we got a call from the school letting us know that they had not attended yet. The principal is worried."

"I work for Mr. Todd," Keith said, "and my boys work here too in the summer." He cast a nervous glance to the older farmer, whose lips were set in a thin line.

"I appreciate that, but the fact remains that during the school day, the boys must be in school. If you have them help here afterwards or on weekends, that's up to you."

"Hell, I stayed out of school to help my pa, and my kids missed school to work on the farm," Jeffrey bit out. "It's harvest time, and I need the help!"

"What you did yourself or with your kids is not the issue here," Grant continued. "The law says that the kids must attend school and on top of that, there are child labor laws that are being broken here."

Jeffrey blustered more about damned laws interfering with a man being able to do an honest day's work while Keith jerked his nervous gaze between his angry boss and the two policemen.

Burt stepped in to calm Jeffrey down as Grant moved toward Keith, motioning the boys to come with him.

"Mr. Montwood, we need to get your boys back in school. So far, they've missed the first two weeks of school, and we don't want them to miss more."

Head bobbing, the smaller man agreed, his hands holding onto the shoulders of both boys. "I know, sir. I agree. They're smart and I want them to finish school, like I never did. It's just that..." his eyes cut over to

Jeffrey, still blustering about the government taking over his life.

"Is he putting pressure on you to have the boys here?" Grant asked.

"He pays well and..."

"And he's indicated that if you keep the boys here to work through the harvest, you'll get more money, right?"

Keith let out a long sigh, answering Grant's question without speaking.

Rubbing his hand over his face, Grant met Keith's sigh. Glancing down at the two boys, uncertainty in their eyes, he knelt to their level and smiled. "Hey boys, my name is Officer Wilder. What's yours?"

Swallowing audibly, the oldest jutted his chin out slightly in pride and said, "Keith Jr., sir, but everyone calls me Junior." His dark hair was slightly messy, but his clothes were clean. His eyes darted over to his dad.

"And you?" Grant asked the other boy.

"B...Bobby," the youngest barely managed to croak out.

"All right, Junior and Bobby. First of all, you have to know that no one's in trouble here. Not you and not your dad. Okay?"

The two small heads bobbled in answer.

"But we do want to see you in school. What grades are you in?"

"I'm in seventh and my brother's in fifth," Junior replied with a glance up at his father, who smiled encouragingly at him.

"What's your favorite subject?" Grant continued to draw the boys out.

"I like math," Junior said. "I'm supposed to be in Algebra this year."

"Whoa, that's pretty impressive," Grant smiled. "But we need to get you in school so you don't miss the first part of what you need to learn."

"I like art," came the shy response from Bobby, as he tried to mimic his brother's bravery.

"All right then, we need to make sure you have the chance to create all the art you want to." Standing, Grant faced their father, who's eyes were filled with pride as much as concern.

"I know I should have made sure they were in school." Lowering his voice, he whispered, "Mr. Todd said that we'd have the crop in last week, but the harvest flowed into this week. I'll take the boys right now."

Grant turned to Burt, who had managed to get Jeffrey to shut up, and said, "Mr. Montwood is going to take the children to school right now, and then he'll be back to finish his work. You might have to hire someone to help these last couple of weeks, but the children will no longer be available." As an afterthought, he added, "And no other children will be available either."

Huffing as he turned back to his tractor, Jeffrey grumbled, "Damned government taking over my farm, telling me I can't hire no kids." Sparing a glance toward Keith, he said, "Make sure you get right back here, and you'll have to work through lunch to make up for the time."

"Yes, sir," Keith agreed, hustling the boys out of the barn.

As Burt called into the station, Grant smiled at the boys. "Listen, me and some friends are starting to work with a youth sports league. Think you'd be interested?"

A flicker of excitement flew through their eyes as they looked to their dad before speaking. Keith's face scrunched for a second, indecision creeping into his response.

"I know some of them leagues cost quite a bit to—"

"No costs involved," Grant quickly said, smiling at the astonished look on Keith's face. "The American Legion is working with the kids and all we ask is for parents to be involved to whatever extent they can. If that's just coming to cheer at a few games, then that's fine. If they can supply some water or snacks, that's good too."

"Can we dad?" Junior asked, his eyes bright for the first time since Grant saw him.

Smiling back, Keith ruffled his oldest son's hair before turning his gaze to his younger son. "Absolutely."

Grant pulled out a business card from his pocket and started to write on the back when he realized he had pulled out the ESMH card. Shoving it back in quickly, he fished for his own card and handed it to Keith after scribbling his phone number down on the back. "Meet us on Saturday morning. If you have to work, then call me and I'll come pick up the boys."

With promises to do that, Grant waved toward the trio as they headed off to their car on their way to school. Turning, he waved to a still grumbling Jeffrey and got back into the SUV with Burt.

Driving back to town, Burt said, "You get the feeling the dad'll keep the kids in school?"

Nodding, Grant replied, "Yeah, I do. And I've got them coming to the ballpark on Saturday, which'll give me a chance to keep my eye on them as well."

Chuckling, Burt joked, "Look at you, being all caring. Who knew you had any domesticated bones in your body?"

Laughing as well, Grant drove into town, passing the coffee shop on the way to the police station. His mirth fled as he thought of the way he and Jillian had parted earlier in the week. His mouth tight, he glanced at Gareth's investigative business on the next street. Harrison Investigations. Grinning, he thought, *I might just have Gareth see what he can dig up on Oliver Dobson.*

Sleep came uneasily that night, as with most nights, as the dreams that haunted Grant returned.

I walked around the vehicle, carefully watching the mirror mounted to the long handle. The wind caught the dust on the road, swirling it around, creating a mini-tornado, just enough to make bomb detection difficult.

The dust covered world morphed into a blonde haired, blue-eyed woman, her hair pulled back in a tight military bun at the back of her head. Laughing and joking. A group sitting around a table, shooting the shit. She reminds me of—

Visions ran into each other...faces...places. Then screams and shouts. Running toward the explosion. A body...blonde hair covered in blood.

Grant bolted upright, sweat pouring off his body as the dark walls of his bedroom greeted him. *Fuck!* The nightmare still had him in its grip as he tried to breathe through the pressure on his chest. Swinging his legs over the side of the bed, he sat for a moment until he was sure his legs would hold him up. Stumbling into the bathroom, he splashed water on his face before filling a glass and taking a long drink.

Lifting his head, he stared at the man in the mirror, hating the haunted look in his eyes. Jillian ran through his mind as he choked back his fear.

The idea of her with someone ate at him, but he just wasn't sure he could go there with her. Suddenly, Mitch's words from the other day came slamming back. *"You need to either let her go completely or decide you want to go for her. Either way, sitting on the fence is only hurting both of you."*

Walking over to his chest of drawers, he picked up the card Ginny had given him and stared at it for a moment. *Problem is, I don't want her to be with anyone else but me. But how can I take a chance on falling in love after...?*

Sucking in a deep breath, he tucked the card into his wallet. Time to make a phone call.

6

Jillian smiled as Oliver carried a large cardboard box up the stairs of the coffee shop. At the top, he returned a smile before setting the box on top of the table she indicated.

"I know I saw the pictures of the pieces you created, but I'm so excited to actually see your work in person," she enthused.

"Well, keep in mind that my pottery is not famous," he laughed, "but I do try to use the elements of where I'm living." He lifted out several bowls, vases, and jars, each fired with the colors of the shore. Some swirled with reds and oranges of the sunsets over the bay and others with the blues and greens of the water.

Lifting one, Jillian reverently held it in her hands. "Oh, Oliver, the colors are beautiful." Glancing to the side, she grinned, "And I know just where I'll display them." Walking over to the far wall, she placed the bowl on top of a wooden pedestal.

Oliver followed her, observing the space with a critical eye. The dark, wood paneled walls glistened with the sunlight coming in from the window. Track lighting was not used at the moment, but was available from overhead, offering a chance for the work to be enjoyed in the evening. Jillian had created a section just for his work, and the various pedestals and glass shelves would show off the pottery to perfection.

"What do you think?" she asked, nervous for his response.

His smile was the answer she craved, and she clapped her hands in glee. "Fabulous! Let's get the others displayed."

They worked side by side for several minutes, giving Jillian time to observe the man working with her. He was much more casually dressed today, wearing nice jeans and a long-sleeved polo. Handsome, he was sure to turn the eye of any woman he met and, if the occasional glances he sent her way were any indication, she was catching his attention as well.

Capturing men's attention had never been a problem for Jillian...it was that she compared every man she met to Grant...and found them lacking. Pursing her lips, she shook her head to dispel the image of Grant from her mind.

"Whoa, are you all right?" Oliver asked. "You don't look very happy right now."

Blushing, she stammered, "I'm...I'm sorry. I...uh... was just a million miles away for a moment."

Once the pieces were in place they stood back to admire them. Turning toward him, she said, "Once I get the woodcarver's work in here and another local artist that creates from sea glass, I'll be ready for our first evening show. I was thinking of hosting a wine and cheese night here at the coffee shop, letting visitors come to enjoy the art."

Oliver's warm gaze landed on her and he nodded his acquiescence. Stepping closer, he kept his eyes on her as he asked, "Your ideas sound wonderful. And, as I promised, I'll get the pottery to you that I've sold so you can send it out through your galleria." He hesitated slightly, rubbing his chin in thought before asking, "Um...would you like to have lunch with me today? I'm not away from the workshop very much, and this would be a treat for me to eat in town."

Jillian's gaze took him in, wishing she felt more than professional interest. *But...nothing. Oh well, a working lunch sounds great.* "That would be fine," she replied, smiling widely. "You can tell me more about your work."

"I've heard there's a good pub in town. Would you like to eat there?"

Jillian plastered on her game face while quickly saying, "Um...actually there's a nice fish house near the harbor. The Seafood Shack. It's got local seafood, and you can look right out on the water."

"Perfect," he agreed and moved back over to the box to clean up the packing materials, leaving Jillian heaving a sigh of relief. *God, the last place I would want to go is Finn's!* She wanted to have a chance to talk to Katelyn before her best friend saw her out with someone. *And I don't want Aiden and Brogan in my business!*

There were times when living in a small town could be inhibiting—and this was one of them.

Soon afterward, sitting at a table overlooking the town harbor, the conversation between Jillian and Oliver flowed easily. The restaurant was known for its local seafood, and sated from her now-empty shrimp basket, Jillian leaned back in her tall chair. She stared at her lunch partner's profile as he was turned, looking out the window. He appeared to be studying the sailboats.

"Do you sail?" she wondered aloud.

Chuckling, he shook his head. "No, never been. I just always liked the lines of a sailboat."

"I never thought about that," she admitted, "but as an artist, you probably see all kinds of things that us mere mortals never notice."

"Probably," he grinned, tuning his face back toward hers. "But I was honestly thinking about how nice it would be to jump in a boat and just sail away. Go wherever the wind takes you."

Casting her gaze toward the bright blue waters of the bay, she said, "Not me. This has always been home."

After they finished their meal, Jillian walked Oliver back to his car, still parked outside her shop. "Thank you again, for the opportunity to show your pottery."

"The pleasure is all mine," he answered, offering his hand toward hers. "And thank you so much for lunch. I don't get out often and being new here, it was a good chance to eat local seafood."

Saying goodbye, she withdrew her hand from his,

but felt the slight squeeze before he let go. Waving, she watched him drive away before returning to the shop, her mind in turmoil. *Why, oh, why can't I be interested in someone like Oliver?*

"We've covered a lot of ground today, Grant," Thomas Peters, the counselor, said as the session was ending, smiling at the former soldier sitting in front of him. "I'm glad you called and pleased you were so open with me."

Grant sat in a comfortable leather chair facing Thomas, the arrangements more conducive to counseling as two friends talking rather than professionally across a desk. The office was neat, with few files on Thomas' desk and walls lined with beach scene pictures that reminded him of the ones he saw in Jillian's galleria.

"I thought I had dealt with everything," Grant admitted, his attention back on the counselor. "But just lately it's become apparent to me that I hadn't."

"Most of us have unresolved issues from all sorts of things in our lives, but especially military personnel. Coming back from war, there are inner conflicts that might surface immediately or may lie dormant for years."

"When I got out, I knew I wanted to continue in police work, but I couldn't face working in Baytown and...well, I couldn't face her."

"What brought you back?"

Grant shrugged momentarily before admitting, "Honestly, when I got back from the war, I saw myself as some worldly guy who needed to be a big city cop. But it only took a few years to realize my roots were here."

"And the woman?"

"Yeah..." Rubbing his hands together, he dropped his chin to his chest. "She's the reason I'm here today. Things happened over there. Things that were...hell, disturbing is about the best way to describe it." Squinting his eyes tightly shut, as though in pain, he said, "But I can't seem to let her go. She's like my other half. I broke it off, pushed her away, said we were just friends, even brought other women around." Shoving back in his chair, eyes now wide, he grimaced. "I've been a total asshole to her thinking that would keep her away from a mess like me, while trying to hide my mess from everyone else."

"I assume it didn't work?"

Shaking his head slowly, he said, "No, not really. All it's done is hurt her and, God knows, she doesn't deserve that pain."

"Did something in particular happen that brought you to the point where you decided to call for help?"

"I can't stand seeing her with someone else. And after all this time, she's finally ready to move on...away from me...and even though it makes me an asshole for giving her mixed signals, I don't want her with any other man." Sighing, he lifted his gaze to the counselor.

Thomas observed the young man in front of him, carefully watching Grant's body language as well as his words. Smiling slightly, he asked, "So, what are you going to do about it?"

Sucking in a deep breath through his nose before letting it out slowly, Grant pierced the counselor with his clear-eyed gaze. "I can be the man for her, but I've got some things to work through. I just need to show her that I'm serious about this. Serious about her. Serious about us."

Nodding, Thomas glanced at the clock on the wall before saying, "You've made a good decision. Recognizing there's a problem is the first step. Being willing to work on it is next. We'll make an appointment for next week and, at that time, you can decide if you're ready to delve into the actual events that occurred in Afghanistan." Gaining Grant's approval, he added, "In the meantime, what's your game plan?"

"I'm going to work with the youth league tomorrow and that'll give me a focus outside my job. A chance to give back to the community that gave me so much. I'll also start talking to my buddies...it's about time I let them know what's going on with me."

"And the woman?"

A flash of the image of Jillian standing on the sidewalk with Oliver, shot straight through him, hardening his resolve. *I'm not going down without a fight!* "I'm going to start showing her that I can be the man she deserves...the one she once loved."

The large, metal tub on the deck held ice and beer, while the lawn chairs had been moved to the grassy yard. The meat on the grill sizzled as it was flipped, juices running down onto the hot coals. Aiden, Brogan, and Zac worked on dividing the equipment list for the kids' teams they were collecting from town sponsors. Callan and Jarrod, another Coast Guard buddy, tossed a football in the yard, while they waited for the others to arrive.

"You don't have a gas grill?" Jason asked, bending over the tub to snag a beer. Twisting off the cap, he drank thirstily before moving over to one of the chairs. Gareth walked up, fist-bumped Jason and grabbed a beer as well.

Grant, standing by the old charcoal grill, spatula in his hand, just glared at the newcomer. "Nothin' tastes like meat cooked over hickory charcoal," he explained as though speaking to a barbeque neophyte.

"Look at him—the grill master connoisseur!" Aiden laughed.

Grant flipped him off good-naturedly, continuing to stand guard over the smoking grill, the scent of sizzling meat whetting everyone's appetite.

Mitch walked around the house, papers in his hands. "Got the AL team signups right here. So far it looks like we'll start off with about thirty kids ranging in age from eight to about fifteen. Some of the older guys play for the high school, but I figure we'll pull in more as we go along."

As the burgers were served, the group settled

around, eating and discussing the upcoming first practice. Ginny ambled around the corner, her face red and sweating, walking with a slight limp.

"Sorry, my car wouldn't start so I decided to combine getting here with my daily run," she panted as she slowed down long enough for one of the men to toss her a bottle of chilled water. "And I tripped on your pothole-filled driveway," she added, rubbing her ankle. Drinking it gratefully, she eyed the applications in Mitch's hands. "We got any girls?"

"Actually, we have three," Mitch replied, "and I figure there'll be more coming."

"Good," she nodded, sitting down. Glancing at the empty plates around, she joked, "Looks like I've got some catching up to do."

Brogan placed a plate in front of her, a large burger with all the trimmings sitting next to a pile of potato chips. Her eyes darted from the plate up to the large man handing it to her, his face unreadable. "I'll have to run more miles if I eat all this."

"You'd blow over in a stiff wind as it is. Eat up," Brogan ordered, as he turned and walked back over to his chair.

Ginny watched his retreat before digging into her burger, but Grant noticed Brogan's eyes drifted often to the pretty police officer.

As the conversation lagged, the warmth of the day combined with full bellies sent a lull over the group. Settling into lawn chairs to finish their beers, Grant sucked in a deep breath, his stomach in knots. As a few pairs of eyes moved his way, he plunged ahead. "I was thinking about what Chester said the other night at the meeting." Looking around the group, he now had all eyes pinned on him but managed to push on. "I thought it was good of him to speak about how things were for him...both in the war and well, you know... after he came home."

He forced his gaze to travel around again, but with relief realized none of them were staring at him as though he had lost his mind. Emboldened, he continued, "I just thought that it might be good to have some of the older ones share...if they wanted to...at each meeting to give some of us younger veterans the benefit of what they learned. It might keep us from making some of the same mistakes."

His palms began to sweat at the silence that greeted him, but Ginny came to the rescue. "I think that's a good idea, Grant."

"None of us came back unscathed," Mitch admitted, "and you're right. We tend to gloss it over."

"And it can eat at your guts," Brogan added, his eyes cast down to the beer in his hand.

"I know I've got things I need to face. Anyway, it was just a thought," Grant said, wanting to take the pall from the gathering. Glancing over at Mitch, he said, "We can bring it up at the next meeting and see who might be interested in speaking."

"Can you imagine serving in the military during World War II?" Aiden asked, leaning forward. "Man, think of how far our technology has come since then."

The conversation became a lively discussion of how

times had changed, and the group settled back into easy camaraderie. Grant let out a silent sigh, glad to have broached the emotional subject without drawing undue attention to himself. *One step at a time.*

An hour later, the group dispersed, leaving Grant and Ginny discussing a case. As she prepared to leave, he walked her around the front of his house, offering to give her a lift. "After all, it was my driveway that caused you to twist your ankle."

"Oh, it's fine now," she protested.

"Come on," he insisted, leading her to his jeep. A few minutes later, he dropped her off at her small house on the north side of town and they stood on her front steps for a minute chatting.

Giving a smile and a wave goodbye, he trotted back down the walk to his jeep, never seeing Jillian's faded smile as she drove down the street on her way home.

On the old, metal bleachers of the Baytown baseball field, Jillian sat wedged between Tori and Katelyn, the tall grass underneath tickling their legs. Two more of their friends, Belle Gunn and Jade Lyons, joined them.

Katelyn looked over and shouted, "Rose! Over here!"

The others turned and saw Baytown's new entrepreneur walking over. Rose Parker had moved to Baytown to open an ice cream parlor. She climbed up the steps of the bleachers swatting at an errant bee and greeted Katelyn before sitting down. Introduced to the ones she had not met, she smoothed her pixie cut back from her face.

"When can we expect you to open, girl? I've been dying to get my hands on your ice cream concoctions!"

Rose offered a tired smile toward Katelyn and shrugged one shoulder. "My bid for the first storefront I wanted was outbid by the new tattoo artist," she explained.

"Jason?" Katelyn asked, surprised this was the first she had heard about it.

"I suppose," Rose replied. "I've never met him. Then I found a nice place further down from Finn's, still on Main Street, but it needs lots of renovations. I've got the money, but the town manager is really riding my ass about getting the work done by certain contractors."

"He can't do that!" Jillian spouted.

Katelyn groused, "I can't stand that man."

"Oh, it's okay," Rose said softly, her gentle smile calming even Katelyn's ire. "It'll happen when it happens." Looking around, she added, "I'm just glad to be out on such a lovely day."

"So, why are we out here on the first day of the practice?" Jade asked, holding her hand over her forehead to shade her eyes, warily observing the rag-tag team of kids running around the freshly mowed and painted field.

Laughing, Katelyn replied, "Because this is Baytown!"

"Huh?" Jade asked, swinging her gaze from the field to the women sitting behind her.

"You're new here, so you'll quickly find out that anytime anything is happening anywhere...it's the place to be," explained Jillian. "And now that the American Legion teams are established, this league will need some people to cheer them on."

"I've always liked coming to see practices," Belle confessed softly, gaining the attention of the others. Shrugging shyly, she tried unsuccessfully to tuck her dark, wayward hair behind her ears. "It gave me something to do besides be at home. So, after school, I'd come to the ball fields and watch whoever was practicing."

Jillian and Katelyn shared a glance, both having often wondered why Belle had hated being at home when growing up. She had been younger and not part of the original Baytown group of kids, but had slowly come out of her shell, joining them now as adults.

"Well, I think it's exciting," Tori pronounced, her gaze following Mitch.

"God, I just hope my brothers won't cuss too much in front of the kids!" Katelyn said as she eagled-eyed the field, her brow furrowed. "Neither Aiden nor Brogan do a very good job of watching what they say."

Jillian tried to pay attention to the conversations around her, but her gaze continually drifted to Grant. Workout shorts and a T-shirt, stretched tightly over his chest and arm muscles, drew her eyes. The men had divided the kids into groups and were working on fundamentals with them. As she watched, she noted two boys hanging near him. Intrigued, she observed how Grant appeared to know them and take great interest as he talked to them. He touched their shoulders, drawing their attention to him when he gave instructions. Numerous times, he crouched down so that he was at their level.

Her lips curved upward as she noticed how the boys appeared to hang on his every word. *I wonder who they are? I've never noticed him with kids before...he's really good with them.*

"What put that smile on your face?" Katelyn asked, breaking into Jillian's musings.

Blushing, she said, "Just watching the kids."

"Yeah, right," came the reply as Katelyn shoulder bumped her. "I wonder who the boys are that Grant is coaching?"

"I recognize the younger one. He goes to the elementary school," Jade remarked, "but I don't know his name. He's older than the kids I teach."

"I've seen them around," Belle added. "They live over near where I do in the trailer park."

Jillian digested the tidbit of information, tucking it away while telling herself she had no interest in what Grant did. *Yeah, right...he's still gorgeous even if he's not into me.* Heaving a sigh as the practice ended, she said, "I'm heading back to the shop, girls. See you later."

Stepping down off the last bleacher, she was startled as a hand reached out to offer assistance. Still standing on the first riser, she came eye to eye with Grant. Blinking under the intensity of his gaze, she bristled. Looking down at his outstretched hand, she placed her hand in his, not wanting to appear peevish. The familiar jolt from his touch zinged through her, irritating her even more. *Why does it have to be his touch that my body reacts to?*

"Jillian," he said politely, his voice whisky smooth.

Making the step down to the ground, she worked to hide the hurt that always threatened to creep out, trying to protect her heart from getting trampled. Pulling her hand back, she looked up sharply as he held fast to her fingers. "What are you doing?" she hissed, glancing around to see if anyone could hear as she dislodged her hand from his.

"If you have a moment, I've got someone I'd like you to meet. Well, actually two someones."

Narrowing her eyes, she was surprised when he twisted around and called out, "Boys! Over here." The two boys that Grant had been coaching so carefully came forward, their shy smiles toward her mixed with their obvious adoration of the large coach.

"I'd like you to meet two friends of mine," Grant said, one hand now resting on the shoulder of the tallest boy. "This is Junior Montwood and," moving his hand to the smaller boy, "this is Bobby Montwood."

Her smile beamed brightly over the boys as she greeted them enthusiastically. "I saw you out there playing. Did you have a good time?"

Junior, trying to emulate Grant's manners, answered her politely while Bobby merely nodded.

"Bobby is interested in art," Grant added, his gaze darting to Jillian's quickly. "I thought maybe sometime you would allow me to bring them to your galleria and let them look around." Grant felt the unfamiliar pang of nervousness, remembering the last conversations he had with her. He really wanted to show Bobby the displayed artwork and wanted to spend time with Jillian. *God, I hope she doesn't shoot me down now. Or at least only shoots me down, not the boys.* As soon as the thought ran through his mind, he quickly dismissed it. One thing he knew—he might have messed up his chances with Jillian, but she would never take it out on a child.

True to her spirit, she beamed even brighter, eyes shining with enthusiasm as she spoke to Bobby. "Would you like to see my showroom? I have all kinds of artists who live close by showing off their art in my building."

Bobby's eyes widened and he darted his gaze between her, Grant, and his brother, nodding all the while.

"I don't know what plans you have this afternoon," Grant said, wiping his palms on his shorts. "I don't have to have the boys home for a while and was going to take them to get a bite to eat and...well..."

Shooting him a curious look, she finished his sentence. "Well, there's no time like the present. I'd love to show the boys the artwork."

Grant released a breath, feeling lightheaded...and lighthearted. "Okay, then. Let's go. We can take my SUV."

"I'll take my scooter and meet you there," she said, looking at the other kids and coaches packing up the equipment. "By the time you get finished, I'll be there and will have the shop opened." Without giving Grant a chance to argue, she waved as she turned around, walking to the parking area. Distracted with her own musings, she did not hear Katelyn's footsteps pounding the gravel behind her as she made her way through the weed-infested lot.

"Hey, slow down!" Katelyn puffed.

Twisting around to see her friend hustling, she slowed down to wait on her.

"I just saw Grant talking to you. What did he want?"

Sliding her eyes sideways, biting her bottom lip, she wondered what Katelyn would think of Grant's plan. She rushed in to say, "He wants to bring those two boys to my shop to check out the artwork."

Katelyn said nothing, but Jillian could feel the waves of disbelief pouring off of her. Sucking in a breath, she said, "What could I say? There was no way I could turn down the kids."

"Uh-huh, and don't you think Grant knows that? I mean what's his game anyway? He throws you in the friend zone forever and now that you finally gave him his walking papers, he's sniffing around." Stopping on the sidewalk, they stood, facing each other. Katelyn placed her hand on Jillian's arm, her voice contrite. "I'm sorry, honey. I just want you to be able to move on from Grant...to someone who'll appreciate you."

The image of Oliver flashed through Jillian's mind. "I know. And...well, I'm working on it." She just wished he made her heart rush the way Grant always had. Plastering a smile on her face, she threw her arms around Katelyn, giving her a hug. "Don't worry...I'm just spending some time with Grant, as a friend, and showing off the art to some kids who might appreciate what I've done."

Ignoring Katelyn's dubious expression, she hopped on her scooter. Puttering down the road, she wondered what Grant was up to. *Is he really just interested in showing the boys my galleria?*

7

If Jillian had any doubts about Grant's sincerity, they flew out the window as soon as she saw Bobby's face when he rounded the corner at the top of the stairs in her shop. His wide eyes swept the room, and his smile beamed.

"Come on over, boys," she encouraged. "You can look at everything up close." She walked Bobby and Junior to each painting, many of ocean dunes, boats in the harbor, pier scenes, or herons and gulls. By the time they made their way to the far side, Bobby was in awe of the other crafts. The woodcarver's work included tiny replicas of gulls, herons, pelicans, and other birds. The metal-work artists' pieces were usually more modern, and Bobby grew bold enough to ask questions about what he was viewing. They made their way to the pottery Oliver had displayed, and the boys were fascinated by the blend of colors in the bowls.

Grant bent to read the artist's information card next to the pottery and "hmphed" as he stood back up. *This was the man Jillian was with the other day.* He said nothing to her, but news of the lunch Jillian had with the new stranger in town had reached his ears.

While Bobby was clearly the one most interested, Junior hovered near Grant as the two of them walked behind Jillian, listening to her explanations as well. Bobby's mouth gaped open as he viewed Lance's perfectly balanced mobiles made from sea glass.

"Have you ever found sea glass on the beach?" Jillian asked him, noting his interest.

He shook his head shyly. "We don't get to the beach much," he replied. "Dad has to work most every day." His face brightened suddenly as he remembered, "We'll get to go on a field trip to the beach this year."

Jillian's heart ached for the little boy who lived so close to the water and rarely got to see it. "Well, sea glass comes from the ocean. It's actually pieces of glass bottles that have been discarded from ships that sail in the bay." Seeing the boys' surprise, she continued. "The glass is broken into tiny pieces that gets tumbled by all the sand and waves before it ends up on shore."

"But they're so smooth," Junior said, leaning closer to inspect the shards, for once moving away from Grant.

"That's because as the waves and sand beat against each little piece, the rough edges get smoothed out. And by the time it washes up on shore, it's a smooth bit of glass."

Holding the boys' attention, she continued, "People can be a lot like sea glass, you know." Seeing their faces upturned toward her, she smiled. "Life can be rough...

just like the waves beating on the glass. But it is from the rough treatment that our edges can be polished out, and we can become as smooth and shiny as what you see here." Squatting down to their level, she held out two pieces of sea glass in her palm.

"Here, take these. Keep them to remember that it is often the difficult times in our lives that shape us into the people we can be."

As the two boys reached out their hands to take a piece of sea glass and hold it reverently in their hands, it was Grant's face that captured her attention as she stood. His normally cavalier manner was replaced by something much more raw, and she cocked her head at him in question.

Blinking rapidly, Grant cleared his throat and said, "Okay, boys, I need to get you back home." His voice, unusually gruff, caught their attention. Junior moved back over to Grant's side with Bobby following much more slowly.

Smiling at the children, Jillian said, "You can come by anytime you want to look at the new work."

The four of them walked back down the stairs and through the empty coffee shop, and she noticed the boys glancing toward the display case of pastries. Smiling, she called a halt to their progress long enough to bag several of the treats and handed them to Junior and Bobby.

Grant watched her, offering a fake pout when she did not hand him one. Rolling her eyes, laughing, she bagged another pastry for him. Handing it over, she felt his fingers linger on her hand, the familiar warmth exuding from their touch.

Grant felt it also, but this time observed the flash of sadness rush through her eyes and longed to take it away. *I've screwed things up with her by pushing her away for so long.* His mind jumped to the sea glass story—one he had heard all his life but had never considered the analogy of the smooth shards to life before. *Leave it to Jillian to teach me something about myself.*

As they reached the door, he told the boys to head on to his SUV and he would join them momentarily. Watching to make sure they stopped at his vehicle, he turned back to the beautiful woman standing in front of him, observing her furrowed brow. The breeze whipped her hair about her head, and he reached out, tucking blonde strands behind her ear and noting her slight shiver at his touch. *She's still affected by me...as much as I am by her. I can make this right...I have to make this right.*

"It was...um...nice of you to bring the boys here," she said, unsure why Grant was standing so close, staring at her.

"They're good kids, and I wanted them to see something beautiful."

"The art is beautiful," she agreed, her gaze lifting to his. "I'm glad they can appreciate it."

His hand slid down her arm, linking his fingers with hers. "It's not the only thing of beauty in here," he said.

The sight of her pinched lips jolted him as she pulled her hand away from his. Before she could back away, he quickly added, "Jillian, thank you for the sea glass story." He watched as she viewed him cautiously, her forehead scrunched adorably as she stared back at him.

Dragging his hand through his hair, making the very front stand up, his breath puffed out. Looking down at his boots for a moment, he lifted his eyes to hers. "Jillian, the truth of the matter is that you make me want to be a better man, and I want you to know that I'm working on it. Kind of like the sea glass."

Reaching back to capture her hand once more, he gave a little tug and rejoiced when she did not jerk it away. "I know I've screwed up. Please don't give up on me. Please give me just one more chance...to prove to you that I can be what you need. I'm getting help dealing with some of the things that happened to me... in the military."

At that, she was visibly startled, her eyebrows raised in surprise. "Grant, I don't know—"

He placed his finger softly on her lips, stilling her words. "Please, Jillian. Just one more chance."

"One more chance for what? To hurt me again? To pull me close just to push me away? No. No," she said, stepping back, needing to put some space between them. Wrapping her arms around her waist protectively, she said, "If you're getting help, that's great, Grant. I'm happy for you, but I told you before...you wanted just friendship, then that's what we can have."

Running his hand through his hair, he whispered, "Is there a chance for more?"

Pressing her lips together in anger, she retorted, "What about Ginny?"

Rearing back, his brows came together. "Ginny? Huh?"

"I saw you two and thought..." she said, now perplexed with his obvious surprise.

Shaking his head, he said, "No, no. She's a fellow officer and Legionnaire. That's all. Honestly, that's all we are."

Searching his face, she knew he was telling the truth. She could always count on Grant to be honest, even if it hurt her feelings.

He took her silence as a good sign and pressed his luck once more. "Please. Go out with me on a date. A real date. I've got evening shifts for a couple of nights, but we can go out on Wednesday night. I'll pick you up at six." He watched her hesitation and held his breath in anticipation.

"I should tell you no," she admitted, but was curious about the help he was getting. Sighing, she knew her heart would always want the best for him. "I'll think about it, Grant," she said, her eyes tormented. "I...I just can't jump in and take another chance."

Disappointed, he swallowed hard, hating the slash of pain he observed in her eyes. *At least she didn't say "no".* Reaching up, he brushed another wisp of hair behind her ear, fighting the desire to pull her in close. "Okay, Jillian, please think about it. Promise?" he pleaded.

Forcing a slight smile, she nodded. "I promise."

Before she could move back further, he leaned

down quickly and planted a kiss on her forehead before he headed toward his SUV where the boys were waiting wide eyed.

Jillian stood rooted to the sidewalk watching them drive away, wondering if she had made the right decision to even consider a date with him.

"I was surprised when you said you wanted to come in this morning," Thomas said, studying Grant as he sat in front of him, his hands tightly clenched.

Grant's gaze was steady as he stared back. "I've been thinking a lot about what we talked about at our last visit, and I don't want to waste any more time."

Thomas let the silence fill the room, giving Grant the chance to speak at his own pace.

"I thought maybe I could take things slow, but the truth is, I need to move forward." Grinning sheepishly, he admitted, "That woman I've been crazy about since we were kids? I'm going to lose her if I don't face what happened."

"You can't rush these things," Thomas warned.

"I know, but I'm ready, and I think the first step is to talk to you about it. Don't know if I'll talk to my friends, but at least I want to talk to you...and then see if I can talk to her."

Settling back in his chair, Thomas smiled encouragingly at Grant. "Okay, I'm listening."

Jillian and Tori sat at a Seafood Shack deck table overlooking the town's harbor, sharing an appetizer and a bottle of wine, relaxing at the end of the day. Jillian presented her with a stack of brochures about Jillian's Coffee Shop and Galleria for Tori to give to the guests at her Sea Glass Inn.

"Oh, these are so pretty! Did you do them yourself?" Tori asked. "I need some updated brochures of my Inn."

Smiling at the compliment, Jillian nodded. "They were simple to design, and then I sent them off to one of the discount printing companies."

As they continued to discuss the brochures, Jillian noticed Grant and Zac walk into the restaurant. The men did not see her, but she had a birds-eye view of them as they approached the bar and sat down.

As usual, it did not take long for the two handsome, single men to attract attention, especially by a couple of bombshell waitresses circling them like sharks. Zac grinned at the blonde closest to him, throwing his head back in laughter as she leaned in, her hand on his arm and her breasts pressed against his bicep. *Yep, encouraging as always.*

Jillian shifted her gaze over to the dark-haired beauty with her hand on Grant's shoulder as her breasts came precariously close to his chest. Instead of laughing, Grant shifted his body away, shirking her hand off him. *Huh?* Jillian leaned back slightly so her view was not obstructed by the other people in the restaurant, and her eyes were not playing tricks on her —Grant was stepping back from the woman's advances.

The waitress gave a little pout along with her shrug and moved on to get the orders. Zac finally disengaged himself from the blonde and the two men sat on the bar stools talking until their take-out order came and they left.

Looking back to Tori, Jillian saw her friend was staring at the men as well, her mouth hanging open.

"Wow," Tori said, looking back to Jillian. "Did I just see what I think I saw?"

Pretending not to know what her friend was talking about, Jillian asked, "What did you see?"

"Oh, come on, dearie," Tori smiled. "I saw you eagle-eye Grant from the moment he walked in." Leaning back in her chair, tossing her long, red hair over her shoulder, she softened her voice. "I admit, I was afraid he was going to flirt and hook up right here, and I hated that for you." Looking back toward the restaurant where the men had stood, she added, "But he never looked at her. I wonder…"

"You wonder what?"

Shrugging, Tori's lips curved slightly. "I know Mitch has mentioned Grant seeming to be more focused lately. I guess everyone has to finally grow up some-time." She reached down to grab another nacho and pop it into her mouth, leaving Jillian to wonder what Grant was up to.

Drop-everything-we've-got-to-talk. The call had made its rounds and now the girls grabbed their plates loaded with sandwiches and chips in Jillian's sun-filled yellow and green kitchen. The all-night gab sessions that began when they were children at sleepovers and continued when they were teenagers had developed into weekly get-togethers. The core group of Jillian, Tori, and Katelyn had now expanded to include Belle and Jade. Today was not on their schedule, but one phone call brought them all together on Jillian's patio.

A circle of comfortable wicker chairs and a settee, all with floral seat cushions, graced her brick patio. Pots of flowers in full bloom sat around the edge and a tall tree provided shade.

Plopping into one of the chairs, Katelyn took a bite of her sandwich and, barely chewing, said, "Spill it."

Jillian's mouth was poised over her sandwich but halted in its path. Her eyes cut to her best friend and her brow crinkled with irritation. "Can't I even take a bite first?"

Chewing, Katelyn shook her head, unable to speak until she swallowed. "Nope. Rules say, you call a special meeting then you need to start talking."

Belle looked over, wide-eyed. "Rules? We have rules?"

"Yeah. The person who needs the meeting can't keep the rest of us waiting, and no calorie counting. We talk, we eat, we drink. Those are the three rules." Katelyn stated firmly.

Tori laughed seeing Belle's big-eyed stare and patted her hand. "Not real rules, Belle. Just...well, you know...um..."

"Oh, for crying out loud!" Jillian said, tossing her

food back onto her plate and setting it to the side. "Okay, here goes." Pursing her lips, she said, "Grant asked me out on a date. I told him no, but then he said he was getting some help with things that happened when he was in the service, so I told him I would think about it." Whatever she expected their reaction to be, she was stunned when no one said anything. Tori leaned back in her chair, a smile on her face. Belle appeared genuinely pleased and Jade, the newcomer to the group, eyed the other women looking for a clue as to how she should react.

Katelyn took a long sip of her lemonade, washing down the bite, before setting the glass on the arm of her chair, its condensation dripping onto the wood. She turned her gaze toward Jillian and stared long and hard at her friend.

"Come on, say something," Jillian begged. "Tell me I'm stupid for even considering giving him one more chance. Or tell me you think it's great. Tell me anything."

Tori, Belle, and Jade instinctively knew the conversation might include all of them, but the undercurrent of heavy emotion ran between Jillian and Katelyn.

After a long, uncomfortable moment of silence, just when Jillian was beginning to think her best friend was never going to speak, Katelyn blinked rapidly to hold back tears.

Sucking in a breath, Katelyn said, "We may have only been in high school, but I loved Philip."

The others sat in stone silence, their food abandoned on their plates. Jillian's face softened as she leaned forward, placing her hand on Katelyn's arm. "Oh, honey," she whispered.

"No, no, I'm all right," Katelyn assured, sighing heavily. "But we didn't get our chance to see if what we had would make it in the adult world." She shifted her gaze over Jillian's shoulder, her eyes glazed with memories. Clearing her throat, she turned back to look at her closest friend. "He may not have come back from the war, but he wasn't the only one affected. I see it in Aiden and Brogan. I love my brothers, but they both have scars deep inside. They deal with it in different ways, but the emotional scars are there."

Tori nodded slowly and Jillian knew that Mitch, though he seemed to have come back unscathed from his tours, bore his own inner wounds. Her eyes shifted back to Katelyn's, as she continued.

"I wanted Grant to come home to you just like I wanted Philip to come home to me." Sighing, Katelyn said, "But when Grant returned and acted like the two of you weren't an item, it pissed me off. He left again to live and work in Virginia Beach, but then when he came back, I thought he was ready to settle down. But I've watched him hold you at arm's length for all that time as he seemed to go for anything and everything around! And now? Now he wants to come back?"

Jillian winced and dropped her head. *She thinks I'm a fool. She thinks I'm setting myself up for more heartache.* A hand landed on her arm, giving a little squeeze, and she lifted her eyes back to Katelyn's as her friend continued.

"But honey, I'm starting to see a different Grant.

Hell, I'm starting to see a difference in all of them. Maybe the American Legion meetings and activities are helping our boys work through whatever they had to deal with."

Holding her breath, Jillian asked, "So what are you saying?"

Katelyn's lips curved slowly into a small smile as she squeezed Jillian's arm once again. "Sweetie, I'm saying that maybe now Grant is ready for whatever you two are going to become."

"So, you don't think I'm crazy for going out with him? Opening myself up for possible heartache?"

"Girl, the only thing that's crazy is not following your heart. I see that now," Katelyn added.

The evening stars dotted the dark sky as the surf reflected the moonlight. Alone, Jillian sat on the sand of the town beach, watching the waves washing up on the shore. This spot was hers, claimed since she was a teenager slipping out to sit on the beach until her curfew. Enjoying the solitude as her mind wandered, she was startled when her phone vibrated.

Checking the caller first, she smiled as she answered, "Hey, mom."

"Hi darling, how are you?"

"I'm fine. How's your trip?"

"New England is beautiful, but we'll be glad to get home in a few weeks. Your father is chomping at the bit to go fishing off the pier this time of year."

"That's nice," Jillian commented.

"Hmmm, you sound distracted. What are you doing?"

"Just hanging out at the beach."

"Oh, I know what that means," her mom replied. "What's going on?" Hearing the silence, she continued, "Come on, Jillian. You sit and watch the waves at night when you have things on your mind. It used to worry me to death, until I finally realized it was what you needed. So, what's got you down at the beach this late?"

Chuckling, Jillian said, "You think you know me so well?"

"It's a mom thing. Just go with it."

"Grant asked me to go on a date," Jillian confessed. "And I keep wondering if I'm just opening myself up to more heartache giving him another chance."

The silence crept through the phone waves for a minute before her mom said, "I wish I could tell you that he won't break your heart again, baby, but only you can decide if the risk is worth it."

"You know the feeling of wanting something so bad you think you can't breathe without it? And yet you know it'll never be yours? Well, that's how I've felt for so long and now, I guess I'm scared. He said that he's getting help with some things that happened when he was overseas. I don't know, mom, but it seems to be making a difference."

"Oh, Jillian, you're going to have to ask yourself which is better—guarding your heart or taking the risk and possibly finding the one you've always needed. There's no right or wrong here. Only you can decide."

With vows of love and goodbyes, Jillian disconnected. Sighing heavily, she watched as a few night birds flew over the water, heading off to roost as ghost crabs came out to scamper on the beach. *Guarding my heart...or taking a risk?* As the moon rose higher in the sky, she stood and shook out her blanket. With a small smile, she turned to walk back to her house, her decision made.

Looking down at her cell phone, she punched in Grant's number. He picked it up on the second ring. Before he had a chance to speak, she blurted, "Okay Grant, I'll go out to dinner with you, but as friends...no date. Just two friends going out."

Silence on the other end of the line greeted her, and she wondered if he were there until she heard a loud sigh.

"Oh, Jillian, thank you, thank you," Grant enthused. "I promise I'll prove to you that you'll never regret giving me this chance."

"O...kay," she replied. "Well, um...I'll see you on Wednesday." Disconnecting, her heart pounded. In fear or anticipation? She had no idea.

Grant stood and looked at the silent phone still in his hand and sucked in a deep breath. Smiling, relief speared through him. *This is my chance. This one I won't screw up.*

8

Grant looked at the clock on the dashboard of the police vehicle and groaned out loud. The timing of the traffic stop could not be worse; he fired off a quick text to Jillian letting her know he was running late due to work. *Hopefully, she'll understand.*

Pulling up behind Burt's police SUV stopped on the side of the main road leading from town, he walked over, eying his fellow officer who had the vehicle's driver standing to the side. The man was arguing loudly, causing Grant's suspicions to rise.

"Check the front seat," Burt said to Grant.

Walking over, Grant peered inside, seeing a gun lying on the passenger seat, partially hidden by a plastic grocery sack. *Yeah, a routine traffic stop for speeding just got a whole lot more interesting.*

As Burt handcuffed the driver, Grant began the search. It did not take long to discover the packets of white powder hidden poorly. *Is this guy stupid, or what?*

Several bags of the powder were wrapped in more plastic grocery bags and sitting in the back seat.

Opening one of the bags, he used his test kit, quickly seeing the change in color on the test strip, indicating meth. Looking over toward Burt, he called out, "Positive for methamphetamine."

Bagging the evidence and calling for assistance from the state police, Grant watched as Burt took the driver into custody, placing him in his vehicle. The state police arrived and assisted Grant with the scene. Impounding the car, Grant had to wait for the tow truck to arrive.

Seeing Jason drive up, Grant grinned. "Didn't know you'd take the job," he greeted.

"Well, seeing as it's the only garage in town and still short-handed, looks like you got me."

Grant watched as the large man hooked up the suspect's vehicle to his tow truck as quickly as possible and, with a wave, Grant was finally able to leave the scene. Sighing heavily, he glanced at the evidence bags in the back seat. *Now, time to process and write up reports. Damn...*

Two hours later, he was just finishing when Mitch popped around the corner. "You 'bout done?"

"Yeah. The evidence is locked up, and I'm just finishing the report now. Burt'll do the traffic report, and I've got the drugs and weapons."

Nodding, Mitch replied, "Good work. I'm heading out, and Mildred's just left. See you tomorrow." Grinning, he said, "And by the way, you've got a visitor. Since you're almost done, I'll let 'em come on back."

Curious about his visitor, his lips curved into a huge grin as he spied Jillian walking around the corner, a picnic basket in her hand. "What's this?"

"Since you couldn't come to dinner, I thought I'd bring dinner to you."

Holding up the report on his desk, he grinned, "Perfect timing. I just finished the report, so we don't have to eat here." Glancing at her basket, he said, "I had planned on wining and dining you, but I don't want that to go to waste."

Her smile was replaced with a serious look as she replied, "I don't want to be wined and dined, Grant. I don't need that."

Standing, he walked around the desk, stopping only when his boots were directly in front of her shoes. Looking down at her upturned face, he reached for the basket. "Then let's go on a picnic."

Meeting his grin, she nodded as she walked beside him, leaving the station. She felt his hand resting on the small of her back as he guided her through the parking lot. Each fingertip burned through her lightweight sweater, and she missed the heat as they reached his Jeep, and his hand left her back to reach for the door.

He hated that he did not have a chance to go home for a shower and change clothes before their date. She appeared fresh in her lacy, pink top and white capris, showing off her tanned legs, and blue sandals with her pink-painted toenails peeking out.

Opening the back door to his SUV, he placed the basket carefully onto the floor to protect the contents.

As he turned, she was reaching for the passenger door, but he quickly reached it before she did. Offering her a hand up, he settled her into the seat. "Buckle up," he ordered gently before closing her door and circling the front to climb into the driver's seat.

"Where are we going?" she asked, as he drove out of town.

Grinning, he replied, "Got a special place." Leaving her in suspense, he took several back roads after they left the main street leading out of town.

Fifteen minutes later, they arrived at the end of a sandy jeep path, pine trees and sea grass dotting the dunes. He grabbed the picnic basket from the back seat before taking her hand and leading her toward the beach. Grinning, Jillian said, "I've lived here my whole life and haven't seen this spot!"

Settling a blanket on the sand before placing the basket on top, he said, "I never knew about it as a kid. I found it when I got back from the Army. I come here sometimes to...be alone."

The thought of him bringing some of his dates here for privacy flew through her mind, but before she could wonder too much, he added, "I've never shared this place with anyone...not even my friends."

Shocked, she tried to hide her smile, but it came out anyway. "Well, then I'm honored."

Sitting on the blanket, he reached up and took her hand, gently pulling her down next to him. "Jillian, you're more than a special friend."

Putting her hand on his chest, pushing slightly, she shook her head. "Grant, you can't play me like this.

We're here as friends. Don't say things like that and then turn around and—"

"No, no," he protested. "I won't."

She observed his expression, seeing nothing but sincerity in his eyes. "You're confusing the hell out of me," she complained. "Let's be honest, you started this only after seeing me with other guys. How do I know you're not just trying to keep me from moving on?"

Dropping his chin to his chest for a moment, he sucked in a huge breath before letting it out slowly. Lifting his gaze back to hers, he said, "Because I don't want you to move on." Seeing her eyes narrow, he quickly added, "Because I only want you to move on with me."

She said nothing, but her heart pounded so hard she was sure he could hear it over the sound of the surf.

He slid his hand from hers, up her arm to cup the back of her neck. His thumb brushed over her silky cheek, watching the blush underneath his finger.

"I'm scared," she whispered.

"Don't be, baby. I know I've done nothing but make you doubt me, but I promise, no more doubts." Seeing her face filled with cautious optimism, he grinned, battling the desire to pull her in ever so slightly to taste the lips he wanted to explore. *Not now...don't rush this.* Letting his hand drop, he twisted his body around to grab the basket. "So, what do we have?"

She missed the warmth of his hand, blinking at the realization she had hoped he would kiss her. Speaking brighter than she felt, she forced a smile, saying, "Okay, we've got some of Katelyn's fried chicken, Tori's potato salad, and my brownies."

"Wow, you enlisted everyone," he laughed as she set the food out onto the blanket.

Shrugging, she replied, "I know how to bake, but my cooking leaves a lot to be desired. Lucky for you, I do know how to utilize my resources."

As he smiled at her explanation, she sat with her legs crossed and her feet tucked underneath her, placing her plate in her lap. Watching as he piled food on her plate, she protested, "I can't eat that much. Everything on this plate will go straight to my hips."

"Works for me," he quipped and added another spoonful of potato salad to her plate. He moved over to peek into the basket and grinned as he pulled out a bottle of wine.

Their conversation remained easy as they ate, the evening shade of the trees near the beach creating a cocoon of privacy. The tide was leaving and Jillian said, "We could walk and look for sea glass after we eat."

His heart became lighter with each minute that Jillian appeared open to him, making him smile. "I can't think of anything I'd like better."

Half an hour later, Jillian bent for what seemed the millionth time to pluck a piece of sea glass from the sand. Grant watched her youthful enthusiasm, wondering how he had ignored it for the past several years. As the sun set behind her the wind caught her braid, whipping it over her shoulder as the loose tendrils danced about her face. The white capris showed off her long, tanned legs and whenever she would bend over, a sliver of smooth skin would peek out above her waistband, drawing his gaze. As she scooped up another one, she twisted around, holding out her palm, showing the bright blue piece.

"Look at this!" she exclaimed. "This beach is great!"

As they continued their walk, he reached over to clasp her hand. He noticed she glanced down at their connection, biting her lip. If she was surprised, at least she did not pull away. The silence between them was only broken by the gentle bayside surf and the occasional sound of gulls calling.

After a few minutes, Jillian peeked to the side, taking in the profile of the man whose face she had watched change from boy to man. Sighing, she looked down at her feet, digging her toes into the sand. Feeling the squeeze of his hand on hers, she looked back up, a question in her eyes.

"What are you thinking?" he asked, his stomach clenching with trepidation.

"Honestly?" She held his gaze, and said, "You have me completely confused. I want to know what's going through your mind. About us. About the past years and now the past couple of days. You told me you weren't good for me, and I don't even know what that means, but it makes me wonder how you suddenly think you are now." She stopped walking and turned toward him, their clasped hands between them. "I need to understand, Grant...if I can trust you."

He looked beyond her toward the woods for a moment, his breath catching in his throat. He thought about his last counseling session and Thomas' words came back to him. *"You have to be honest with yourself first and then honest with those you may have hurt. Then, and only then, can you move forward and learn to give into the fear of love."*

"The fear of love," he whispered, his eyes moving from over her shoulder to her face.

She observed him closely, not sure she heard correctly, but the warm look on his face held her attention.

Sighing, he replied, "I thought I was ready for the military when I left here after high school, but it... things were a lot harder than I expected. I liked it... liked the camaraderie...a lot like being here with the guys. But when you get close to someone and if... when...something happens, it can really mess with your mind."

Jillian had no idea what he was referring to, but sucked in her lips as she watched him struggle with the words.

"I'm not ready to go into the details, but what happened over there affected me and when I came back, I pulled away from you. I even tried to put distance between us when I took the job in Virginia Beach but, well, I guess Baytown always called to me to come back." He held her eyes, lifting his hand to cup her cheek. His rough thumb grazed her soft skin again and a small smile played about his lips. "I guess I'm not really answering your concern, am I?"

"You don't have to tell me anything you don't want to," she replied softly, realizing the reasons behind her friend-zone freeze had been more profound than she anticipated. "We can um...just take things as they come—"

"No!" he rushed, his thumb still caressing, but his gaze jumping between her eyes. "I want to move forward. I'm not content to sit back and just think that one day I'll get my shit together only to find out that you've moved on."

The six years since Grant had returned from the military flashed through her mind, a wince of pain slashing across her face. Her gaze held his as she saw, for the first time, the look of fear in his eyes. *He was always just Grant...my cocky Grant. I never understood there was something painful he was hiding.* No words were spoken for a long moment as she pondered what he was asking. *He wants me to be patient. He wants me to trust him. He wants me to put my broken heart aside and give him just one more chance.*

Reaching up, she placed her hand on his shoulder for balance as she lifted up on her toes. Leaning in, smiling at his wide-eyed surprise, she kissed him. Soft and gentle, the barest brush of lips. As she settled back on her feet, his hands on her waist, steadying her, he let out a sigh of relief before breaking into a smile. The smile that captured her heart, many years before.

The drive home was silent, but comfortable. The huge, full moon hung over the bay, its reflection shimmering on the undulating surf, sparkling like diamonds. He reached over the console and linked his fingers with hers, gaining a smile.

Pulling into her driveway, he wished the drive had taken longer, unwilling to give up her company. But he knew, the time was not right. *If I go in, I won't come out until the morning, and she deserves a man who's ready to give her everything.* Her soft voice broke through his thoughts.

"Do you want to come in for a while?"

Giving her a wistful smile, he silently let go of her fingers to alight from the jeep, walking around to open her door. Linking fingers once more, he walked her up the steps onto the Victorian porch. Stopping at the front door, he halted her hand as it reached for the keys.

"I'd love to come in, Jillian, but I'm not going to... tonight." He watched her head tilt to the side in silent questioning and, lifting his hand to cup her face, he continued, "You deserve a man who can give you everything and that includes all of himself. I'm working on it. I promise. But we're...I'm...not there yet."

Jillian, rooted to the porch, her heart pounding in her chest, stared at his face. His expression, a mixture of eagerness and uncertainty. Her lips curved into a smile as her fingers clutched his shirt, pulling him closer. Licking her lips, she noted his eyes drop to her mouth and her grin widened. "You know I want you, Grant. It would be foolish for me to pretend otherwise." Her smile slowly faded as she added, "But you're right. I know we need to take things one step at a time."

Holding her closely, his thumbs caressing her silken cheeks, he lowered his lips to hers. Moving his mouth over hers, he reveled in the petal soft texture mixed with the delicious taste of chocolate and wine. Licking her lips, he took advantage as she opened her mouth to groan. Swallowing her slight noises, he plunged his tongue in, immediately taking the kiss from sweet to white hot.

She clutched his shirt tighter, pulling up on her toes as she tried to draw him closer. Sucking his tongue deeper into her mouth, she felt his chest growl against her fingers, the noise jolting straight to her sex. Dropping one hand to her waist, he pulled her tightly into his body, his crotch pressing into her stomach.

Noses bumping as they angled their heads back and forth, each tried to find the perfect alignment for maximum contact. Gasping, clawing, climbing. They finally pulled apart, their expressions wild and stormy.

Her chest heaved as he touched his forehead to hers, both stunned by the force of their contact.

"Well," he said, clearing his throat. "I...uh..." Unable to think of anything to say, he closed his eyes, breathing her in.

"Yeah," she whispered, unwilling to take her gaze off of him. Finally, she slid her head to the side and laid her cheek on his pounding heartbeat, her hand circling his waist.

He rested his chin on the top of her head, his mind whirling. He remembered as teenagers they had been able to go at it like weasels, once he had finally gotten the nerve up to ask her out. With her cousin being his best friend, it had taken a lot for Mitch to finally not threaten to beat him up for asking her out. *But then, Mitch never knew we lost our virginity to each other in the back seat of my dad's old pick-up truck! I wonder if she remembers—*

"Do you remember your dad's truck?" she whispered, her face still tucked against his chest.

Grinning into her hair, he chuckled. "I was just thinking the same thing," he confessed.

Jillian wanted to look into his face, but blushing, she kept her head down. Having other ideas, Grant lifted her chin with his fingers, peering into her blue eyes. Seeing the emotions swirling in their depths, he said, "I remember everything about you."

Sucking in a shaky breath, Jillian nodded. "Me too."

They stood for a moment, the night's dark silence cloaking them from the rest of the world. Their gazes held as sorrows remembered and promises made, all with a look, were shared between them.

Stepping inside, she locked the door and turned out the lights as she made her way up the stairs to her bedroom. Walking over to the bright green curtains, she pulled one panel back and peeked outside. She watched as he backed out of her driveway, her eyes following him until his taillights were no longer in sight. Sighing heavily, she dropped the curtain as she turned around, facing her room. As she eyed her bed, it appeared lonelier than ever.

9

"When you gonna let me outta this dump?"

Ginny passed Grant in the hall outside of the holding cell, her eyes rolling as she shook her head. "Your turn. I've listened to his mouth all morning."

"He give us anything on who he's working for?"

"Nope, but says he's got some big-shot lawyer coming to get him out."

Grant's gaze jumped back to hers as he asked, "Bail set?"

Ginny grinned mischievously and replied, "Mitch talked to the DA this morning. She says the judge will deny bail since Isaac, in there, is a flight risk."

"Hell yeah. That, and the fact he had over a hundred thousand dollars worth of meth in his car."

"Chief Freeman will be down to pick him up later. She'll take him to the county courthouse."

A loud voice carried through the station again. "Where the hell's my lawyer?"

With a wry grin, Ginny patted Grant's arm before heading down the hall. "Like I said, it's your turn."

Grant watched her walk out of the station then turned to head into Mitch's office, seeing the Chief sitting behind his desk. "You have to listen to that guy all morning too?"

Mitch's angry glare was his answer. Before Grant could respond, Mildred stepped into the office. "Chief? The prisoner's lawyer is here."

Grant and Mitch shared an eye-brow lift before they both turned and headed to the small conference room. Inside, a short, slightly-balding man in a brown suit sat, his briefcase open in front of him on the table. Before they had a chance to introduce themselves, he peered at them over his glasses and began talking.

"Officers, I'm here on behalf of my client, Isaac Canton. I have the paperwork to make his bail as soon as the judge sets it." He pushed several papers toward them, his lips turned down in a bored expression.

"And you are?" Mitch asked, still standing with his arms folded across his chest, his glare matching Grant's.

Narrowing his eyes, the man said, "I assumed the receptionist told you who I was. I'm Stanley Martino. Attorney for Isaac Canton." He pulled out a business card and pushed it across the table toward them.

Mitch and Grant sat down, both silently observing Stanley. The only sound heard was the ticking of the old clock on the wall behind them and the lawyer began to squirm slightly. "Gentlemen—" he began.

"Isaac seems to be a rather low-on-the-totem-pole

kind of drug carrier," Grant observed. "How did he come by your services?"

Bristling, Stanley retorted, "Everyone's considered innocent until proven guilty, officer. I'm sure you're aware of the right of each citizen—"

"How'd he get your number?" Mitch cut in, glancing down at the card. "Says your office is in Baltimore. That was a nice little drive for you this morning. Coming all the way down here for your client." He hesitated before adding, "Unless he already had you on retainer. Or did his supplier?"

Standing, Stanley scowled at both men before saying, "I have nothing to say to you other than I'd like to see my client."

Silence filled the small room for a moment, before Mitch turned to Grant. "Would you show Mr. Martino to the holding cell area?"

Grant shoved his chair back, the metal legs screeching over the tile floor. "Right this way," he said, before turning and moving out of the room. A few minutes later he walked back into Mitch's office, closing the door behind him.

Mitch's lips were pressed tightly as though not trusting what would come out. Grant talked for the both of them. "I don't like it. Isaac's got connections with that much meth in his car, and Stanley just happens to show up."

"I'm gonna have Gareth dig into the lawyer, see what his background is."

Grant hesitated for an instant before admitting, "I was going to see him today anyway. I'll talk to Gareth if you'd like." Seeing Mitch's eyebrow raise, he slumped into the chair in front of the desk and said, "I was going to have him take a look into the new potter that's sniffing around Jillian."

Chuckling, Mitch said, "And just what are you hoping to find? A counterfeit potter?"

Blushing, Grant shook his head. "I don't know, maybe something unsavory? Like he's got a bunch of women or didn't pay his taxes. Oh, hell." Blowing out a puff of air, he confessed, "He's suave and I could see him trying to turn her head."

"And you think you'll pale in comparison?"

At that, Grant ground his teeth in frustration, sucking in a quick breath through his nose. Before he could reply, Mitch just shook his head and said, "Go on, but do me a favor. Tell Gareth to look into Stanley first."

"Sure thing," Grant nodded, relieved to have the conversation over with. He felt foolish enough without Mitch's ragging on him.

Twenty minutes later Grant sat inside Harrison Investigations with Gareth in his small conference room. He noticed the front reception area had a desk, but no receptionist. Gareth scribbled the information about the lawyer on his yellow legal pad. "I'm assuming you guys ran a check?"

"Yeah, but the lawyer is clean from what we can tell in our database. It's just too slick that a low-life drug runner has that kind of attorney on speed-dial."

"Unless?"

"Unless the drug runner is not so low-life or the

attorney is on retainer for whoever is in charge of running the operation," Grant finished.

"Okay, I'll see what I can dig up on the lawyer while you all work on Isaac Canton." Gareth started to close his pad of paper when he noted Grant shifting in his seat uncomfortably. "You got something else for me?"

Looking Gareth in the eyes, Grant nodded. "Yeah, and this is on me, not the department."

Lifting his eyebrows, Gareth said nothing as he opened his pad to a clean sheet of paper. "Okay, whatcha need?"

Rubbing his chin for a moment, he pulled out a folded piece of paper from his pocket and slid it toward Gareth, who took it from him. Unfolding it, Gareth stared at the name written before lifting his gaze back to Grant.

"You want me to check out this person? Oliver Dobson?"

"Yeah. He's got a pottery place just north of here and I'd like to know more about him."

Nodding slowly, Gareth wrote the name and address down on his pad before looking backup. "You want the usual background or you looking for something in particular?"

"Just the usual," Grant said, his gaze dropping to the table as he worked his mouth to the side as though tasting something sour. "I...well, he's going to be working closely with Jillian and I'd rather...uh...make sure about him."

Gareth watched Grant's unusual demeanor

crumble as he talked about Jillian. Smiling, he replied, "No problem. I'll check him out and get back with you."

Standing, Grant nodded and walked to the door before turning back and adding, "And...uh...I'm assuming Jillian won't know about this, right?"

"You're the client," Gareth said. "Total confidentiality."

"Thanks, man. Work on the slimy lawyer first and then you can work on this."

"Shouldn't take too long for either," Gareth said, walking him to the front door.

Grant stepped back out on the sidewalk, rubbing his chin again. He felt a pang of guilt, going behind Jillian's back to check on one of her clients, but had to admit that he also saw the man as a possible competitor. *It'll be fine. What she doesn't know, won't hurt us.*

"How's it going in there?" Oliver asked, calling into the studio workshop.

"Fine, Mr. Dobson," the young woman's voice answered. "I'm almost ready for the final firing but would like you to check it out first."

Oliver walked into the room, seeing two potters bent over their clay splattered wheels and one standing next to the kiln, holding an exquisite vase. With a smile and a nod toward the two, he headed to the kiln, his gaze on the colors and design. "Aubrey, that's wonderful. You've added the layers to look like a sunset over the water."

She beamed up at him and nodded. "This was my fourth attempt, but I think I've finally figured out what I like."

"I saw your little camper out there," Oliver said, "Are you staying for a bit?"

"Yeah, if you don't mind. It saves me from traveling back and forth, as long as you don't have a problem with me camping out nearby."

"It's fine with me," he replied, smiling.

The older man sitting at the potter's wheel looked up and asked, "Are we going to be able to show our work with the galleria in Baytown?"

Clapping his hands before rubbing them together, Oliver's face split into a grin. "Yes. The owner's name is Jillian Evans, and she has a perfect little place for our work. A coffee shop downstairs and a local artists' galleria upstairs. The building is an old, restored store and is beautiful. And, as I was hoping, she'll be handling the shipping of our pieces to wherever we sell them."

Aubrey crinkled her nose as she glanced over her shoulder toward Oliver. "I've been handling my own shipping, so it'll be nice to have someone else do that. I'm also thrilled to have a place to show my work, but will anyone but some locals and tourists see it?"

"Ms. Evans has plans to have some extra showings, like a wine and cheese night. She will invite some people from the larger Virginia Beach area as well as from Maryland. It'll be nice exposure. Plus, she said she had a few other ideas to showcase the work."

Walking from the studio into his office, he gratefully took off his coat and tie. Settling into the chair behind his small, cluttered desk, he pulled out Jillian's business card. Dialing as he smiled, he called her number.

"Jillian's Coffee Shop and Galleria," she answered.

"Jillian? It's Oliver."

"Hi!" she greeted enthusiastically. "What's up?"

"I told the artists who are interning with me about your shop and, well, I was thinking about you and wondered if you had any interest in seeing our work here?"

"Come to your studio? Oh, I'd love to! When were you thinking?"

"How about tomorrow? I'll be here all day, so it really wouldn't matter when."

"The breakfast rush is over by ten a.m., so I could easily get away after that. So why don't we say eleven-thirty, just to be safe."

Grinning into the phone, Oliver agreed. "Tell you what, after you see the studio, I'll take you to lunch."

"Um...okay. I'll see you tomorrow."

Standing, he continued to smile as he changed into his work clothes, tying an apron around his waist before heading into the studio.

———

As Grant walked toward the police station, he noticed Stanley climbing into his car and backing out of the parking lot. Stepping inside, Grant witnessed the normally unflappable Mildred grumbling about the "insufferable, rude, obnoxious" attorney.

Passing her by, he headed back to Mitch's office. "How did it go?" he asked.

Mitch's irritation was as fierce as Mildred's, but he held onto his temper. "Says his client borrowed the car and had no idea the drugs were in it."

"When I ran the tags, it was registered to him, so how the hell is he saying the car was not his?"

"Claims he sold the car a couple of days ago to a someone on Craig's list but was able to borrow it back yesterday to make a trip to see his sick brother in Virginia Beach."

Grant's eyebrows raised as he barked, "So, how stupid of a criminal are we dealing with? When Burt pulled him over, he had the gun in plain sight. Did the lawyer have anything to say about that?"

Shaking his head, Mitch rubbed his hand through his short hair. "I tuned him out after the first minute. Anyway, I told him the hearing was tomorrow, and he could present his side to the judge then. But," he grinned, "I've talked to the DA, and she's raring to go on him. Says the judge will go along with what her recommendations are as well."

"Good," Grant sighed, relaxing his stance. "But don't you figure Isaac is a small fry? Can we figure out who he's running drugs for?"

"I'm working with the state police and the other Chiefs on that," Mitch confirmed. "I'm convinced Isaac is just a runner and, while the kingpin isn't around here, I don't want them using our city as a thoroughfare for their drugs."

Nodding his agreement, Grant tapped the door-frame twice and said, "I'm getting ready to head out on patrol. Catch you later."

After checking the public beach, he was driving down Main Street when he saw Bobby and Junior coming out of Jillian's shop. She was standing on the sidewalk, still talking to the two boys, as he drove up and parked.

Climbing out of the SUV, he grinned as the two boys ran over to greet him. "Hey guys, what're you two doing down here?"

Junior ducked his head and said, "Bobby wanted to come see if Miss Jillian had more art, so I came along to keep an eye on him."

"You wanted to come too," Bobby protested, his innocent face turned toward his brother in surprise.

Quickly stepping in, Jillian said, "Well, it was a treat to see both of you." She smiled at them before lifting her gaze up to Grant. "I told them that if they wanted to earn a little money, they could help me out sometimes after school."

Grant flashed a look of gratitude toward her, admiring the way the sunlight glistened off her blonde hair flowing down her back with only a sparkly head-band holding it away from her face.

Junior tapped Bobby on the shoulder and said, "Come on, we've got to get home."

Both Grant and Jillian looked down sharply at the two boys. "I thought your dad dropped you off. How did you get here?" she asked, her eyes narrowed in concern.

"Naw, we got the bus driver to bring us here." Junior reached inside his backpack and pulled out his cell phone, saying, "But it's okay. Dad knows we came here."

"Boys, go hop in the SUV, and I'll take you home. It's way too far for you to walk."

The two boys looked up at Grant, huge smiles on their faces, before they called out goodbyes to Jillian and ran down the sidewalk.

Grant turned back to her, one hand on his hip, and said, "I was stopping by anyway to see if you wanted to do something tomorrow. I'm off during the day and only have the evening shift, so I thought we could have lunch or something."

Jillian looked at his eager face and could not believe the poor timing. *Good grief, I've wanted Grant to ask me out for years and now I already have plans.* The thought jumped into her mind to call Oliver to reschedule, but she quickly dismissed it. *Nope, this is business.*

Sucking in her lips, she answered, "I'm so sorry, but I can't. I've got plans. I'm driving up north tomorrow."

Blinking rapidly, Grant reared back slightly. "Up north?"

"Yeah, I'm...uh...well, Oliver invited me to see his studio." She watched in fascination as Grant's face morphed from eager anticipation to confusion to anger —all in a few seconds time.

"Oliver?" He wanted to protest but could not think of anything to say that would not make him look like a jerk. Before he could respond more, Jillian continued.

"It's just a business meeting. He thought I might like to see his studio and some of the interns that will be supplying artwork."

Slowly digesting this information as he attempted to tamp down the rush of jealousy, he said, "Oh, so there'll be others around."

Laughing, Jillian said, "Yes. I get to see where he and his students create their work. I'll be going up tomorrow morning."

"Well, then you should be back in time for us to have a late lunch," he prodded.

Biting her lip, she hesitated before adding, "Well, he asked me to lunch after the tour."

A flash of jealousy reared its angry head, but he worked to hide it. "Okay, well then I guess I'll talk to you when you get back." Leaning over, he kissed her lips. He meant to only brush against hers, but the instant their lips touched, a flame sparked, and he snaked his arms around her waist, pulling her closer. It took all his willpower not to take the kiss into erotic territory, fighting the desire to plaster her body tightly to his. Finally, he pulled back slightly and smirked at her flushed cheeks, plump swollen lips, and lust-filled eyes. Grinning, he knew it was a Neanderthal move to claim this power over her, but seeing her acquiescence made him want to thump his chest.

Before he had a chance to revel in that experience, she gave him a slight slap on his chest instead. "Just what are you smiling about?" she asked. "You look like a caveman who's about to drag me off to his lair."

Throwing his head back in laughter, he squeezed

her waist. "Busted," he admitted. "I can't help it, Jillian. I felt like I just got my head out of my ass when it comes to you, and now you're having lunch with someone else."

"It's just business," she protested. Sliding her eyes upward, she added, "Kind of like when you're with Ginny. There's nothing there, so it's just business."

"No way," he countered sternly. "Ginny and I are partners, neither has any interest in the other. But *Oliver*? I think he has a very personal interest in you!"

Reaching up, she cupped his strong jaw with her hands and brought his mouth back down to hers. With a gentle kiss, she said, "No, he doesn't. But don't worry, there's really only ever been you."

The feel of her fingers on his face, the gentle touch of her lips on his, and her soft confession warmed his heart while bringing a fresh wave of guilt that he had spent so long pushing her away. Mitch's words came back to haunt him. *I have hurt her.* Sighing, he jolted when she brushed her lips once more against his.

"Grant, stop it. No going back. From now on, we move forward."

Smiling down at her, he could not agree more.

10

The fuchsia blooms of the crepe myrtle trees were vibrant against the green leaves and the brilliant blue sky. Jillian smiled in appreciation of the colorful early fall as she drove along the main highway that cut straight through the Eastern Shore from the southern tip in Virginia north into Maryland. Farmland bordered both sides of the road while crepe myrtle trees lined the edges. Winding her way through another small town, she came to a gravel driveway, the name on the mailbox stating *Dobson Pottery*.

At the end of the drive an old building sat, paint peeling off the sides. A large, sliding door was partially open in front, so she parked her car on the gravel near the entrance. Alighting, she smiled as Oliver stepped out to greet her. She noted his relaxed stance in what must be his work clothes—stained cargo pants, long-sleeved T-shirt, and muddy work boots. He was just pulling off a thick cotton apron, wiping his hands, as he approached.

"Hey, did you have any trouble finding us?" he asked, reaching out to shake her hand.

"No, no, your directions were perfect." Smiling as she looked around, she said, "This place is bigger than I thought it would be."

Shrugging, he explained, "I got a good deal. I needed a place to bring the kilns, which take up a lot of space. An old garage or barn would have been great, but it was hard to find just that without having to buy a lot of land. I found this place and spent several months setting it up."

"I can't wait to see it," she exclaimed, following him inside. As her eyes adjusted to the interior light, she saw four pottery wheels, three with people working at them.

"Let me introduce you to my interns," he said. "Aubrey and Jonas are from the University of Maryland's Art School and Mike is a potter who rents my space and use of my kilns. Guys, this is Jillian. She will be showcasing our work and handling shipping from now on."

Aubrey looked up and smiled as her hands continued to work the clay, the soothing motion creating what appeared to be a large vase. "Nice to meet you, Jillian," she called out before turning her concentration back to the wheel.

Jonas was just finishing his piece and Jillian paused by his wheel to admire his deft fingers as they made the fluted edges on his bowl. His boyish enthusiasm was contagious, and she laughed as he wiped his cheek, leaving a large streak of wet clay.

Mike, grey-haired, grizzled, and bent over his wheel, gave her a swift nod before returning to his work.

As they passed from the front wheel room into the back area, she saw three kilns set up. Oliver talked excitedly about the process and showed her some of his newer work.

"I've got some new shipments packed up and ready for you to send out for me," he said. Seeming to be suddenly unsure, he rushed, "If that's okay?"

"Absolutely," she assured. "I'll get the galleria labels ready and can get them shipped tomorrow."

Letting out a sigh, he nodded. "Thank you. It relieves me to have someone I can trust to take over the shipping aspect of my work. And," he grinned, "gives you some exposure as well."

"Speaking of exposure, I'm organizing the first showing in the galleria. I'm leaning toward a Saturday night in two weeks. Now that I've seen your place here and your interns working, I'd love to have them come as well."

"Sounds perfect," he agreed. "Let me know as soon as you have the details." Looking down at his clothes, he said, "If you give me a few minutes to go to the house, I'll get cleaned up real quick, and we can head to lunch."

She watched him jog to a small house toward the back of the studio and turned to meander to the front. Making small talk with the interns, she discovered more about them and Oliver's work.

"Were you an art major, too?" Aubrey asked.

"Oh, goodness no. I love local art and since I have a business where I can showcase it, the situation works for all of us."

They continued to chat for several more minutes until Oliver reappeared, now in clean jeans and a button-down white chambray shirt. His hands were slightly red from the scrubbing. He smiled as he escorted her to his car. "There's a nice restaurant in the nearby town."

"That sounds fine," she agreed, glancing sideways at the man behind the wheel. *Handsome, accomplished, owns and operates his own business...but no sparks.* She quickly chastised herself for even having those thoughts, but then just as quickly accepted that there was nothing wrong with acknowledging that her sparks only ran toward Grant.

Minutes later, as the host showed them to a table in the corner of the small, Italian restaurant, she felt Oliver's fingers pressing on the small of her back. Eyes wide, she involuntarily stiffened. *Oh shit, could Grant be right? No, no...Oliver is just being a gentleman.*

"Are you all right?" Oliver asked. "You seem a little flushed." He held her chair and scooted her up to the table.

Muttering, she said, "Yes, yes, I'm fine. It's just a bit warmer than I was prepared for today." Thankfully, the rest of the meal passed without incident as they talked about the area, their businesses, and the upcoming wine and cheese event at the galleria.

"I have sold a few pieces of your work to some of the tourists," she commented. "I'm keeping track of them and will send you an itemized list along with your payment at the end of the month."

"Perfect. For the pieces I've boxed up, if you just add your logo and send them to the address I have on each box you can deduct the cost of shipping from my sales payment."

"I can do that easily with a spreadsheet," she said, but then cocked her head to the side. "Are you sure it wouldn't be cheaper for you to just send them yourself?"

Shaking his head, he said, "I have no desire to deal with that aspect." Rubbing his fingers on the table, he added, "Essentially, I'm an artist. I totally hate the business aspect of dealing with sales, taxes, and shipments."

Laughing, she said, "I'm the total opposite."

"That's why we make such a good pair," he said softly, his eyes never leaving hers.

Swallowing deeply, her gaze shot down. *Shit, that did sound like a come on.* Clearing her throat, she lifted her eyes and said, "Well, here's to great business partners." She noticed a flash of disappointment in his eyes, but neither remarked on it.

Clinking their wine glasses, they finished the meal in easy camaraderie. She made sure to stay a step ahead of him as they made their way back to his car. Once at the studio, she noticed the lights were off. "I guess the interns have gone home for the day?"

"Yes, they have no set hours. I guess I don't either," he joked. Coming to her car, he said, "I've got the boxes in the back. I'll put them in your car."

It only took a few minutes to load the boxes packed with Oliver's ceramics, and afterwards they stood awkwardly by the driver's door of her car.

Sticking her hand out, she thanked him for lunch, but glanced down nervously when he held her hand a moment longer than she wanted. Turning, she opened the door but hesitated as he put his hand on her shoulder.

"I'm really glad you came today," he said, his gaze holding hers. "I'll see you the next time I bring more pottery to town, and make sure to give me all the details about the showing."

"Righteo!" Jillian called out, inwardly wincing at her goofy choice of words. A minute later, pulling out onto the main road heading south back toward Baytown, her mind raced. *Oh Lordy, I hope Oliver isn't getting any ideas other than being business partners!*

Grant stepped into the ever-empty reception area of Harrison Investigations. Assuming Gareth was in his office, he called out, the PI's response from the back room giving credence to his assumption.

"Man, you need to get a receptionist," Grant said, seeing Gareth poke his head out from his office, waving Grant back.

"I've got someone in mind, but I need to get a little more work before I try to hire them." Gareth motioned for Grant to take a seat. "I sent some info to Mitch this morning about the lawyer, and he'll go over it with you all later. But I knew you were anxious to see what I could find, at least initially, on Oliver Dobson."

Grant's senses were instantly on alert as his eyes pierced Gareth. His heart pounded thinking about Jillian not only doing business with but spending lunch with the artist. "What'd you find out?"

"I don't know if you'll consider this good or bad... but so far, he's clean. He's just exactly what he seems— an artist."

Leaning back, Grant's breath left him in a *whoosh*. Before he could ask more, he halted as Gareth held his hand up.

"Now, this is just preliminary, but his credit is good, his education checks out, the purchase of the studio he's working out of had no unusual elements to it...from first looks, he's just an artist. Graduated from the Maryland Institute, College of Art, majoring in ceramics. Interned and worked in New York City for a couple of years before coming back to the Maryland area."

The two men sat, the silence stretching between them, causing Grant to shift in his seat for a moment. Finally, letting out a sigh, he shook his head slowly. "I look like a fool, don't I?"

"Why? For wanting to make sure Jillian's not getting involved with someone shady?"

"Yeah, but I didn't have you check out any of the other artists in her galleria."

"None of them appear to be interested in her as more than a shop owner," Gareth added, a smile playing about his lips.

Grant jerked his eyes back up to Gareth's and said, "Did it show that much?"

Shrugging, Gareth replied, "I saw them at lunch at the Seafood Shack a while back. I could tell Jillian was just having a good time with no one in particular, but Oliver had an interested look on his face."

Grimacing, Grant nodded, "I figured as much." Running his hand over his face, he added, "Hell, who could blame him?"

"I take it you two have history."

"Yeah, we do." There was no reason not to admit it to Gareth since the town knew most of the Baytown Boys' backgrounds. "Childhood friends, teenage relationship. I did four years in the Army and came back determined not to tie her to my nightmares."

Gareth stared at the fellow Legionnaire and felt a pang of sympathy for Grant's situation. "I hear you, man. I was lucky...I came out of the Air Force, proud of my duty but fairly unscathed; have some friends not so fortunate."

The two men shared a look before both nodded and Grant stood. Sticking his hand out, he shook Gareth's hand firmly. "Thanks for the work. How much do I owe you?"

"Don't worry about it now," Gareth said. "I'll bill at the end of the month."

With a jerk of his head, Grant stepped back out onto the sidewalk, sliding his sunglasses on his face. *So, he's just as he seems...an artist with an interest in my girl-friend.* Pinching his lips together, he had to admit that

Jillian was not officially his girlfriend yet. *Time to remedy that!*

Grant stopped by the station, even though he did not have duty until the evening shift, wanting to hear Mitch's report on Stanley and Isaac. He arrived just as Ginny and Burt entered as well, and the trio found Mitch and Sam already sitting at the conference table. The officers settled quickly, and Mitch opened the file in front of him with a smirk.

"Just to let you know, the Easton Police Chief sends her regards, thanking us for Isaac's company—"

"Thank God he's there and not here!" Mildred interrupted, walking into the room to grab a cup of coffee. The others barely hid their grins as she banged around the pot, leaving quickly with her steaming beverage.

"I think Mildred just spoke for all of us," Sam said, shaking his head.

"The mouth on that prisoner got on everyone's last nerve," Burt agreed.

Nodding toward the file on the table, Grant asked, "What did Gareth come up with?"

Pulling out the papers, Mitch replied, "Stanley Martino is an attorney that practices in Baltimore, but is also licensed in Virginia. That's not unusual for lawyers who live near state borders. He owns his own practice, and Gareth did a search of his latest cases. He's a defense attorney...used to have his own commercials on TV and radio."

"Ambulance chaser?" Ginny asked.

"Kind of," Mitch agreed. "Seems he touts himself as the defender of the oppressed."

"Oppressed!" barked Sam. "There's nothing oppressed about that mouth we had in lock-up!"

Rubbing his forehead, Mitch agreed, before continuing. "Gareth looked into the man's finances, and it appears he keeps some clients on retainer; they make regular payments into his bank accounts. And a few of those have been under observation for drug running. So far, there's nothing illegal coming up on Stanley... just unsavory."

"So, he makes himself available for drug kingpins running drugs up and down the East Coast, swooping in when one is caught? And that's not illegal? How fucked up is that?" Grant growled.

"Agreed," Mitch stated, "but everyone has a right to legal counsel and there's nothing illegal about defending someone."

The group sighed in unison, angry faces set in stone. "I've got a bad feeling that the Eastern Shore is going to see more and more of this, so stay sharp," Mitch added. "Not only on traffic duty, but when watching our youth as well."

"Got a group that hangs around the town park, just at dusk," Sam said. "The mayor hates it. Says it makes townsfolk not want to walk in the evenings at the park. I've been keeping an eye on them, but so far, they just seem like kids wanting a place to gather."

"Makes them a target," Grant commented.

Mitch nodded. "Agreed. So, keep an eye on it."

The meeting broke up, but the tense expressions remained on everyone's faces. Grant headed back out, deciding to see if Jillian was home from her trip. Driving by her house, he was pleased to see her just pulling into her driveway. Battling jealousy coursing through him at the thought of her lunch with another man, he parked behind her, his heart leaping as he observed her smile when she turned around and saw him.

"Hey!" she called out. "Whatcha doing here?"

Matching her grin, he climbed out and stalked over to her, not stopping until his boots were planted in front of her sandals. Towering over her, he wrapped his arms around her, pleased as she immediately slid her arms around his waist.

"Just thought I'd stop by to see if my girl was home yet," he declared, his voice not giving in to the nervousness he felt by claiming her. Kissing the top of her head, he waited anxiously for her reply.

Tipping her head back, she cocked her eyebrow. "Your girl?"

Grinning at the lighthearted tone to her voice and the gleam in her eye, he nodded. "Yeah, my girl."

"Hmph," she mumbled, planting her face into his chest. "That's kind of presumptuous of you."

Tightening his arms, he replied, "Maybe. But we've...well, I've wasted too much time as it is."

The two stood in her driveway under the shade of one of her large trees, allowing the breeze to blow around them as they continued to hold each other tightly. Jillian had to admit, it felt right, but she hoped she was not, once more, placing herself in the way of heartbreak.

11

Choking on terror, Grant jerked up, kicking his legs out in his tangled sheets. Heart pounding, sweat dripping off his face, he brought up his knees, resting his head on his forearms. Having confessed his nightmares to the counselor, Thomas had encouraged him to talk to Jillian. Lying in bed, the sunrise just barely peeking in through the window, he wondered how to go about doing that. *I thought a time might naturally open up and the words would flow easily.* But so far that moment had not happened.

Swinging his long legs over the side of the bed, he sat with his head resting in his hands, elbows propped on his knees. Sucking in a deep cleansing breath, as Thomas had taught him to do when he felt anxious, he realized he needed to man up. Grabbing his phone off the nightstand, he started to call Jillian before looking at the clock. *Damn, it's only six a.m.* Hesitating for a moment, he figured she was already awake since the coffee shop opened at seven.

Pressing the button, he listened as her phone rang twice before she picked it up, sounding more chipper at six o'clock than a person should be at that ungodly time.

"Hey, Grant. Kind of early for you, isn't it? What's up?" she asked.

"I wondered if you'd like to go to dinner with me tonight. We've got an AL baseball practice this afternoon, but I could pick you up afterwards." Rubbing his hand over his chin, he felt the unfamiliar pang of nervousness.

"Sure," she said, her voice now soft and low. "I'd like that."

Letting out a slow breath, he smiled. "Great. I'll pick you up as soon as I can get home and showered. It'll be around six or so."

"Grant..." she hesitated, "why are you calling so early?"

"Just couldn't sleep. Talk to you later...and Jillian? Thanks." Hanging up, he flopped back on the bed, the ceiling fan blades slowly rotating overhead, their calming motion steadying his heartbeat.

Word had spread about the teams the American Legion had created for children and the bleachers were filling up with parents as well as townspeople. Jillian, Tori, Belle, and Jade sat near the bottom, watching as some of the Legionnaires coached from the sidelines now that there were enough children to form teams.

Ginny had recruited Katelyn to assist with the girls, who were playing on the co-ed teams. Shouts from the stands cheered on all of the children, with each child getting a turn at bat. Jillian watched as Grant worked with some of the younger children, keeping her eyes on Junior and Bobby. Smiling as Bobby made a hit, she screamed as loud as some of the parents when he ran to first base.

"So..." Tori began, turning to look at Jillian. "How're things going with Grant?"

Smiling a little crooked smile, Jillian glanced to the side, seeing the concerned look on Tori's face. "Good, I think," she admitted hesitantly. "It's kind of weird...I'd given up hope that we'd never be more than friends, but he seems to really want to be more now. At first, I thought it was just because Oliver asked me out."

"Grant did get jealous when you came to our engagement party with someone else," Tori reminded.

"Oh, don't worry. I haven't forgotten," Jillian said, a flash of irritation passing through her eyes. "I'm trying to take things slow. Although..." she giggled, "I almost jumped him the other night and asked him in!"

Laughing, Tori said, "Well, it's not like he's new in your life. You two have a lot of history." Her mirth slowing, she added, "I just don't want to see you hurt."

Nodding, Jillian agreed, "I know. That's what Katelyn's worried about." After another moment of cheering, she added, "He told me that something happened when he was in the Army that had a profound impact on him, and he hinted that it was the reason why he backed away from me when he came home."

"So, what's different now?"

"He's been talking to one of the counselors in town."

Eyes wide in surprise, Tori said, "Oh, wow, Jillian. That's wonderful."

Cheering all around jolted the women out of their conversation and their focus jumped back to the field. Jillian saw Grant standing between third base and home plate, yelling for Bobby to run as the little boy's legs pumped as fast as he could go, sliding safely into home, scoring a run. She jumped up and down on the bleachers, screaming his name, watching as Grant hoisted Bobby up on his shoulders.

As they retook their seats, she felt Tori's hand on her leg, and she looked over at her friend.

"I'm rooting for you two, you know," Tori said, a beautiful smile on her face.

Snorting, Jillian said, "You just want everyone to be as happy as you and Mitch ."

"True...but I really think Grant knows what he's been ignoring and hopefully, getting help, will send him straight back to you."

Turning back to watch him down on the field, she gazed speculatively, thinking of the deep secrets he carried. "I hope so," she whispered.

That evening Grant pulled into Jillian's driveway, his nerves forcing him to check his tie in the side view mirror once more before walking to the front door.

Sucking in a big breath, he let it out slowly, willing his heart to stop pounding quite so loudly. *This is it. I can do this. I can tell her everything—*

In the middle of his pep talk, the door opened, and Jillian stood there, smiling as she saw his hand raised to knock. "Hi!" she greeted, staring at the eye candy standing on her front porch. Dressed in navy slacks paired with a crisp, light blue shirt and a mauve tie striped with navy, he appeared utterly different from the sweat-soaked coach with dirt on his blue jeans earlier at the game. And yet, she thought both images equally sexy.

He peered down at the woman in front of him, as familiar to him as his own image, and yet even more beautiful than when he had seen her a few hours before. Her blonde hair was pulled back from her face with a jeweled clip, allowing the waves to cascade down her back. Her lithe body was encased in a red dress that clung to her curves, stopping just above her knees. The modest neckline was accentuated with a few gold-fili-gree necklaces. Her long, tan legs ended in strappy sandals, the four inch heels bringing her eyes level to his mouth .

Warmth pooled deep inside as he looked at the classy woman standing before him. "Hi yourself," he greeted, bending down to place a gentle kiss on her lips. "Ready to go?"

Nodding, she turned to lock her front door, and his jaw almost hit the floor. Her demure dress dropped into a deep V in the back, leaving her silky skin bare for his —and any other man's—perusal. "What the hell do you have on?" he barked. "Or rather, what don't you have on?"

Glancing over her shoulder, she gazed in wide-eyed, mock innocence. "Why Mr. Wilder, don't you like it?"

"Dammit Jillian, you know I do, but so will every other red-blooded male between the ages of thirteen and a hundred!"

Turning back around, she cocked her hip and threw her hand out. "This is a perfectly acceptable cocktail dress, suitable for an evening out at a nice restaurant. Neither my boobs, nor my ass cheeks, are showing." Irritated at his continued tight-lipped grimace, she added, "And may I just say that the women you've been escorting around town have been dressed in far more provocative and downright slutty clothes!"

"That's unfair! And you're not like those women, who meant nothing to me!"

"And that's supposed to make me feel better?" she snapped.

Rubbing his hand over his face, he sighed. So far, they were only five minutes into the date, and it was not going the way he had hoped. Releasing his breath, he agreed. "I apologize, Jillian. You are beautiful and, to be honest, I'll feel jealous with every other man's eyes on you tonight."

They stood awkwardly on the porch, staring at each other, for a long moment. Nodding, she turned and unlocked the front door, slipping back inside before he had a chance to react. His heart dropped, fearing the date was over before it had begun. "Jillian—"

The door re-opened and Jillian walked back out,

this time with a black, lacy shawl draped about her shoulders. With no other explanation, she looked up, a smile on her face that no longer reached her eyes, and said, "Are you ready?"

Dropping his chin to his chest, he closed his eyes for a few seconds before lifting his gaze back to hers. "I'm sorry...really sorry," he said.

Uncertainty filled her face as the anger fled from her eyes. Giving a little shrug, she mumbled, "It's okay."

Placing his hands on her shoulders, he fought the urge to pull her into his body because he wanted to see her face, peer into her eyes, and make sure she understood what he was going to say. "It's not okay that I made you feel less than what I should have made you feel. You are beautiful...so fucking beautiful. And that dress is killer. You look classy and gorgeous, and any man would be proud to have you on his arm. And that you're giving me the chance to prove to you that I can be that man? Baby, that makes this evening so special."

Seeing the warmth return to her eyes, he slid his hands from her shoulders around to her back, tucking her closely to his front. "No one, and I mean no one, has ever meant what you mean to me." He felt her stiffen for an instant and prayed he was choosing the right words. "I'm ashamed to admit this, but everyone else was...well, I've never had a relationship that went beyond the physical. I was running...that's all, just running."

Leaning back, she looked up, her brow knit in confusion. As much as she hated discussing the revolving door of women he had had over the past couple of years, she wondered what he meant. "Running?"

Kissing the top of her head, he said, "We're getting out of order. I wanted us to do dinner, have a nice time, and then...uh...well, talk."

Seeing the little boy expression of uncertainty now in his eyes, she sighed. "You're right. Let's do that, shall we?" Holding out her hand to him, she smiled as he linked fingers with hers, and they walked to his jeep.

It only took a few minutes to drive to the Sunset View Restaurant and as they followed the host, Grant took her lacy wrap and grasped the top, gently pulling it off her shoulders, exposing the back of her sexy dress as they walked. Jillian gasped, glancing back at his grinning face, loving the heat of his fingers as they possessively lingered on her skin right above her waist. Knowing he was staking his claim for any other man in the vicinity, while allowing her to show off her beautiful dress, she smiled as he settled her into a seat.

The town's elegant restaurant sat right on the bay, earning its name from the glorious views of the sunsets each evening. An hour later, after the dinner had been consumed, the wine drunk, and the dessert sampled, the couple rose from the table after witnessing the sunset over the bay along with the other appreciative diners. Stepping outside, the cool breeze had Jillian quickly replacing the wrap on her shoulders as she snuggled closer into Grant's embrace.

"It's a little chilly to walk on the beach—," he surmised, but before he could continue, she interrupted.

"How about you come to my house?" she offered, her eyes sparkling.

Bending to kiss her lips, he nodded. A few minutes later, they parked outside the refurbished house with the wide Victorian porch. Entering, she kicked her heels off immediately. "Can you open some wine while I change?"

Agreeing, he slipped off his tie and unbuttoned the top of his shirt before rolling up the sleeves. Sliding off his shoes, he padded on socked feet into the kitchen to find the wine, glasses, and opener. He looked around in curiosity, having never been inside, but was not surprised by the burst of color that so represented Jillian. The green and yellow kitchen was warm and cheery, just like her.

By the time he heard her feet on the stairs, he had two glasses poured. Halting, he watched as she appeared, her bare toes peeking out from black yoga pants, a slouchy, pink sweatshirt, falling off one shoulder. He sucked in a quick breath, unsure at that moment which was the sexier Jillian—the makeup, hair fixed, little red dress wearing woman...or the fresh faced, hair in a sloppy bun, comfortably-clothed beauty in front of him. He quickly decided they were both stunning.

"Is that for me?" she asked, nodding her head toward the wine glass in his hand.

Giving a mental shake, he grinned. "Yeah," he said softly, handing it to her. "Can we sit?"

She led the way into her living room, sitting on one side of the sofa, immediately tucking her legs under her and facing him. She allowed him to choose to sit where he would feel the most comfortable but was secretly pleased when he joined her on the sofa at the other end. Placing his wine glass on the coffee table, he twisted his body so that he was facing her.

They sat in easy silence for a moment before he finally sighed and ran his hand over his chin. She recognized the mannerism as one he performed when he was deep in thought, so she remained quiet, sipping her wine.

Finally, he looked up and blurted, "I've been seeing a counselor." Holding his breath for a second, he continued to gaze at her, seeing nothing but acceptance. *It's time. It's now or never,* he thought.

12

———

Jillian watched Grant's strong jaw flex and relax a couple of times as he struggled with how to begin. Wanting to ease his tension, she leaned forward and placed her hand on his knee, giving a reassuring squeeze. His gaze dropped to her hand and a small smile slipped out, remembering days from their youth.

"Do you remember when I struck out, losing the baseball game when I was in ninth grade?" He lifted his eyes to hers and watched as her lips curved into a slight grin. "I was so pissed and took off running, leaving my friends behind because all I wanted to do was kick myself. But a few minutes later you found me at the end of the town pier. You didn't say a word, but you plopped down next to me and just sat. After a while, you placed your hand on my knee, and I felt the anger slip out of me with that one gesture."

"I remember." She watched him for a moment as he got lost in thought. "And now?" she prompted.

He linked his fingers with hers and rubbed his

thumb on her tiny hand. "Feels the same," he admitted. Leaning his head back against the sofa cushion, his gaze wandered over to the mantle where framed pictures were placed haphazardly—some of Jillian's family, some of the girls, and one of the whole gang of Baytown Boys and the girls at a bonfire at Mitch's grandfather's beach house.

"Those were good days," he said, nodding toward the pictures, seeing her nod her agreement from the corner of his eye. "Easy...full of friends and fun times. I cared about you then, after I finally got over the fact that my best friend might beat the crap out of me if he found out we were together." The sound of her light giggle shot straight to his heart. "But, like most of us raised in this tiny town, I wanted to get out. I thought about a scholarship to play ball but loved the idea of joining the military first. Hell, all the others were doing it, and it made sense. But I never expected it to change me...mark me."

"Can you tell me what happened?" her soft voice carried across the space between them. A long silence filled the room as Jillian waited to see if Grant would open up.

"Basic training was no problem for me and Mitch," he began, "and we even did our Military Police training together." Giving a little shrug, he said, "Afterwards, we got sent to the warzone, even to the same base. The first tour was bad but doable. I ended up working the gates of one of the important locations. Part of my job was to train others on how to safely search a vehicle for bombs before they entered the facility. I made Sergeant and my next rotation took me to Afghanistan. I was doing the same thing, made new friends and was proud of the training I was offering. It was there, that I met a girl."

At those words, Jillian's heart froze. The only movement was her chest as it rose and fell with her breathing. Her mind quickly reached back, and she knew that he was still communicating with her at that time with promises of coming home. Swallowing, she clamped her mouth shut, forcing the desire to scream down deep.

He felt her stillness and quickly glanced up at her face as she struggled to maintain a calm façade. "No, no, it's not what it sounded like," he rushed, inwardly cursing at his bumbling. "I just meant that I met a female soldier, and we became very close. But not like you're thinking!"

He squeezed her fingers, willing her to relax so he could get through the rest of his tale. "She was married...had a little girl back here in the states where her husband lived. They'd met in the Army, married, and then he got out of the service, and she had one more tour to complete before moving back. She reminded me so much of you..." He let the last words hang for a moment, the image of the blonde-haired, blue-eyed soldier with the ready laugh filling his mind.

"Her name was even similar...Julie. She was funny and could tell a wicked joke. Most of the time her blonde hair was pulled back in a tight, regulation bun, but when she was off duty, it would flow, and when I saw her from the back, I could swear I was looking at you." He sought Jillian's gaze once more and let out a sigh of relief as her face appeared more relaxed.

"She was smart, and we became friends...just friends. I was loyal to you, and she was loyal to her husband. In fact, sometimes when she video-chatted with him and their daughter, I'd just stare from across the room, and hope that one day you and I would have that kind of relationship."

The silence once more descended as the two sat with their own thoughts. Grant struggled with what to say next—how to explain the root of his nightmares and the beginnings of his descent into stepping away from the woman sitting with him. Feeling the light pressure from her fingers on his, he sucked in a quick breath only to let it out slowly before continuing.

"I cared a great deal for her...never sexual...but a deep friendship. My counselor has helped me realize that for people in traumatic situations, strong emotional bonds can be formed quickly; although most times they don't last once the situation is over...but some do. I even thought about what it would be like to introduce you to her and her family once we got back."

He let go of Jillian's fingers, sliding his sweaty palms up and down his legs. She flexed her fingers, instinctively missing the warmth of his touch. Needing something to do with her hands, she reached for her wine glass, taking another sip as he stared into space, his lips pressed together. *What happened over there, Grant?* She wanted to vocalize the question pounding inside her head, but swallowed the wine, now bitter on her tongue as she waited.

"It was routine," he said, his voice now a hoarse whisper. "A truck came in, and she walked over to do the undercarriage inspection with the long-handled mirror. Routine. Just a truck with supplies. I didn't even walk over—she and another soldier were on duty." Sucking in another deep breath through his nose, his chest began to move up and down more rapidly as the image filled his mind.

Jillian, fear now eating away at her, reached back over to touch his leg, but he jumped up from the sofa and paced to the fireplace, resting his hands on the mantle.

"The explosion didn't detonate as it was supposed to. If it had, we'd have all been dead. It would have blown the whole gate area to smithereens and all of us in the vicinity."

Jillian's eyes widened, the idea of Grant not coming back alive hitting her in the gut. *He could have been like Philip!* Forcing her breathing to steady, she watched his shoulders slump in defeat but had no words to help him face his demons as his tale continued.

"The bomb partially detonated and destroyed the back of the truck only...not the front or the gas tanks. Fire and metal exploded from the back...just where Julie was standing. It was organized chaos as we secured the area so I could get to her." His voice now low and rasping, he shook his head as he stared at his feet. "I got to the back, and she was lying in the dirt. Her blonde hair, out of the bun, was streaming behind her bloodied body. I rushed to her, rolled her over, and...and..."

"Oh Grant," Jillian blurted, jumping from the sofa and rushing over to him. Encircling his waist from behind, she laid her head on his back, nestled between his shoulder blades. "I'm so sorry."

He continued, pulling out of her embrace and stalking a few feet away before swirling around to face her. "She looked so much like you...reminded me so much of you. She represented the part of home that I missed the most. Jesus, she had a husband sitting at home waiting for the love of his life to come back. A daughter who wanted to have her mommy hug her. And she was blown. The. Fuck. Up!" He roared the last part, his hand sweeping the mantle, knocking the pictures crashing onto the floor.

Jillian stepped back as the glass shattered at her feet, but it was nothing compared to the shattered anguish on his face. Instinctively stepping forward, she halted as he shouted for her to stop. Before she could react, he stepped over the carnage and scooped her swiftly up in his arms, protecting her bare feet from the glass. Sitting back down on the sofa with her in his lap, he buried his face in her neck, his voice still hoarse. "It was like looking at you, there on the ground."

Jillian wrapped her arms around his body, holding him as close to her as she could. *Oh, Jesus. Oh, Jesus. I had no idea!* A sob broke through the silence and his body bucked into hers, causing her to tighten her arms even more.

"I missed her so fuckin' much...as a friend...but I swear, all I could see was you. It was the realization that when you love someone, and something happens to them..." his voice trailed off for a moment before continuing. "I accompanied her body to the states and watched as her husband, holding their daughter, cried over her casket." He shook his head against her and moaned, "I thought, I can't do this. To love someone and lose them...the risk is too great."

Jillian said nothing, knowing no words would make his turmoil any better. She held on tight, willing her warmth and strength to seep into his body. Murmuring nonsensical words of comfort, she rubbed her hand up and down his back, releasing a held breath as she finally felt his body easing.

She knew he had to be exhausted because she was tired beyond belief and had not had to relive the trauma. Her thoughts swirled as she held him, understanding seeping into her consciousness. *He wasn't rejecting me when he came back as much as he was running from the fear of loving me.* Unsure what to do with the new information, she cupped his face, wiping a tear with her thumb.

"Come on, Grant. Let me put you to bed."

He wordlessly allowed her to rise and grasped her hand as though holding on for dear life. Avoiding the glass on the floor, she led him up the stairs to her bedroom. Grant, for the first time he could remember, slipped off his clothes and under the covers without attempting to make a pass at the woman he was with. Fatigue pulled at his very being, and he was barely aware of the bed dipping slightly as Jillian joined him, her arms once more wrapping around his body.

"Sleep," she whispered. "I've got you."

For the first time in years, Grant fell into a deep sleep, nightmares held at bay.

The morning sun peeked through the slats in the blinds, casting stripes of light across the bed. Grant woke slowly, his normally keen instincts sluggish. Blinking a few times, he looked around, the colorful curtains and unfamiliar furniture coming into view before his gaze landed on the sleeping beauty resting next to him. *Jillian's bedroom. Damn!* Flopping on his back, he thought to the previous evening, the heat of embarrassment flowing through his veins. *Jesus, what must she think of me?*

A light touch on his cheek jolted him and he jerked his head to the side. Jillian's wide blue eyes were pinned on him, her pink slips curved into a smile. Her soft voice sent tingles throughout his body with her simple greeting. "Hey."

"Hey, yourself," he replied, his voice raspy and his focus unable to tear itself away from hers.

"How'd you sleep?"

He thought for a few seconds before responding truthfully. "Really well. Like probably the best in years." Peering closely at her, he watched for signs of disgust but found none.

Her smile widened as the hand on his cheek continued to stroke his face. "I'm glad. I'm glad for a lot of things."

Steeling his courage as he rolled to his side to face her, he stayed silent, willing her to explain.

"I'm glad you finally sought help. I'm glad you trusted me, shared with me." Her fingers continued to move over his stubbled jaw, loving the feel of his morning beard. Her brow crinkled in concern as her gaze held on to his. "Grant, I'm so sorry about your loss...so sorry you had to go through that. And so sorry you had to hold it inside all these years—"

"No, no," he rushed, interrupting as he reached out to pull her close. "I'm the one who's sorry. Sorry I never faced what happened or tried to see how it affected me...and you." Closing his eyes for a long moment, he said, "I can't believe I wasted so much time with you by pushing you away. Thinking that not having you in my heart would be better than having you and then possibly losing you." Her fingers continued to massage his jaw, and he sighed in pleasure before admitting, "I'd rather have a moment loving you than a lifetime of never having you with me."

Her heart leaped at his words, and she moved quickly, pulling him in for a kiss. Latching onto his lips, needing the kiss to live, she angled her head as their noses bumped.

Grant, taking the kiss from mild to wild, plunged his tongue into her mouth, exploring her taste. He was intoxicated from the kiss and wondered how he had ever resisted her. *I was a moron!*

"No, you weren't," she said into his mouth, and he realized he had spoken aloud. Leaning back, he separated from her for an instant to see the light in her eyes.

Her hands grasped both of his cheeks as she emphasized, "You were not a moron, Grant. You were a man traumatized and trying to deal with it on your own. But you don't have to anymore...you have a counselor...friends who'll help...and me. Especially me."

"I need you to forgive me," he whispered. "Forgive me for pushing you away. For hurting you. For flaunting other women in front of you to keep from feeling anything—"

"Shhh," she said, understanding his need for forgiveness but not wanting to hear any more. "I do forgive you Grant, but I want no more talk of other women when you're in my bed. I want there to be only me...no past."

Feeling a weight lift off his chest, he rolled over, pinning her underneath him. Keeping his weight on his forearms, he gazed down, eyes twinkling as he searched her face, finding sincerity. Dropping a kiss to her lips again, thoughts of any other woman from the past flew from his mind. *This needs to be right. Maybe it's not the best time—*

"Stop thinking and start kissing," she ordered, tugging on his bottom lip with her teeth, eliciting a grin from him.

"Yes, ma'am," he said, nuzzling her nose just before plunging back in. Holding her face with his hands, he sucked on her tongue as his lips assaulted hers. He memorized the petal soft texture and the intoxicating taste as his lips moved over hers. Hating the material between them, he rolled to the side just long enough to jerk the offensive clothing down his legs and onto the floor before slipping his hand to the bottom of her huge T-shirt, his gaze asking permission to take it off. Before she could reply, his hand stilled...she was wearing his old high school football shirt. *Jesus, all these years...she still has it.*

Glancing down to see what he was staring at, Jillian realized he noticed what she slept in. Too late to be embarrassed, she gave a little shrug. "It's comfortable," she offered, before a small grin slipped out. "So is your basketball T-shirt and your baseball T-shirt."

He wanted to roar, pound his chest, and shout from the roof that this woman was his — but instead he whipped her shirt up and over her head, tossing it to the floor. His hands and mouth found her immediately, and she arched into him with a soft sound that made rational thought difficult.

She wiggled underneath him, reaching to help, but his hand stilled hers. "No," he murmured against her skin. "Me."

"Okay, caveman, can you speak in a full sentence?" she joked, her hands grasping his shoulders.

He paused just long enough to glare down at her as he finished undressing her himself. The glare dissolved the moment he looked at her. *Long, tanned legs. More curves, in all the right places, than she had in high school. Wavy blonde hair flowing across the pillow. And those sky-blue eyes staring right at me. Right through me. She knows my secrets and is still here.*

She wrapped her legs around his waist in a silent invitation he had absolutely no intention of ignoring.

He took his time with her, learning what made her

gasp, what made her writhe, his attention utterly focused until her body gave way beneath him and his name broke from her lips. He watched her face as it washed over her, unguarded and beautiful, and felt something fierce and humbling move through his chest.

When her eyes slowly found his again, her lips curved into a lazy, satisfied grin. "Hey," she said.

"Hey, yourself," he replied, his smile matching hers. Then his head swiveled, searching the room. "Where're my pants? I need a condom." His search halted as she grabbed his face in both hands and held it close to hers.

"I'm on the pill...and clean," she confessed. "You?"

His breath left him in a whoosh. "Yeah. Tested for work, and I've never gone without. Never." He searched her eyes in the morning light. "Okay?"

"Yeah, okay," she grinned just before squeaking as he captured her lips, kissing her thoroughly and without apology.

He moved over her slowly at first, savoring every sensation, privately terrified he wasn't going to last.

He gathered himself and found his pace, and she met him with equal urgency. Her hands moved over his back, her body rising to meet his, the two of them finding a rhythm that felt less like something new and more like something remembered. The tension between them built in waves, electric and relentless, until she was clinging to him and he was holding on by pure stubbornness.

"Baby?" he managed.

"Oh, yeah," she breathed back.

He shifted, giving her exactly what she needed, and her whole body answered. His name was on her lips, and her arms pulled him closer as she came undone around him. That was all it took. He followed her over the edge, every muscle in his body drawn taut, his forehead dropping to hers.

He collapsed, landing with somewhat more force than intended. A grunt rose from underneath him.

"Sorry," he mumbled, rolling to the side, taking her with him so she was tucked, half draped over his body.

The two lay together, neither speaking as they fought to catch their breath, their bodies slick with sweat. Chests heaving in unison eased as their heartbeats slowly ceased their erratic pounding. Jillian, her legs tangled with his and her hand on his chest, slid her fingers though the soft hair there.

As the air cooled their bodies, Grant leaned down and snagged the covers, jerking them up, making sure to tuck her tightly as his arms wound around her. Brushing her hair back from her face, he smoothed his thumb over her blushed cheek before rubbing it across her kiss-swollen lips. He knew he had never seen a more beautiful sight.

Smiling, she sighed softly as she watched his eyes roam appreciatively over her face. *This man...I fell in love with him when I was a little girl...and he's now in my bed... in my arms.*

"Whatcha thinking?" he asked.

Giving her head a little shake, afraid to jinx the moment, she said, "Nothing."

He cocked his eyebrow as he responded, "Woman, I can tell when your mind is whirling."

Grinning, she playfully slapped his shoulder. "Oh, you can, can you?" The silence settled between them for a comfortable moment before she confessed, "I was just thinking that having you here is everything I ever dreamed."

Closing the scant distance between their lips, he kissed her softly. "Me too, babe. And the only place I ever intend to be." Leaning back slightly, just enough to hold her gaze, he added, "Thank you...for listening...for forgiving—"

"Shhh," she placed her fingers over his lips. "I'm here for you. No thanks required. You need me, I'm here. Always."

With that, he rolled her on her back, showing her just how much her vow meant to him as the sun rose higher in the sky.

13

"Liam Sullivan has discovered a meth lab in his jurisdiction."

Mitch made the announcement from the Accawmacke Sheriff to his officers in their morning meeting, creating grumblings from all around the table.

"Any connection to Isaac?" Grant asked, scanning the information handed out by Mitch.

"Not sure at this point...they're still working the scene. State police, as well as the FBI, are there."

"The route coming through the Eastern Shore is longer," Ginny stated, "but is the fact that it's less populated the draw?"

"Seems to be," Mitch agreed, before looking behind her with a smile at the new arrivals. "Hannah. Colt. Good to see you."

Grant twisted around, greeting the two people walking into the room. Colt Hudson served as the Sheriff of North Heron County, which surrounded Baytown, and Hannah Freeman was the Police Chief of the small town of Easton, the county seat. Colt, tall and lean, had the outward demeanor of an easy-going cowboy, but taking that at face value was a mistake to anyone who crossed him. A former Army Criminal Investigator, he kept his sharpshooter gaze on his county, protecting it. Hannah was only about five feet, five inches, with dark hair and dark eyes. Her curves looked good on her and belied her power. As a black belt, she had no problem taking down a suspect in her town.

The group slid their chairs around the table, making space for the newcomers to join them.

"Thanks so much for our newly incarcerated prisoner," Hannah joked, referencing to Isaac. As the county seat, Easton held the jail. "He's a real charmer. And such a quiet man."

The others laughed ruefully, pitying her and glad they no longer had to deal with his loudmouth.

Grant eyed them, knowing there was a specific reason for the two fellow law enforcement leaders to make the trip to Baytown, but before he could ask, Colt explained.

"We're tasked by the State Police to be extra vigilant, which," he eyed the group, "I know we all are. But some of the drugs we thought were just being run through our counties are now being made here."

"I was just telling them about the meth lab in Liam's county," Mitch confirmed. "What does the FBI say?"

"It's no secret we've got the poorest, or close to the poorest, counties in Virginia," Colt continued. "It makes for a perfect setting to bring in drugs, make them, sell them, transport them, use them. Poverty makes people willing to do a lot just to get food on the table."

Hannah added, "One thing I've learned is that the drug cartels like places that are poor not only because it's easy to find people willing to work for the cash but also work cheaply. It's a win-win for the drug cartels and the people willing to haul for them."

"Isaac give up anything?" Grant asked. "Or his slick lawyer?"

At the mention of Stanley, Hannah rolled her eyes. "Oh God, if I have to listen to that man anymore, I won't be responsible for what I might do!"

"I've got a PI doing some checking into him, to see what we're dealing with," Mitch added.

"I've got a feeling his shit's tied into the drug money as well but, so far, on the outside at least, he just seems to be an ambulance-chaser attorney for drug dealers, spouting their constitutional rights. But I'll be interested to see what your PI can dig up. Who are you using? Gareth?"

"Yeah."

Nodding, she smiled. "Good man. My brother and I were both in the Air Force and he served with Gareth. Said he was glad he came out here after getting out."

Ginny's face brightened. "I didn't know you were former service. I was with the MPs in the Army."

Hannah and Ginny shared a look, one that Grant was sure spoke volumes about being a female in the military that most men would never understand.

Turning back to Colt, he asked, "Besides the meth lab, what else do they suspect?"

"Kids," Colt bit out. "Using fucking kids. They're cheap workers, need the money, and worst of all, are considered expendable."

The thought of Junior or Bobby being used by drug runners made Grant's blood boil. "Fuckin' hell," he growled. He thought about how being in school kept them from working on the farm, a place that could possibly make them easier targets for earning fast cash. Sucking in a sharp breath through his nose, he leaned back heavily in his seat as he let it out.

"You thinking about some of the kids?" Burt asked.

"Yeah."

"I heard the Legionnaires were working with kids and ball teams," Hannah said. "I haven't been to a meeting yet, but I'd like to check it out."

"Absolutely," Mitch said. "I've been wanting to reach out to the other law enforcement personnel in the area who have served." Leaning over to grab some brochures lying on the counter, he handed a stack to both Hannah and Colt as they stood to leave. "Can you give these out for me?"

"No problem," Colt agreed, his ready smile back on his face. "Me and some of my crew will be at the next meeting as well. And if we can get some kids up in the northern part of the county to play, you can have more teams."

With goodbyes said, Hannah and Colt left the station, leaving the Baytown officers still mulling over the problem of the at-risk youth.

"I'm the next one on rotation at the school programs," Burt said, "I'll see if I can ferret out any information."

Grant thought about the migrant children often used in the fields, much the way Junior and Bobby were. Speaking up, he told the others about the two kids. "Their dad is trying to do the right thing, but it's hard."

"I think that's why the Legionnaire program is so important. We need to keep these kids in school and in programs that'll help."

"So," Mitch stated, placing his fists on the table as he stood, his sharp gaze pinning the collection of law officers, "keep your eyes and ears open. While I hate like hell Liam's jurisdiction had a meth house, I do not want that shit in this town!"

Stanley drove from Easton, frustrated that the judge refused to set bail for Isaac, calling him a flight risk. His phone rang on the console, and he glanced down, grimacing as he saw who was calling. Picking up, he faked cheerfulness. "Juan! Good to hear from you!"

"Cut the shit," the harsh voice growled back. "Why the fuck is Isaac still in that shithole jail cell?"

"Now, Juan, you know how he is. He's got a mouth on him, and he's managed to piss off just about everyone who's come in contact with him, including the judge. They refused bail, citing he's a flight risk. Don't worry, I'll—"

"Don't tell me what you'll fuckin' do," Juan Munoz argued. "You just remember that you work for me."

Sucking in a sharp breath through his nose, Stanley pinched his lips. *I'm the educated attorney and I'm stuck working for an asshole cartel leader...* As he let his breath out slowly, he thought of the money he made with them and assumed his placating demeanor once more. "I understand Juan, but I'm working on it. I've advised him to stay quiet and hang on. I've filed an appeal in the courthouse and—"

"Don't worry about Isaac anymore," Juan interrupted. "I've got more important things for you to deal with. The lab in the county north of where Isaac is being held just got raided last night. I want you to get with our contact and make sure that they're covered."

"You must be joking, right? If you want to keep using me as your clean-up attorney, you've got to play this smarter, Juan! I can guarantee I'm being investigated as we speak. That's why we're on a burner phone, and we'll keep being on a burner phone. You take care of the contacts, and I'll try to keep the legal end of your business from falling down around your head!" The silence was frightening, and Stanley grabbed a fast-food napkin from the passenger seat of his car and wiped his brow. Just as he was about to apologize, Juan spoke.

"You're right. Get on back to Baltimore and see to the legitimate side of your practice. We better not have any more fuckups like Isaac to deal with for a while."

Breathing a sigh of relief, Stanley disconnected before pulling off at a gas station. Standing in the sunshine, pumping gasoline, he wondered for the millionth time if the money he made with the cartel was worth it...but then decided with his life on the line, he had no choice. He wiped his brow again, more out of desperation than the heat.

"Hey, girls," Jillian called out. "Come on up!" She smiled as the three women rounded the wooden railing at the top of the galleria stairs and headed toward her. Katelyn and Tori immediately walked up to her, and Belle paused to admire paintings displayed on the walls.

"How's it going? Do you need any help for the showing?" Tori asked, sitting down at the little, round table next to Jillian.

"Here's what I have planned, so tell me what you think?" Jillian replied, sliding into a chair in between Tori and Katelyn. She twisted around to see Belle still wandering around the room, her eyes taking in each piece. "Do you like them, Belle?"

The dark-haired beauty smiled shyly, answering, "Oh, my God, yes. I'm not artistic at all, so I'm always in awe of what others can create."

"Same here," Jillian laughed. "I have no artistic ability in the least, but I do know what I like and seem to have a knack for finding others who like it too."

Belle joined them at the table and Jillian began. "I've got some RSVPs from several buyers in the Virginia Beach area and as far north as Baltimore. The two artists whose work is over there," she pointed to the back wall, "are bringing in pieces that are a bit more original than what we have displayed here for the more touristy crowd. And most of the artists will be here that night."

Pointing to the other pieces, she said, "The artists making the sculptures will be here, too."

"What about Lance? Will he come for his sea glass work?" Tori asked, knowing Mitch's friend and newest Baytown resident's penchant for isolation.

Jillian shook her head, her mouth turned down in a sad frown. "No. I asked, but he's not about to come into a crowded room full of strangers." Shrugging her shoulders, she added, "But he's bringing in a few more pieces for me to show."

"And the handsome potter?" Katelyn asked, arching her eyebrow as a smirk crossed her lips.

Jillian gave a pretend glare toward her friend, while admitting, "Yes, the handsome Oliver is coming as well. He's bringing more of his interns' work."

"How do you think Grant's going to react with him here? He's not exactly the sharing type, is he?" Tori asked, thoughts of his behavior at her engagement party flying through her mind.

Jillian sucked in her lips, a crease forming on her forehead. "Grant knows that I'll be working with Oliver...and other men. Hell, Lance is every bit as gorgeous as Oliver."

"Yes, but Lance isn't giving vibes that he'd like to be with you."

Sighing, Jillian declared, "Well, I'll just have to

make sure Grant knows that I'm with him and to stuff his jealousy! After all, I had to stuff mine when he paraded his bimbos for the past couple of years!"

"So, are you guys really together now?" Belle asked. Seeing Jillian's nod, she smiled, "That's so romantic. It's like a fairy tale."

"Fairy tale?" Katelyn snorted. "More like a version of romance disasters!"

"No, no," Belle insisted. "You know, young lovers torn apart and then finding their way back together." She gazed fondly at Tori, adding, "Like you and Mitch."

Jillian patted Belle's hand and nodded. "You're right. To me, it is a fairy tale come true." Turning to look at the others, she said, "Now, let's talk food!"

For the next hour, the quartet planned the menu for the Galleria Wine & Cheese Event, their lighthearted laughter heard by the coffee shop patrons below.

14

Grant stood with Ginny, Burt, and Burt's wife near the end of the food table, keeping an eye on Jillian's first Wine & Cheese with the Artists event. The coffee shop downstairs held the bar while the food laden tables were at the top of the stairs so that patrons could sample the cheese, fruit, and desserts as they wandered around, admiring the artwork.

"Earth to Grant," Ginny called out, elbowing him in the abdomen.

"Umph," he grunted as he whipped his head around to glare at the pint-sized officer attired in a cocktail dress and heels. "What'd ya go and do that for?"

"Because you haven't stopped shooting daggers at that artist standing over there next to Jillian for the past ten minutes."

He had not been able to relax since seeing Jillian upon arrival, gorgeous as always, but in a sexy cocktail dress. He had to admit it was pure class. In fact, the dress was modest from the front with a simple neckline that scooped down but did not show much of her cleavage. He had no idea if the blue material was silk, but it flowed off her figure and landed mid-thigh. Paired with her high-heeled black pumps, she looked beautiful... *and totally fuckable.* And when she turned around, he groaned once more. The back of the dress dipped way below where he thought her bra strap should be and yet, there was nothing but satiny skin showing.

"Just making sure everything is going well," he lied. Standing there pondering what lingerie contraption was worn underneath Jillian's dress, he barely heard Ginny as she spoke again, rolling her eyes.

"Uh huh," Ginny laughed, walking away with her plate filled. "Keep telling yourself that."

Aiden and Brogan walked up, sampling the hors d'oeuvres as well. Brogan watched Ginny walk away, his eyes glued to the beautiful officer, her hair down for the first time he could remember.

"Who's the guy with Jillian?" Aiden asked.

"He's fuckin' not with Jillian!" Grant growled, moving his head back so he could keep Oliver in his sights. "He's an artist who happens to have some work here, that's all."

Aiden and Brogan shared a grin. "Hmm, sure looks like he's with her," Aiden continued, egging his friend on.

"Fuck you, man," Grant said, huffing as he stuffed another bite-sized egg roll in his mouth.

"Wait, I think he just put his hand on her waist," Aiden commented, unable to contain his laughter when Grant almost toppled over in his attempt to see through the crowd.

"Cut it out," Brogan said, although his own laughter almost drowned out his words. "Grant, my boy, now that you've got your head outta your ass and finally made it official with Jillian, you're getting a taste of what she's had to put up with."

Hanging his head for a moment, he nodded. "I know...and that doesn't make it any easier." Looking over, he watched Jillian step away from Oliver, putting a small display case between them. Her gaze shifted around until it landed on Grant's, her smile blinding as it beamed toward him. "She's good," he said, knowing he trusted her explicitly, "but I wish I could say the same about ol' Oliver there."

Across the room, Jillian smiled at an art dealer from New York as he looked at Oliver's pottery. "I have to say, it's such an honor to have you here," she said, trying to hide her giddiness.

"I was visiting a friend in Norfolk who was coming tonight and thought I might be interested. I love the colors in Mr. Dobson's work."

"They are beautiful, aren't they?"

"Do you sell directly, Mr. Dobson?" the man asked Oliver, who was standing next to Jillian.

"I do, but I ship through Ms. Evans' galleria here. I find it is easier for me not to have to deal with that aspect. She also handles the payments."

Smiling up at Oliver, she continued to let the two men discuss his work as she made her way over to Lance's display.

"Is the artist not here?" asked a rather large woman squeezed into a tight-fitting cocktail dress. Her plate was balanced precariously in one hand while the other was fingering one of his perfectly balanced mobiles.

"No, unfortunately he was unable to be here tonight," Jillian explained smoothly. "Are you interested in his work?" Her eyes grew wide in horror as she watched the plate of food tip toward the work he had on the display stand. At the last second, the woman righted her plate, but not before Jillian's heart nearly pounded out of her chest in fear of the sticky hors d'oeuvres landing on Lance's delicate work.

The woman's husband came over, looking reproachfully at his wife, while engaging Jillian in a discussion of the art. A writer for a southern artisan magazine, he wanted to arrange a time to talk to Lance about his work as well as do an article about Jillian and the Galleria. His wife's almost-disaster forgotten, she excitedly discussed dates and times for him to visit again.

Several minutes later, she felt Oliver's presence near her side, closer than she was comfortable with. She had not said anything to him about seeing someone, but then, neither had Oliver made any attempts to ask her out again. Now, she was regretting not having Grant nearby as Oliver sought her attention. Offering him a quick smile, she moved through the crowd, stopping to greet visitors and checking in with her assistant keeping track of sales.

"Didn't think you'd be able to pull this off."

Turning, Jillian stared into the face of Silas Mills,

the town manager. Forcing her lips to smile, she said, "Well, I'm pleased to surprise you."

He scanned the area, assessing the crowd. Nodding toward Jason, standing with Zac and Callan on the other side of the room, he said, "Who knew the town mechanic would even own a suit."

Jillian's eyes bugged out as she whirled around, "You need to keep your opinions—"

Interrupting, he continued, "You have another one of these, we need to see about doing it at a time when other businesses can be open as well."

"This is for the artists, not me," she bit out between pinched lips, inwardly groaning as the mayor approached.

"Got a nice little thing going here," Corwin Banks said as he and his wife stepped into her path. Corwin, the longtime mayor, loved anything that brought class to Baytown, as long as it did not bring in what he referred to as *the wrong crowd*. "I didn't want a lot of artsy-fartsy hippies around, but this is real, real nice." He and Silas moved away, heading toward the food table to replenish their plates when Phyllis Banks, the mayor's long-suffering wife, offered Jillian an apologetic smile.

"I'm afraid my husband wouldn't know art if it jumped up and bit him on the ass," Phyllis said, stone sober, arching her brow. "But I would like to thank you for this soirée."

Jillian tried to stifle her grin at Phyllis' comment about Corwin and was grateful when the woman turned away before Jillian's giggle burst forth.

Suddenly, she felt someone's arm slide around her waist, and she was startled.

"Hey, sweetheart," the familiar voice sounded in her ear. Immediately relaxing against Grant's strong body, she turned her face up to his.

"Hey, yourself," she greeted.

His gaze left hers for only a few seconds to survey the crowd before settling back on her face. "How's it going? Everyone seems to be having a good time, and it looks like your assistant is keeping busy."

"Yes! It's great," she enthused, her face glowing as she leaned more into him, lifting one foot and wiggling it slightly.

He looked down, tightening his grip on her waist and asked, "You okay? What's wrong?"

"I bought a new pair of shoes for this and haven't broken them in, and my feet are killing me," she whispered.

"Well, as soon as it's all over, I'll take you home and give you a foot massage."

She whispered, "Is that all you'll give me?" Grinning up into his leering face, she laughed out loud.

"Are you all right, Jillian?" Oliver asked, moving to stand in front of her and Grant. "Do you need a chair?"

Grant stiffened at the insinuation that he was not taking care of her needs, and replied, "Don't worry. I'm taking care of my girlfriend."

Now it was Oliver's turn to startle as his gaze jumped between Jillian and Grant. "I...I see. Well good. Uh...I just wanted to make sure you were all right." He turned and walked toward his display cases where several people were gathered around admiring his work.

Jillian glared at Grant. "You didn't have to say it that way, you know."

"What are you talking about?"

Keeping her voice low, she said, "You know exactly what I'm talking about. You couldn't have been plainer if you lifted your leg and pissed on me!" She started to pull away but found his grip on her waist kept her in place.

"Babe, I'm sorry," he said, his voice caressing her ear.

Studying his face, she pursed her lips for a moment before accusing, "No, you're not!"

Sliding his hand up her back to cup the back of her head before pulling her forward, kissing her forehead, he admitted, "Okay, not really. I'm sorry I upset you, but not sorry that everyone knows we're together now."

"Oliver wasn't being a problem," she protested.

"And now I know he won't be."

Huffing, she pulled away only to be brought back for a quick kiss on her lips. Offering her a wink, he let her go so she could continue to work the room while he made his way over to Mitch and Tori.

An hour later, Jillian had just finished discussing Lance's sea glass work to another prospective dealer when she felt a presence at her back. Turning, she saw Oliver standing awkwardly, his eyes shooting between her and the other side of the room.

"Hi, Oliver. Are you all right? I've had a lot of

interest in your work," she commented, wondering if he was concerned.

"No, I'm fine," he said. "I just...uh...well, I wanted to thank you for all your help. And," he shifted his gaze around again, "I also...I didn't know you had a boyfriend. I hope I didn't make things awkward."

Smiling, she laid her hand on his arm. "Not at all. To be honest, Grant and I are newly...well, not exactly new." Scrunching her nose, she shook her head and laughed. "I guess I'm not exactly sure how to describe us!" Seeing his look of confusion, she quickly added, "I've known him all my life and we had been very close at one time. But it's just been very recently that we've started dating." She hoped her explanation made sense, but even to her ears she sounded flighty.

Before she could say anything else, he smiled and patted her hand. "It's okay. I get it." Glancing around again, he added, "But I have to say, he's a very lucky man."

She stared at the handsome man in front of her, knowing he did not make her heart stutter the way Grant did, but glad for his friendship, nonetheless. "Thank you, Oliver. And I'm glad we're in business together...and friends."

He flashed her a wide smile and nodded, before saying, "I think I'll mingle. Who knows? One of your beautiful friends might take pity on this poor, starving artist."

Throwing her head back in laughter, she watched him move across the room toward several ladies near his pottery, just as she saw Grant moving back toward her.

"Hey, babe," Grant's voice caressed her, while keeping his gaze on the retreating back of Oliver. "You need anything?"

"I think it's about to wind down," she said. "This has been really good, honey. I hope I can do more...but not too soon. I'm exhausted and we still have to clean up afterwards!"

"I'll help," he promised, his hand sliding along her back, his fingers itching to dip beneath the fabric to her bare skin. Forcing them to settle at her waist instead, he knew this was not the time or place, but he was excited at the thought of peeling the dress off her later.

It was in the wee hours of the morning by the time Grant and Jillian made it home. After all the guests had left, Jillian closed her books and, with the help of Jason, Zac, and Katelyn, quickly cleaned most of the shop. She had chattered excitedly about the evening's success and Grant's chest swelled with pride over her accomplishments.

Her coffee house staff would be in later to take care of the rest of the cleanup, so she finally locked the door and almost fell into Grant's jeep. Opening her door, she squealed as he swept her into his arms.

"Let's get you off those tired feet," he said, carrying her easily into her house. Refusing to set her down once inside, he bent to close and lock the front door before carrying her immediately up the stairs.

Sitting her on the side of her bed, he knelt in front of her. Sliding his hands down her silky legs, he slipped her strappy heels off, kneading and massaging each foot.

"Oh, God," she moaned as he worked the kinks out. The excitement of the evening had worn off, replaced with exhaustion.

"Not God, just me here," he joked, "but you can call me anything you want."

Laughing, she flopped back on the bed, her tired body beginning to come alive under his magical hands. As he finished with each foot, she raised up on her elbows. "You got anything else you want to massage?"

Lifting his eyebrow, he cocked his head to the side. "Sweetheart, you have got to be completely worn out."

"I am, but I'm never too exhausted for you."

His body, already primed and ready to roll, fought the urge to pounce on her as she lay, an open invitation on her lips. Her blonde hair, now out of its intricate style, flowed across the comforter. Her sexy dress that had held his attention all evening was now up around her hips, showing off a delectable pair of black, lacy panties. But then he noticed the drooping of her eyes. "How about a nice hot shower instead?"

She thought for a second then grinned a slow, sly smile. "Sure, but as tired as I am, I think you'll need to wash me off."

Chuckling, he shook his head as he stood. "Girl, you don't have to convince me to get you wet, naked, and in my arms!"

He scooped her up again and walked into the master bathroom. Jillian's house was not large, but it had been remodeled by the previous owners and one of their projects had been enlarging the master bath by incorporating an extra walk-in closet from the hallway. Now, the room sported not only a soaker tub, but a large, separate shower as well. Grant flipped the water on before setting her feet onto the plush floor mat.

Stilling her hands, which had begun to slide the side zipper of her dress down, he shook his head as his eyes flared with lust. "Oh, no, babe. I've been itching to peel this dress off you for the past six hours. Do not take that pleasure away from me."

Grinning, she held her hands out of the way, allowing him to slowly unzip the dress from underneath her arm, down along her hip. As the material parted, he viewed her black, lacy, strapless bra peeking from the side. With his hands on her shoulders, he slid the silky dress down her arms, over her waist and hips until it pooled at her feet. His gaze dropped, seeing her clad in only the silky undergarments, his breath catching in his throat. For an instant, he thought of the years wasted chasing other women in an effort to erase this woman from his mind, but he had never succeeded. *Thank God!* Remorse slammed into him, having felt her acceptance and forgiveness, not altogether sure he deserved it.

Her hand lifted to caress his cheek, and he was startled at the touch.

"Hey," she said softly, stepping closer to him.

Sucking in a cleansing breath, he replied, "Hey, yourself."

"Are you okay? You seemed to drift away for a moment."

He closed the distance between them, his finger trailing along her arm up to her neck, where he pulled her in for a kiss. Soft and sweet. "I'm fine," he replied. "In fact, with you...I'm perfect."

Stripping quickly, he followed her into the shower, smoothing the shower gel suds over her curves as he massaged the evening's stress from her muscles. Then christening the shower, they worshipped each other's bodies, their cries of passion filling the room. An hour later, curled together in bed, Jillian fell into an exhausted, albeit sated sleep, as Grant tucked her slumbering body tightly into his.

15

"Hey guys, you ready to work?" Jillian called out.

Bobby and Junior bounded up the stairs, carefully placing their backpacks over to the side of the room. Their eyes landed on her and both grinned.

"What are you two smiling about?" she asked, her hands on her hips as she stared at her young helpers.

"We were trying to figure out what you'd be wearing today," Bobby blurted before Junior nudged him.

Looking down at her bright pink yoga pants and purple T-shirt, she said, "What's wrong with what I'm wearing?"

"Nothing," Junior rushed to say, blushing.

"We like your pretty colors," Bobby announced, a wide smile on his face.

"Whatcha need us to do?" Junior asked hurriedly as Bobby walked over to the new artwork stacked against the wall.

"Eager for your first payday?" she laughed.

Nodding, he made his way directly to where Jillian

was kneeling by some boxes. Bobby, as always, checked out the new paintings first, carefully studying the artwork. Jillian smiled indulgently at both boys before explaining what they needed to do.

"Mr. Dobson has brought in some boxes that need to be shipped out and some that have pieces to be placed in his display cabinet to replace the ones sold."

A week had passed since the successful Galleria event and Jillian had been pleased to have the artists send in more work. Junior looked down at the five cardboard boxes on the floor and asked, "Which is which?"

"Good question," Jillian answered. "The ones with a mailing label already addressed on them are to be shipped out. You will need to place one of my Jillian's Galleria return labels here," she said, showing him where to affix the sticky label in the corner. "And then these that have no mailing label on them are for us to open and display."

Turning to look behind her, she smiled at Bobby, who was still staring at the pictures. "Come on, Bobby. Work first and then you can look at the new things that have come in."

Within a few minutes, the boys had the mailing labels on the correct boxes and were busy carefully unpacking the pieces of pottery for her to place.

Later, as they sat doing their homework in the downstairs shop, Grant walked in, calling out his greeting. "Boys, you about ready to go?" Gaining their nods, he said, "Give me a minute and I'll be ready."

"Gonna go kiss your girl?" Junior asked, grinning at Bobby.

Turning around, Grant pretended to throw a stern look with his hand on his hips. "Yeah. You got a problem with that?"

"Naw," the two boys said in unison.

"Just don't take too long," Junior added. "We've got a bedtime, you know."

"Everybody's a wise guy," Grant joked, taking the stairs two at a time. Turning the corner, he saw Jillian bent over a box, her tight pants stretched across her delicious ass, and he groaned as his dick twitched against his zipper. "Geez, babe, you're killing me."

Standing straight, Jillian turned around, eyes bright with a smile on her lips. "Hey, sweetie. Did you say something?"

Knowing the boys were in earshot, he simply shook his head as he stalked over and placed his hands on her hips. "Just came for a kiss before I take the boys home and head to the AL meeting tonight."

Tipping her chin, she offered her lips. "Are you coming over afterward?" she asked, hope in her voice.

He had slept at her house almost every night since the Galleria event and she wondered if he would keep it up or return to his home.

"Yeah, I'll be there, although I need to stop by my place tomorrow and check on things."

"We could go together," she suggested. "I could spend the night there, if you wanted."

His heated grin was her answer as he brushed her lips quickly. "The boys are just downstairs, so I'll keep this G-rated, but tonight, expect the X-rated version."

With a laugh, she waved goodbye as he jogged back down the stairs.

"I thought it would be different," the grizzle-bearded man said, appearing uncomfortable as he stood at the podium. "When we were in the bush...in Nam..." he hesitated. "We used to say that if we could just live, then the rest of our lives would be easy." Shaking his head, he continued, "We were wrong. The America we left wasn't the same one we came back to." After a long pause, he added, "Or maybe we were the ones who had changed. All I know is no one thanked me for my service, like they do now. Got married, had kids...then began to drink to try to get the nightmares outta my head. Lost my wife. She took the kids. Even after all that, I didn't know to get help. Wish I had." He opened his mouth a few times, as though to say more, then finally shook his head again as he made his way back down to his seat. The room was eerily quiet before Mitch continued the meeting.

The officers of the American Legion had taken Grant up on his idea to ask other members to talk about their experiences, if they wanted, and the idea had been well received.

Once the meeting ended many of the members migrated over to Finn's Pub. Sitting at the bar, half listening to Aiden and Brogan quibble over the Legion-naire's children's teams, he barely noticed when Ginny slid onto the barstool next to him. Glancing to the side, he saw her gaze piercing his.

"Got something on your mind?" he asked.

"You're different," she stated matter-of-fact.

Rearing back slightly, he repeated, "Different?"

Sucking in a breath, she nodded slowly. "Calmer. Hell, even happier. Finally getting with Jillian instead of chasing bimbos in skirts. So yeah...different."

He wanted to argue, but knew Ginny would see right through him. And upon reflection, he realized he did not want to deny her observations. *And the reality is that I owe it in large part to her.* Twisting slightly on his stool so he faced her, he admitted, "You're right. And thank you."

With a tilt of her head, she waited for his explanation.

"The counseling. The ESMH group. I called them," he said. Seeing her eyes widen in surprise, a small smile spread across her face. "I've got someone I talk to now."

"It seems to have really helped," she said softly.

Nodding slowly, he rubbed his chin. "Yeah. Made me face some things I hadn't wanted to face. And that, in turn, gave me the strength to talk to Jillian."

Lifting her eyebrows, she said, "And I take it that went well."

Chuckling, he agreed, "Much better than expected." Uncomfortable talking about his feelings, he took a sip of his beer. "So, we're together now and have a chance to move forward while dealing with the past."

Patting his arm, she grinned. "I'm glad, Grant."

She turned to slide down from the stool when his question stopped her.

"What about you? Are they helping you with whatever's buried inside of you?" he asked, observing her startle as she sucked in a quick gasp of breath, a flash of bleakness passing through her eyes. With a sad smile, she slid off the seat, reaching back to take her beer in her hand as she walked away.

Grant watched her for a moment before turning away, noticing Brogan's gaze following her as she made her way over to a table of friends.

Finishing his beer, he was anxious to get home to Jillian. *Was I ever one of the first to leave the bar? When did that happen?* Grinning, he knew the answer.

Grant walked into the police station the next morning, ready to start his day shift, but halted in his greeting to Mildred as he heard Mitch's voice from his office shouting, "God dammit! How the hell did that happen?"

Mildred's eyes widened behind her glasses as she cast a worried look toward Grant and the others quickly gathering. The officers hustled toward the back, meeting Mitch in the hallway.

"Conference!" Mitch growled, leading the way into the conference room.

Grant sat quickly, as did the other officers, each pair of eyes pinned on their Chief. Mitch's face was uncharacteristically flushed, and his lips were pressed into a tight grimace.

"Isaac Canton is dead."

Eyes wide, Grant's reaction was, unsurprisingly, the same as the others.' "What the fuck?" Their eyes darted around before settling back onto Mitch's for an explanation.

"He was being taken from the jail over to the county courthouse, since his lawyer was appealing bail, when a shot rang out. Long distance rifle."

"Holy shit," Sam cursed, shaking his head. "This doesn't happen around here."

"Execution," Grant stated, not needing Mitch's head nod to confirm. "What's Chief Freeman doing?"

Mitch grimaced again, "Hannah's pissed as hell. Her officers on the scene immediately took cover and called for an ambulance while others were sent looking for the sniper. Got the State Police and Colt's deputies looking as well. Gone...fuckin' gone."

"It's early," Ginny said. "They'll get him."

"What I'd like to know is where was slick-shit attorney Stanley when this happened?" Grant asked.

Burt leaned forward and said, "I was just getting ready to ask the same thing."

"Seems he was on the courthouse steps, not close to the defendant at the time," Mitch explained.

"So, our connection to drug running through the Eastern Shore is dead before his big mouth was able to tell us anything," Grant surmised.

"He was definitely a liability for them, that's for sure. The FBI and DEA are looking further into his contacts now, so we'll see what they dig up. In the meantime, stay on the lookout for any more evidence of drug dealing in our jurisdiction. Gareth is still digging into the lawyer. He's dirty with the cartel, I just know it."

"What the fuck were you thinking?" Stanley screamed into the phone, his voice strident with adrenaline. "I was right there! Are you crazy?"

"Problem solved," Juan stated.

"Did you not hear me? I was right there!"

"Yes," Juan said, "And you couldn't have done it, and with your reaction, you weren't expecting it. You're safe, so stop bitchin'."

Stanley tried to slow his pounding heart while wiping his sweaty hand on his pants. As shaken as he was, he knew Juan was right. Isaac's mouth was a danger to them all, and now the danger was gone. Pulling in a ragged breath, he asked, "What about the gunman?"

"Gone...for now. But if he's caught, he's dispensable. Knows nothing. Just paid to do a job. So, stop worrying like some ol' woman. We've got bigger fish to fry than that mouthy prick who got himself stopped and had a fucking gun on the seat next to him."

"That was stupid," he acknowledged.

"Taking care of Isaac also made a statement," Juan said. "Anyone else carrying for me better keep their shit together or they'll end up like him."

He stayed silent, his calculating mind working furiously, as well as his self-preservation. *How much do I now have in my overseas account? I could easily disappear. Maybe practice law in the Caribbean.* "Sure, sure, that makes sense," he eagerly agreed. "Now that Isaac doesn't need me, I'll head back to Baltimore."

"You do that," Juan said. "And I'll let you know as soon as you're needed again."

"Right," he agreed, disconnecting and tossing the burner phone into the passenger seat next to him. Passing a North Heron Deputy SUV sitting on the side of the road, his eyes shot down to his odometer. *Good, under the speed limit.* Keeping his foot steady on the gas pedal, he wiped his sweaty brow, eager to make it back to his home. *It may be time to start packing!*

"Oliver?" Jillian, sitting at the small desk in the corner of the galleria, held the phone with one hand while scribbling new orders with the other.

"Jillian, how nice to hear from you," his pleasant voice replied. "What's up?"

"Since the showing, I've had some new orders come in from several people and wanted to let you know." She rattled off what she had accrued and asked if he and his interns would be able to deliver.

"That should be no problem," he said. "I want to thank you so much for your help. I'll have more for you to ship to New York as well."

"Oooh, that dealer who came to the event must have really liked your work."

"He seems to be very interested. I'll get those to you for shipment later this week."

"Perfect." Disconnecting, she sat, staring off into space as she tapped her pen against the tabletop, wondering who she could set Oliver up with. She had a number of single friends, all wonderful women. *Katelyn? God no, she'd eat the easy-going artist alive in one day! Belle? No...too shy. They'd end up sitting for hours, neither saying anything. Jade. . .Rose. . .*Thinking of some of the newer teachers in the area, she finally shook her head and walked down the stairs to get more coffee, a smile on her lips as thoughts of her own relationship with Grant raced to the forefront of her mind.

Oliver pounded the clay in front of him after he dipped his hands in water to allow them to caress the mound.

"You okay, boss?" Aubrey asked.

He glanced to the side, hating that he had not hidden his scowl. Sighing, he looked back down only to see he was already misshaping the new vase. Starting over, he nodded but kept his eyes on his work. "Yeah."

"Were you on the phone to the guy in New York again?" she queried. "That's a good thing, right?"

Hating to talk about the situation with an intern, he simply replied, "He wants more, and I told him we would try to supply what he needs." Oliver did not need to look over at the young, eager woman to know she did not understand why that request was a problem. "I told him art is hard to churn out...we're not a production company."

She nodded, but said, "It seems like a good problem to have, though. You know, more demand than supply. And I'll certainly step up what I'm doing to help. We'll have lots to ship to them."

He bit back the sharp retort that was on his lips, knowing his problems were his own. *Supply. Demand. Shipments. More and more work.* As he forced his concentration on the clay in front of him taking shape, his hands smoothing over the material, he allowed the spinning wheel to lull his mind toward a calmer place.

16

The two kayaks glided along, creating ripples on the calm, early morning surface of the Chesapeake Bay. A heron stood perfectly still at the edge of the water, waiting for its chance to catch a crab. Gulls flew overhead, occasionally diving into the water for fish. The sun cast the water in sparkling diamonds as the breeze gently rocked the kayaks.

Grant watched the pink craft in front of him, a grin spreading across his face. *Only Jillian would have a hot pink kayak.* He admired the tanned skin of her back, the ties of her black bikini top the only material in the way of his unadulterated view. Her hair, braided and hanging down her back, was held out of her face by a bandana, the same color as her kayak.

Looking over her shoulder, she flashed a white-toothed grin, recognizing his leer as he eyed her. "Why, Mr. Wilder. What is on your mind? And don't tell me it's water safety!"

Laughing, he admitted, "Busted. But it's your fault.

Here I am, trying to be a gentleman, and one look at you and all I can think about is getting you out of that tiny bikini and burying myself deep inside your—"

"Grant!" she interrupted. "Keep your mind on your paddling!"

"I'd rather bend you over and paddle your sweet ass," he smirked, pulling alongside her. The two held their oars still as he leaned over, kissing her lips. Balancing the kayaks, he knew he had to keep the kisses short and sweet, not at all what he wanted to do. "Next time, let's use the paddle-boards. Well, actually, one paddle-board. You can work on your tan, and I'll paddle us around and admire your body."

Giggling, she leaned back, holding his gaze. "You're a goof, you know that?"

Holding his hand over his heart, he retorted, "A goof? You wound me, woman! I've never been called that before."

"Oh yeah? And what did all your other women call you?" As soon as the words came out of her mouth, she grimaced, wishing she could pull them back in. The last thing she wanted to do was think of his previous hook-ups.

Grant saw the doubt in her eyes and sighed, tight-lipped at the thought of his previous actions hurting her.

"I'm sorry," she said, forcing a smile on her lips. "It was a dumb thing to say." She lifted her oar in her hands, moving to dip it into the water, when his hand landed on hers. Looking over, she waited to see his reaction, her stomach rolling with nerves.

"Babe, I'm the one who's sorry," he admitted, reaching up to cup her cheek. "I hate like hell that I made such bad decisions in an effort to try to distance myself from you. If I could take it all back, I would."

Her features softened as her lips curved slightly, this time the warmth reached her eyes. "You don't need to apologize, Grant. We weren't together then and," her eyes shifted down to their clasped hands before lifting back to his, "we're together now. That's all that matters."

He leaned over, his lips dipping to hers. Soft and slow, he felt her silky skin, relishing her taste of berries and cream. As he pulled back, he saw the sunrise glistening off the surface of the water sparkling in her eyes.

"Anyway," she grinned, looking around, "this morning is too beautiful for anything other than joyful thoughts." With a giggle, she cried out, "Race you!" as she used her oar to push his kayak away from hers before whipping around and beginning to paddle furiously toward the beach.

"Oh no, you don't!" he called, and within a few strokes was right beside her once more. Laughing, they stayed side by side until they were close enough to the shore to climb out, dragging their crafts behind them, up the wet sand and over to the blankets they had left.

Bending over to grab a towel, Jillian heard Grant groan, and she turned to see what the matter was. *He's staring at my butt. I should have known! Well, I'll just give him a little show!* Repeating the motion, she bent again, teasing him as she slowly toweled off her legs.

A slap on her wet bottom had her jumping forward as she twisted around in shock. Rubbing her stinging ass cheek, she stared wide-eyed at his smirking face. "You...you...I can't believe you did that," she accused, hating to admit she was turned on as she noticed he was too.

Stalking toward her like a panther after its prey, he did not stop until his arms snaked around her waist, one hand dropping to smooth over her left cheek. "Retribution for wiggling that perfect ass when you know I can't do anything about it right now." Pressing against her as he pulled her closer, he said, "But if you're ready to go home and play, just let me know."

With that, he took her lips, searing them with white-hot flames as he licked, nipped, sucked, and plundered her warm crevices. Jillian wound her arms around his neck as she gave a little hop, wrapping her legs around his waist. She felt his heat with only the bathing suit material between them, now wondering if that had been her smartest move.

"Guh huhm," she mumbled against his lips as she pressed closer to him.

Assuming she had just ordered him to go home, he slowed the kiss, willing his dick to behave. Pulling back, he said, "You got it, babe, but first we've got to load the equipment."

She groaned at the interruption, the sound shredding his resolve to wait. He quirked a brow and, with a quick nod from her, bent to snag the blankets from the sand, one hand securely around her waist. Quickly glancing around the private beach, he easily carried her behind the first dune he saw before dropping the blanket onto the sand.

Her lust-filled eyes held his as he gently lay her down on the blanket. Shooting a look around, she determined no one could see them and relaxed as she lifted her arms up toward his shoulders, pulling him down on top of her.

Grant peered closely into her eyes, checking to make sure she was really all right with what they were about to do. "You okay, babe? We can head home."

Her smile lit his world as she closed the small space between their lips and tightened her hold on his shoulders. As he rolled slightly to the side to take his weight off her, she said, "Only thing I'm worried about is getting sand up my...um...well, you know." Blushing, she burst into giggles.

Unable to hold back his laughter, he pulled her closer and said, "Then I'll just have to make sure the only thing in your, you know, is me!" Before she could reply, he sealed his lips over hers once more, kissing down her neck as his hands found the edges of her bikini top.

Her body arched into him, her fingers winding through his hair as his mouth and hands moved over her with focused attention. He slid his hand down slowly, finding her warm and ready for him.

He took his time with her — deliberate, unhurried, learning every sound she made and exactly what drew them out. Her head pressed back against the blanket as her body responded to him completely, the soft give of sand beneath them and the morning breeze the only things anchoring her to the world. She felt herself unraveling, boneless and breathless, until he finally eased back and watched her drift.

Her hands moved lazily over the hard lines of his back and shoulders. "Mmmm, I love your shoulders," she murmured, eyes closing as her fingers continued to roam.

"My shoulders?" Grant lifted up on one arm to see if she were kidding, but her expression was soft and unhurried as her hands kneaded the muscles of his neck and upper back.

She opened her eyes, focusing on the man she loved lying half on top of her, his weight comfortable and right. "Yeah," she whispered. "You've got great shoulders."

He kissed her lightly. "Now you're the goof...but an adorable one." Shifting over her, he settled against her and said, "Let's see if there's another part of my anatomy you think is great."

He moved the fabric of her bikini aside and freed himself from his trunks.

Grinning, she grasped his shoulders tighter, fingers digging in as she replied, "Oh, I'm already a big fan."

He cupped her face in his hands, kissing her deeply as they moved together. His mouth said everything his words hadn't, and his body following the same rhythm. Whatever restraint he'd been holding onto dissolved entirely. She was all he could feel, all he wanted to feel, and he gave himself over to it completely.

She held on to him, her hands moving over the shifting lines of his back and shoulders as the tension between them built and tightened. *Jesus, what this woman does to me.* He wanted her with him when he fell and reached between them to make sure of it.

She shuddered, her fingers pressing hard into his shoulders as the wave crashed through her — warmth radiating outward in every direction, her whole body alive with it. His own groan followed close behind, low and unguarded, as he poured himself into her completely.

He barely managed to shift to his side before going still, his heart hammering against hers in the warm morning air.

They lay on the blanket, sweaty bodies quickly cooling with the breeze across the dunes, both breathing rapidly until, slowly, their bodies recovered. Staring into the blue sky, afraid to look into his eyes, Jillian whispered softly, "I love you." Unable to hold them back, the words simply slid from her heart to her mouth. Biting her lip as they floated between them, she barely had time to wonder what he thought before he leaned up on a forearm and peered down at her, blocking the white clouds passing overhead.

Reaching out with his free hand, he brushed scattered strands of hair behind her ear, while some still blew about her head like a halo. Caressing her cheek with his thumb, he admitted, "I fell in love with you years ago, Jillian Evans. And then I let life...and nightmares...keep us apart. But my love for you is still there...still strong...and here to stay."

Sucking in a quick breath as his words slid into her being, her lips curved into a slow, sweet smile. Reaching up, she caressed his jaw, holding his gaze.

Just then, the wind picked up slightly and Jillian felt the sting of wind-blown sand hitting her body and she snapped her legs together tightly. A crease appeared on her brow as she bit her lip. "Uh...Grant? I hate to ruin a perfect moment, but um...the wind is blowing sand up my...*you know*."

It took a second for her words to penetrate, but then his eyes widened, and he moved quickly. Pulling his trunks up, he leaned down and tied her bikini bottoms back at the sides as she shifted her top to cover her breasts once again.

"Well, we need to take care of that problem," he announced with a grin as he stood and offered her a hand up. Grabbing the blanket, he linked fingers with hers and they jogged back to the kayaks. It took several minutes to carry them over the dunes to where his jeep was parked, but they had them tied on top as quickly as they could.

"Come on, sweetheart," he said, as he led her around to the passenger side, assisting her up. "We still need to take care of your, *you know!*"

Giggling, she rolled her eyes as she shifted uncomfortably on the seat, the small amount of sand in her bikini beginning to chafe. Eyeing him as he jumped into the driver's seat, she said, "What are we? Twelve?"

"You started it," he laughed, pulling away from the dune and back onto the road. "I'm just following your lead."

Within a few minutes, they pulled into her driveway and jumped down from the vehicle at the same time, jogging toward the door. Once inside, she shrieked as he scooped her up and headed up the stairs.

"I swear, I should get used to you carrying me to the shower by now," she said, holding on to his neck. Once inside the bathroom, she slithered down the front of his body as his arms loosened. With a wink, she turned and flipped on the water, letting the warmth fill the room.

Stripping, they entered underneath the shower-head, letting the water flow over their bodies, washing away the residual sand.

"So, I take it you're not a fan of beach sex?" he asked, his soapy hands roaming over her body.

Turning to face him, a smile on her lips, she replied, "Sex with you anywhere, anytime...perfect."

"Well then, let's see what you think of shower sex."

Grant drove the Baytown police SUV through the early morning streets, his thoughts returning to the delights of the previous morning spent with Jillian, first on the water, then on the beach, and then in her shower.

Hearing dogs barking as he turned down one of the streets, he saw Mrs. Malton on one side of the road holding onto her dog as it strained toward the other side where Mr. Royer and his dog were walking. *At least they're staying on opposite sides of the road!* He slowed and down his window as he came to Mr. Royer. "Good morning! How goes the walking?"

"As long as she stays on her side, we're fine!"

Waving to Mrs. Malton across the street, he choked back his grin when she snubbed him. Grateful the town was quiet as he finished his patrol, he glanced at the clock. Knowing he had an early morning presentation at the elementary school, he left the town and drove toward the county school.

The main highway cutting through the Eastern

Shore was a four-lane road with a grassy median. As a school bus in front of him slowed, he watched carefully as it came to a stop to pick up children, knowing both lanes on their side needed to halt as well.

A black car with dark, tinted windows all around, coming from behind, ignored the school bus stop sign and lights, passing quickly. Flipping on his siren, he waited until the school bus dropped its sign before he pulled around, keeping the car in his sights.

Calling it in, he had Mildred radio for assistance from the North Heron County sheriff and the state police. Driving fast, but cautiously, he was glad the traffic was almost nonexistent on the road. *Come on, prick, pull over!* Furious at not being able to see the license number from the vehicle, he lost sight of it as it rounded a curve. Speeding forward as he came out of the curve, he grinned in victory as he saw a North Heron Sheriff's cruiser SUV jerking in behind the black car, entering the high-speed chase. Within a minute, the SUV managed to maneuver the pursued vehicle off the road, dirt and gravel flying beneath its tires as it ran into a ditch. Grant called in the tags and got the name of the suspect—Tyrone Johnson. Calling in his location and status, he stalked over to the black car, his boots stamping into the ground.

Glancing into the trunk as the State Trooper popped it open, he viewed two dark duffle bags, each stuffed and full. Snapping on gloves, the State Trooper unzipped the bag, revealing plastic bags full of white powder.

"You can't look in there!" Tyrone yelled. "I was just out to get my coffee. I didn't do nothin' wrong!"

"Colt," Grant acknowledged, as he was joined by Sheriff Hudson, who proceeded to lean over to see what else was in the trunk. The State Trooper unzipped the second duffle bag and revealed a multitude of handguns. Picking one up, he turned to Grant and Colt commented, "Serial number's been filed off. Probably off all of them."

"He's gonna kill me! The mother-fucker's gonna kill me!" Tyrone, handcuffed and on the ground, began screaming.

Grant, jaw tight, called in to Mildred just as more law enforcement vehicles pulled up. Stepping back, since he was out of his jurisdiction, he turned to Colt. "I witnessed him speeding by a school bus stopped at a bus stop, so while that may be secondary to all the evidence here," he said, jerking his head in the direction of the trunk, "I still want that added to his charges. I do not want this piece of shit to get away."

Colt nodded before moving over to the suspect, just being lifted to his feet, still struggling against his handcuffs.

"Who are you afraid of?" Colt asked, his hard eyes pinned on Tyrone.

Tyrone's lips tightened into a grimace, but he held his tongue, shaking his head. Giving a little shrug, Colt said, "I'll just be putting you in the county jail...same cell as a recent drug runner had."

Tyrone's eyes grew wide with fear as his chest heaved with each breath. "You gotta take me somewhere different, man," he begged. "He'll off me just like..."

Grant moved closer, listening as Colt continued. "Who? You give me one good reason to listen to anything you've got to say."

Tyrone leaned forward, his voice dropping. "You know. You know what'll happen to me."

Another shrug, and Colt spoke as though he did not have a care in the world. "I don't know anything unless you choose to enlighten me. Then, and only if I determine what you say has any merit, we may consider a scenario other than the one the last drug runner had that was caught here."

Tyrone held on to his silence until the officer was pressing on his head to assist him into the back of the cruiser. "Wait, wait!" he called out, looking over at Colt and Grant. "You get me some protection and I'll," he swallowed deeply, his eyes darting around, "give you what you want."

With a curt nod toward the officer, Colt and Grant walked back toward their vehicles. "Hate like hell he passed a school bus, but sure as fuck glad you were right there," Colt said.

"I was pissed just about the traffic violation, but as soon as I saw the all-tinted windows, I wondered if he didn't have some reason to be flying down the road this morning—besides just wanting to get to his coffee."

Colt snorted, shaking his head. "Well, I guess Tyrone's Starbucks is just going to have to be delivered to the county jail."

"Hey, Mr. Policeman," the young child's voice called out. "Can you show us your gun?"

The small children sat in a semi-circle on the floor as Grant perched in a too-small chair, all eyes glued to him as he cleared his throat. Not about to draw his weapon from its holster, he attempted to answer the first grader's question before being peppered by the next but was unsuccessful. "Well, I—"

"You ever shoot anyone?"

"Do you look at blood and guts under a microscope like they do on TV?"

"My daddy says it's okay to race down the road as long as there ain't no damn cops around."

"Richie!" Jade hushed the child, reprimanding his language. "You do not use that word even if you are quoting your father!"

Grant, looking at the clock, was glad when he realized his time was up. Standing, he waved goodbye to the small children, startled when one little girl ran over and hugged him around his knees.

"I'm glad you came, Mr. Policeman," she said, her wide blue eyes and blonde ponytail reminding him so much of a much younger Jillian. "And I can say no to drugs too."

Grinning down at her, he patted her head before moving into the hall with Jade. Dropping his head back to stare at the ceiling for a moment, his mouth opened to speak but nothing coming out. He then looked back down at the pretty, brunette teacher and asked, "How on earth do you do it?" Placing his hands on his hips, he shook his head as she laughed softly.

"I love this age," she admitted. "They're fun, inquisitive, and not cynical."

"They're inquisitive for sure!"

Patting his arm, she said, "You did fine, Grant. Thank you so much for coming by today."

He turned to shake her hand when he heard, "Officer Wilder!" from around the corner. "You're coming to my room next, and I've been sent to escort you so you don't get lost!"

Bobby bounded over, his enthusiasm contagious as Grant greeted him. With a wave backward to Jade, he followed Bobby to the next classroom, grateful to have a chance to speak to the older children. An hour later, as he was leaving the school, Jade came jogging after him.

"Grant!" she called out, breathless as she came to a stop in front of him. "I've got an aide watching my kids," she explained. "I wanted to tell you that after you left, one of the girls in the class told me that her older brother talks about using drugs. I have no idea if it's true, but when I questioned her, she seemed to know what she was talking about. Her name is Karly. Karly Hubbard."

"Damn," Grant said, pulling out his small notepad. Writing down her name as Jade gave it to him, he then asked, "What did she say?"

"Just that her brother, who dropped out of school, is always arguing with their mom, talking about his friends. She says he's gone a lot and when he comes back, he's got money. She's overheard her brother and mom fighting and it seems that last weekend, she heard her mom say the word drugs."

Grant's gaze sought Jade's as his mind ran through the possibilities. Taking down the child's information, he thanked her.

"No, thank you for talking to the kids today in a way that helped them understand," she said. "If you hadn't, I don't think she would have told me what was going on."

Climbing into the cruiser, Grant headed back to the police station, a headache beginning to form. *Jesus, I'm tired and it's only eleven-thirty!*

Walking into Stuart's Pharmacy and Diner a few minutes later, Grant smiled as he saw Jillian sitting in a booth waiting for him. Thinking of the little girl from the school who had reminded him of the Jillian of years ago, his heart skipped a beat at the woman she had become. Her blue eyes twinkled as he dropped a kiss on her lips before sliding into the red, vinyl covered booth, sighing heavily.

"That doesn't sound good," she said, a small frown forming. "Tough morning?"

Nodding, he replied, "Oh yeah. High-speed chase down Highway 13, followed by the arrest of another drug runner, then spent a few hours at the elementary school and got a lead I need to follow up on."

Eyes wide, she leaned forward, running her fingers

over his arm. "I'm sorry, honey. I'm glad you called, so I could meet you here."

Looking at her sitting across from him, Grant knew why he fought the attraction for so long but wished he had pulled his head out of his ass sooner. Her soft touch. A gentle smile on her warm, concerned face. Her rockin' hot body showcased in a light green sweater and skinny jeans that had his tired body sitting up to take notice. *Damn, I wasted a lot of years fighting this.* He linked his fingers with hers as Katelyn made her way over.

"Hey, lovebirds," she called out. "What'll it be?"

Grant looked at Jillian and grinned, the memories of many times sitting in the same booth when they were teens filling his mind, and, by the matching grin on her face, she remembered, too. "We'll both have cheeseburgers, mine with everything and hers with no pickles or onions. Mine with fries and hers with onion rings, so we can share. And two chocolate milkshakes."

Katelyn threw her head back in laughter. "Geez, that's a blast from the past!" Walking away, she called over her shoulder, "Nice to have you two back!"

Grant's eyebrows lifted as he watched their dark-haired friend walk away. "I thought she was against you giving me another chance," he said, looking at Jillian's beaming smile.

"You remember what I like to order here?" she asked softly, her smile reaching her wide, blue eyes.

"Yeah...like it's part of me," he replied. Jerking his head back toward Katelyn, he prompted, "Katelyn?"

Lifting her shoulders in a slight shrug, she said,

"Katelyn loves me. She's always wanted the best for me."

"And she thinks that's me?" he asked, unable to keep the incredulity out of his voice.

"Well, for a while, no," she admitted, "but recently… let's just say that she's willing to give you another chance."

Giving a tug on her hand, he pulled her toward him as he leaned forward, meeting her in the middle of the space. "All I needed was you giving me just one more chance, sweetheart," he whispered against her lips before sealing them with a kiss.

18

Grant observed the faces of his fellow officers, his voice tight with anger as he read his report about the morning's activities and subsequent arrest. As he finished reciting the facts, he pushed the report away and said, "I'm telling you, that guy was scared. Scared shitless. But Colt played him perfectly."

Looking over to Mitch, Ginny said, "How's Hannah doing?"

"She's pissed the shooter hasn't been found. I was afraid the press would be all over a prisoner getting gunned down on the courthouse steps," he admitted. "And it seems as though the big news stations couldn't wait to report about it."

"Well, this guy was scared as fuck to be going to the same jail."

"Think Colt'll get him to talk?" Sam asked, going for his second cup of coffee before plopping back down in his chair.

Nodding, Mitch said, "Colt is former Army CID. He

was an investigator—and a damn good one. I can see him making this guy crack."

Rubbing his hand over his face, Grant said, "There's more to report from this morning." The other officers' eyes turned toward him, and he told them about Jade's student from the classroom lesson. Pulling out the piece of paper with the child's information written down, he said, "I'm gonna start checking into this, Mitch, but I already recognize the address. It's in the trailer park on the north side of town."

"Damn," Burt cursed. "Those new owners have done a good job of cleaning that place up. Hate to think there's a problem there."

Sam added, "I was on the force when you all were in high school. Those trailers used to be run down and nothing but drug infested shitholes." He sighed deeply before recanting. "Well, not all of them. Some were just homes to good people who needed cheap housing, but a whole section of the park was a den of depravity."

Burt said, "The previous owner died, and a new one bought the park. Cleaned out the old trailers and has worked at keeping it fairly nice. I hate like hell to think that someone's running drugs there now."

"I'll see what I can find out without endangering the child. Don't want anyone to suspect that she's told us anything."

"Right," Mitch agreed, "but keep us in the loop."

The metal chairs scraped against the tile floor in unison as the group dispersed to their duties.

Grant slowed his SUV as he drove through the trailer park while school was still in session. Mowed lawns and flower beds surrounded quite a few of the closely packed trailers, including the one Junior and Bobby lived in. Passing a neat, white, double-wide trailer with dark-blue shutters, he viewed bird feeders, a bird bath, and wind times tinkling in the breeze. Smiling, he appreciated the care so many of the residents took in their homes. When he was a teen, he knew many of the trailers were unkempt as transient residents moved through. As he wound his way toward the back section, the older trailers stood, some with torn screen doors and garbage bags sitting just outside the front steps. *Looks like the new park owners are only able to clean things up a bit at a time.*

Making his way back to the front section, he stopped outside the Hubbard's home, observing the freshly painted shutters and flowers lining the front walk. His boots crunched on the gravel as he walked to the front door, surprised as it was flung open before he had a chance to knock. A thin woman appeared, her eyes narrowed on his face before her gaze slid down to the police logo on his shirt and then to the badge on his belt.

"What do you want?" she asked, wrapping her stick-like arms around her waist, as though to ward off bad news.

"Just checking the neighborhood, ma'am," he replied.

"Ain't never heard of no cop just checking unless

they got somethin' they're after. We rent this place, pay our bills, and ain't had no trouble with the law."

Nodding, he glimpsed inside the trailer behind her, noting the cleanliness of the interior matching the neat exterior.

"There's been some talk about young people and possible drugs in the area, ma'am, so I'm just patrolling and making sure I get to know more of the citizens."

Her eyes narrowed again, sizing him up. "I live here with my daughter. Husband works railroad construction and he's gone most of the week...comes home on weekends. My stepson lives here, too."

"Does he go to school as well?"

Grant watched as a flash of irritation flew through her eyes before they narrowed on him again. "Nope. He's outta school."

"He work around here?" She rocked back slightly, and he wondered if she was going to slam the door in his face. He kept his expression neutral, hoping she would keep talking.

She lifted her bony hand, smoothing back her hair held in a tight ponytail. Licking her lips, she shifted her gaze down before mumbling, "I don't know where he works. He's an adult and don't answer to me. He comes and goes. Helps out with rent and stuff, so I don't ask him too much."

Taking a step backward, Grant smiled and nodded. "Well, it was nice to meet you. By the way, I'd like to invite your daughter to the ball field in town this Saturday." He pulled a card out of his pocket and held it out toward her in his fingers.

Her hand began to reach for the card, then hesitated, her brow crinkled as her eyes narrowed on him again. Finally, she plucked it out of his hand and looked it over carefully.

"American Legion? I heard some others talking about their kids playing. My Karly don't like ball too much."

"She wouldn't have to play, but she could watch and make some new friends. I'm sure some of the kids in her class will be there as well."

Chewing the inside of her cheek, the woman sighed. "I've had some medical bills and there's not much left over for her to do too much outside of school—"

"There's no charge for anything. It's all funded by the American Legion."

Her eyes widened for a second before the corners of her tight mouth turned up slightly. "No...no cost?"

"Nope, and we've got people who can pick her up if you're working or something."

Her head jerked in a short nod as she stepped back inside her house. "All right," she declared. "That's neighborly of you."

With a wave, he called out, "Nice to meet you." Walking back to his cruiser he stopped at several of the houses around, but only found one other elderly man at home. Heading back to the station, he detoured as he saw Gareth walking from his truck into his office.

"Hello?" he called as he entered the reception area. Hearing Gareth yelling from the back, he stepped into the PI's office. "Hey, man, how's it going?"

"Good, good," Gareth replied. "I'm glad to see you. I was just going to head over to talk to Mitch, but I got another call to check out, so can I give the info to you?"

"Sure," Grant replied, sitting across from him. "What's up?"

"Got a lead on that lawyer Mitch was interested in —Stanley Martino."

Attention snared, Grant leaned forward, his forearms resting on the desk. "I'm all ears, man."

Nodding, Gareth pulled out a folder from the plastic file holder on his desk. "The attorney's got some interesting bank account transactions that I've been able to dig into. Doesn't make him guilty of anything, but it's interesting, nonetheless. Seems that up until about three years ago, he was an ordinary attorney making ordinary money, nothing remarkable at all. He opened his own defense practice, not too big, and his bank deposits reflect that—nothing concerning there. Then, about two and a half years ago, he made a rather large deposit; only nine grand, but still a nice amount. Realistically? Okay, that could have come from selling a car, some stocks, hell, even some property. And, in this day and age, that amount wouldn't even trigger the IRS's interest or qualify for a Currency Transaction Report."

"But..." Grant prodded.

"About six months after that, he made another nine grand deposit. And did so about every other month for the rest of the year. He even set up an investment account at his bank for the deposits. So, I went on to check out his clients over that time. Although he had been defending a variety of clients, from spousal abuse to drunk driving to grand theft to embezzling, he suddenly started representing some arrested for drug distribution that caught my attention. It wasn't like he was defending some doctor accused of passing off prescription drugs, but a couple of real lowlifes."

Gareth shuffled a couple of papers in the file before continuing. "Okay, here they are—got a list of some of these clients. Since it's public record, they weren't too hard to find. Now, what struck me is that he's getting so much money at once, seemingly from these guys caught on drug distribution—which, again, is not his typical clientele—but this clientele doesn't appear to be able to afford anything better than a public defender... and yet, here they have the money to not only pay a private defense attorney, but somehow pay him well."

"What was he able to do for them?"

"For a couple, he managed to get 'em off on technicalities. Several got reduced sentences."

"And the money?" Grant probed further.

"Can't find the source. There was no bank transfer of funds. No check. It appears they were all cash deposits. Even though they were somewhat regular, they were less than $10,000 each, so they didn't trigger a Currency Transaction Report. Then, about a year ago, they stopped. With some real digging on my part," he cleared his throat and, with a self-deprecating grin, said, "looks like he may have set up an account in the Caymans and has been depositing even greater amounts there—thus avoiding the CTR and any suspicious looking activity on his part."

Grant leaned back, mulling over the possibilities. "So, he starts representing some drug dealers that could not possibly cover his expenses but somehow manage to and then some, opens an off-shore bank account to keep this on the down low... he's got to be at the beck and call of someone able to afford all this."

"Yep, that's about the crux of the matter," Gareth agreed. "Anyway, I was about to take this over to Mitch and just got a call for another client, so if you don't mind, I'll give the report to you and let you share it."

"No problem," Grant acknowledged, his hand reaching across the table toward the file Gareth was sliding forward.

Gareth blinked as he shook his head, saying, "I didn't even ask why you came in."

"Well, it's not like you didn't have anything to go over with me," Grant chuckled, "but yeah, I wanted to ask if you've ever done any surveillance in the trailer park on the north side of town."

"Some," Gareth nodded, his brow crinkled in interest.

"Got a tip that there might be some drug activity going on—either with some teens or even older. I'm checking out a lead on Jermaine Hubbard."

"Don't know that name and don't have any specifics, but I'll keep my ear to the ground for you."

Standing, the two men shook hands before Grant picked up the folder from the desk. With 'goodbyes' and 'good lucks' between them, he drove back to the station to update Mitch on the findings.

"Where are you?"

Stanley cringed at the harsh voice on the other end of the phone. Sucking in a quick breath, he responded, "I'm in my office, where I'm trying to get some work done." He looked out of his condo's front window, almost afraid of someone lying in wait for him in the street. Not seeing anyone, he turned back to the open suitcase on the bed and continued to fill it with clothes —everything he could possibly need for an extended vacation in the Caribbean.

"Your work is to be working for me," came the sharp retort.

"You are not my only client, Juan," he said, hoping his voice carried more authority than fear, although the fear was choking. "And it was one thing to defend the occasional person on your...*payroll*, but now it's getting to be too frequent. I'm sure I've got people that are checking on me. I'm a legitimate defense attorney, for Christ's sake!"

"You are on my payroll, you royal prick," Juan bit back. "I pay you well to be available for me."

Knowing it was a risk to keep antagonizing Juan, he sighed heavily as he replied, "What is it? What now?"

"Another piece of shit runner got caught. Talk to him but let him know he'll get the same treatment if he's not careful."

Plopping down on the side of the bed, his shoulders slumped. "If I go back to the same hick town, to the same hick jail, talking to the same hick cops...you don't think the Feds will be all over that?"

"Just do it. Make it work. And I promise this'll be the last time we have this problem in that hick town."

The silence hung between them for an uncomfortable moment until he finally agreed, squeezing his phone in his hand after disconnecting. Rubbing his hand over his face, he dialed his secretary.

"Margery? I'm almost ready to leave. You've got the keys; I'll need you here tomorrow morning. I've left detailed instructions for both you and the movers. The furniture goes to my sister in New Jersey, and my books and the rest of my clothes are to be packed up and shipped to the address I provided. If anyone asks, tell them I'm on an extended family emergency. The Simons Law Firm is a well-established firm in town, and they are taking you and any of my outstanding clients, so you'll be well cared for."

After saying goodbye, he closed the suitcase and called for a taxi to come to the back entrance of the condo building. Rolling his three suitcases out, with his laptop case slung over his shoulder, he stood at the door looking back one last time. With an angry grimace, he closed and locked it behind him.

19

Jillian heard the soft whimpering first, before feeling Grant's body tense. Rolling over, she carefully placed her arm around his waist, hoping her touch would calm whatever he was fighting in his dream.

Grant woke suddenly, his breathing harsh as his body jerked against something. Unable to sit up, it took a few panicked seconds to realize his arms were pinned by Jillian's soft, warm body.

"Honey, it's all right." Her quiet voice instantly soothed his racing heart as her hand gently lay on his chest. She watched as he swallowed deeply several times, her fingers lightly tracing his muscles and shoulders.

With one hand still underneath her body, he threw his free hand across his eyes, unwilling to let her see his terror. *Jesus, how did my nightmares change? And why?*

"Will you tell me what it was about?" she asked, her fingers now playing with the smattering of soft chest hair. "Please...it might make you feel better."

Dropping his arm from his face as he twisted toward her, he stared silently before pulling her forward and placing his lips on her forehead.

She waited, knowing he needed time to process the dream and how much he would tell her. "Was it your regular nightmare?"

He shook his head, afraid to tell her what terrors had crept into his dreams, but one look at her determined-to-help face and he knew he needed to talk about it. Even his counselor had agreed that talking about the nightmares would help him process them, therefore giving them less control.

"It started the same as always...the truck rolling up, dust billowing out from behind," his voice was raspy as he sucked in another breath. "The explosion...the ground shaking...everyone ducking as metal flew out in all directions." Letting out his breath, he closed his eyes, willing the scene to disappear. Speaking again, he added, "The slow-motion walking over to Julie...it seemed to take forever and then seeing her as I always have..."

"Okay," Jillian said, her voice barely above a whisper, glad he was sharing and not shutting her out. She waited a moment, then touched his sweaty face gently as a prompt to continue.

"But this time, when I got there...it was different."

"Different?"

Grant nodded, his body a mixture of taut and dismay, and yet he craved the feel of her light touch. "She wasn't wearing her fatigues. She was wearing something bright."

Jillian's eyes widened, her own heart picking up speed as she anticipated where his dream was taking them.

"When I rolled her over, it wasn't Julie." He clutched her jaw, his rough thumb rubbing over her cheek, reminding himself the woman in his arms was alive and well.

"It was...me?"

His nod was the only answer and for a second, Grant feared she would leap from the bed in horror, insisting he leave. "I—"

"Oh, baby," she crooned, her lips finding his, kissing him lightly before pulling back to grasp his face. "I'm here, I'm fine. It was just a bad dream. I'm not going anywhere and nothing's going to happen to me!" She pulled his body in tightly, scooting up in the bed so that his head pillowed against her chest, rocking him.

He allowed her this measure of comfort...hell, he reveled in it. After years of waking up alone with his night terrors, he pulled her closer, hearing her heart beating steadily against his cheek. His fears of vulnerability dissolved as the reality of her touch ignited him. Desperation to bury himself deep inside her overrode all other thoughts.

Leaning back, he cupped the back of her head, bringing her forward until their lips met—a slow, easy kiss until his heartbeat increased again, but not in fear. Drowning in her taste, the texture of her lips, the scent of her hair, he slid his hands down to the hem of her nightshirt, his fingers itching to touch her bare skin.

Jillian instinctively knew what he craved, knowing

nothing makes someone feel more alive than connecting intimately. She leaned up, separating just enough to pull her shirt over her head, tossing it to the floor.

He gazed at her for a moment, undone by the trust she placed in his hands. He gave himself over to knowing her — the right touch, the right moment — bringing her pleasure with the focused devotion of someone who had been waiting a long time to do exactly this.

The sensation built and spread as they moved together, hands exploring, legs tangling, until she rolled over and landed on top of him.

She straddled his hips, the moonlight falling over her beautifully, her long blonde hair loose around her shoulders. He gazed up at her like she was something he couldn't quite believe was real.

"Please," she begged.

"Please what?" he teased.

"I need you. I need all of you," she said, her head falling forward, pinning him with her gaze.

"Take what you need," he answered, his hands moving up to cup her warmth against him.

"What about what you need?"

His eyes moved up to her face and a slow, easy smile curved his lips. "Baby, you are what I need."

Determined to chase away his nightmares, Jillian shifted over him, and they came together slowly, her breath catching.

Grant wanted to close his eyes and simply feel, but he fought the urge, keeping his gaze trained on the beautiful woman giving herself to him. Her hands found his shoulders, and the memory of her telling him she loved them surfaced with a quiet warmth. Her fingers pressing in as her blue eyes, shining with understanding and acceptance, humbled him completely. Her normally sun-kissed skin glowed pale in the moonlight. But it was her lips, parted around a soft groan of pleasure, that finally undid him.

He grasped her hips, and they found their rhythm together. She held on to him like an anchor, certain she couldn't support herself otherwise, and she didn't care. *As long as he's making love to me.*

The tension between them coiled tighter and tighter. She was breathless and trembling as his gaze moved over her face as though he needed to be sure she was still with him. She was. Completely.

She flopped onto his chest, both of them breathing hard into the cool night air, hearts pounding, unable to speak or move for several long minutes.

Jillian finally pushed up off his chest and grinned down at him. "Feel better?"

"Hell, yeah!" he chuckled, his nightmare replaced now with the reality of her draped across him. As his laughter faded, he cupped her face in both hands, his thumbs moving gently over her skin. "Baby, the idea of you being taken from me is my worst nightmare."

"I'm here," she whispered, leaning down to touch her lips to his. "And I'm here to stay. There's no danger here...nothing to fear. I love you...I never stopped loving you."

He closed his eyes against the pain, grimacing for a

moment as the weight of all the wasted years hit him once more. But he had to let that go. He drew a slow breath, opened his eyes, and felt the warmth of her forgiveness move through him like something healing. "I love you too, Jillian. With all my heart. And with everything I have to give, I vow to protect you and love you for the rest of my life."

With a flip he rolled her over, holding his weight on his forearms, his lips finding hers with everything he had left to give. Ready for round two, the sound of a vibrating phone on the nightstand barely crept into his consciousness.

"Bab fo," she mumbled against the onslaught of his kiss.

"Mmmm?" *It can wait!* Not willing to slow the passion, he moved his hips.

"Baby," she said, out of breath as he kissed his way down her jaw. "Phone."

The phone vibrated again, seemingly more insistent as he allowed its intrusion to interrupt his kiss. Reaching over he answered curtly. "Yeah?" A pause. "Shit, Mitch."

Jillian watched as his face morphed from passion-interrupted irritation to shock.

"Right, be there in fifteen." Hanging up, he looked down, his eyes full of regret. "I'm sorry, but—"

"You've got to go," she finished for him, a rueful smile on her lips. Touching his mouth with hers, she said, "It's okay, honey." Pulling back slightly, she reminded, "Just remember...I'll always be here when you get back."

Rolling off her body, he stalked into the bathroom and came back out a few minutes later, quickly throwing on his khakis and BPD polo. Jillian turned to the side, her head propped up on her hand, watching him get ready. As he fastened his gun holster, she was reminded of what he faced on the job.

"Will you be all right?" she asked. A reminder of the prisoner that had been gunned down on the courthouse steps of Easton a week earlier bolted through her. The realization that the sleepy little Eastern Shore was not immune to the ills of the world made her stare at him, wide-eyed with fear.

Bending over, he kissed her once more, this time ending with a smile. "No worries, babe. Now that I have you to come home to, I'll be fine."

Fifteen minutes later, Grant pulled his SUV off a long drive on the north side of town, close to the county line. The drive wound around toward the beach where he pulled into a clearing next to the dunes and parked beside a number of other law enforcement vehicles. Mitch and Burt were already there, and Ginny pulled in right behind him.

Observing as Zac exited the back of the ambulance, he hustled over to the group standing at the top of the dune. Hearing a noise from behind, he saw Ginny and Sam approaching as well as Colt's Sheriff SUV driving up.

Stalking over to where Mitch stood with Burt, he

looked over the dune, his gaze immediately latching on to the body lying on the beach. *Male, dark suit, hands tied behind his back, obviously shot in the head. But who the fuck is it?*

20

Before Grant could ask the identity of the body, Mitch turned, his mouth set in a firm line, eyes hidden behind the same reflective sunglasses they all sported.

"It seems our intrepid attorney, Stanley Martino, has met an untimely demise...and was left here on our turf."

"Executed," Ginny huffed as she reached the group and scanned the carnage.

"Yeah," Grant acknowledged. "Left here as a warning to us?"

"More likely a warning to anyone around working for this gang not to mess with them."

"But why him?" Burt asked, hands on his hips, his stance matching the others'.

Colt interjected, "Just got a call from the FBI in Baltimore. Seems Mr. Martino was attempting to leave the country. His condo is packed up and movers were inside loading the furniture according to Martino's instructions. His secretary has been located and she indicated he had tickets to the Caribbean, leaving last night from Baltimore Airport. When questioned, she admitted it had not been a planned trip as far as she knew, but he called her two days ago with instructions for his practice to merge with Simons Law Firm...at least his legitimate clients. She wired money to his Cayman account, got the tickets, and was in charge of forwarding some of his belongings that were going to be put in storage."

"Fuckin' hell," Grant cursed, his words echoed among the others standing around, watching the crime scene being processed.

"From what we can see," Mitch continued, "it looks like he was killed somewhere else and brought here, taken over the dune, and dumped." He looked at the deputies from North Heron as they began to work the scene, before turning to his group. "Help where you can, but just know that when the FBI arrives, they'll take over."

As the others began to investigate, Grant could not drag his eyes away from the body on the beach. The gender was different...the clothes were different...but as the body was rolled over, all he focused on was the destruction. His back hit the nearest tree as he closed his eyes tightly, praying the image of his nightmare with Jillian as the victim would flee from his mind. Hoping the tree would hold him up while protecting him from the probing eyes of all around, he felt a body near his as a quiet voice asked, "You okay?"

Knowing it was Ginny, he sucked in a cleansing breath before opening his eyes. "Yeah."

She nodded, no more questions forthcoming, giving him a moment to compose himself. Continuing to observe the crime scene processing, she noted, "Weird, isn't it? Like dumping something right at our back door."

Grant, his head cleared and his fingers itching to search the area, nodded. "Mitch and Colt will find out everything 'cause, while the Feds are stepping in, I've got a feeling that whatever's happening, it's been brought to our back door for a reason. And I'll bet that last runner we arrested won't open his mouth for a deal now." With one last glance toward Stanley's body, Grant turned away and noticed two all-black SUVs driving up as he stalked back to Mitch. "Now that the Feds have shown up, I'm going on patrol. We've got a game later and I've got some investigating to finish on a possible suspect in the trailer park."

"Oliver, these are amazing!" Jillian called out as the artist brought one more box upstairs to her. She hefted a large bowl, the various blues fired into the pottery capturing the sunlight streaming through the window. Junior sat cross-legged on the floor, making a rudimentary list of each piece she unwrapped, while Bobby stared up in awe at Oliver, who ruffled his hair as he walked by.

"Here is the last box to be mailed," he said. "This one is to California and the others are to a dealer in Texas."

"I'll take care of them this week," Jillian promised. "What do you have in them?"

He looked up quizzically, his eyes wide. "In them?"

"Yeah, silly. The boxes? Are you shipping more pieces like this bowl?"

"Oh, oh. Sorry...my mind was somewhere else. Um...yeah, there are a couple of vases and bowls... all mine. Sometimes I sell pieces that my interns make, but only locally."

"Do those dealers mind getting pieces from the interns instead of you?" she asked, cocking her head to the side. "I thought they would only want your work."

"There's only so much I can produce myself, so if the intern is working under me and their techniques are the same, I consider them as coming from my shop and sell them as such. Each artist is given fair credit, of course, but they are listed as being under my tutelage. I thought I'd keep them local for the time being, branch out later on maybe—if the artists are interested in that. Don't worry, the buyers know what they're getting and pay accordingly, on a scale."

Shrugging, Jillian smiled. "Well, good! More for both of us then!"

Oliver met her smile, his gaze holding on her face before sliding over to the boys. "Who are your helpers?"

"Boys, come over here and meet Mr. Dobson, our potter. Oliver, these are two young men who work for me after school some days. This is Junior and he's a whiz at helping me catalog the items coming in." She stood behind Junior, her hands on his shoulders as he stood with straight posture, his hand coming out to shake Oliver's.

"And this," she continued, moving behind his star-struck brother, "is Bobby, who is a budding artist himself and a true fan of your work."

"Well, it's nice to meet a fellow artist," Oliver said, bending down to Bobby's level.

The boys moved to carry Oliver's boxes to the desk while Jillian watched them, a smile playing at the corners of her mouth.

"You seem to get along with them really well," Oliver commented, turning back to her.

"They're good kids and love helping. Junior is great with your packages to be sent off. He makes sure the labels are attached correctly and that we have them going to the right place."

"He keeps track of where they're going?" Oliver asked, his eyebrows raised. "I mean, I'm not trying to be a problem, but—"

"Don't worry," she assured, smiling up at him. "I oversee everything and just allow them to help."

Placated, Oliver sighed in relief. "Good, good. I just wouldn't want the artwork to go missing."

"No worries. Listen, Oliver," she said, stepping closer to him. "I was wondering if you would like to come to one of the American Legion games. There're lots of towns people there, and I have some friends that you could meet. We often go to Finn's Pub afterwards and you would be able to...uh...well, you know? Meet some more people." Jillian realized she was stammering but did not know how to set him up with one of her girlfriends if he was never in town.

"I...don't know," he replied, his brow furrowed as he shifted his eyes from her face to the window behind her. "Meeting other people would be nice, but I've got no idea how long I might be in the area."

"Oh...I thought you were here to stay?" Searching his face, she found no answers as he continued to avoid looking directly at her.

About to question him further, they were interrupted by a shout from downstairs.

"Boys! You ready to go?" Grant yelled, instantly lighting a fire under Junior and Bobby who jumped up and ran to the top of the stairs. Within a few seconds, Grant rounded the corner, grinning widely at the two youngsters with enthusiastic greetings of their own.

He twisted around, his eyes searching for Jillian but landing on Oliver first. Hiding his scowl, his boots clomped loudly on the wooden floor as he made his way to Jillian, his heart lightened by the welcoming smile on her face. She stood on her toes offering him a light kiss, one that he was more than eager to accept, before he turned back toward Oliver, keeping his hand on her waist.

The two men nodded their greetings but sized each other up in the way men do—barely disguised testosterone behind firm handshakes.

Sucking in a breath, Oliver glanced over at Jillian, saying, "Um...I guess I'll head on out now. I'll have a few more boxes to send to you by the end of the week."

"Remember, the invitation is always open," she said.

"Children's games are on Saturdays, but if you're working you can come by later to Finn's Pub." Wiggling her eyebrows, she smirked, "And I'll be sure to introduce you to some of my friends."

Chuckling, Oliver waved at her before heading down the stairs, pointedly avoiding Grant's stare.

"What was that all about?" Grant asked, pulling her in closer.

Nodding toward the boys, she shook her head slightly, offering him another light kiss only. "I was just being neighborly."

"Is that what you call it?"

"Grant, stop acting jealous," she fussed, keeping her voice down, but noticed the boys were oblivious to their discussion. "I feel bad, that's all. I'm actually trying to set him up with some of my single friends."

Grinning at her explanation, he bent down to whisper, "Okay, no more jealousy, I promise. And if you can play matchmaker so he won't feel like competition, that'd be fine with me."

Her forehead scrunched as she turned her face up toward his. "Competition? You are so silly sometimes! He's not competition. There is no competition. Only you," she finished, her hands planted on her hips, her foot stamping a staccato on the floor.

"Boys? Don't look," he ordered loudly before grabbing her around the waist, pulling her even closer.

"What are you—mmphh!"

Shutting her up with a deep, wet kiss, albeit one regretfully without tongue, he still heard the boys giggling in the background and knew it was the right decision. Leaning back, he peered down, pleased to see her half-lidded eyes, rosy lips, and dreamy expression.

He kissed the end of her nose and said, "See you at the ball field, babe. Boys? Let's go." With that, he, Junior, and Bobby tromped down the stairs, leaving Jillian ready to find her girlfriends. *Well, I need a testosterone-free zone for a bit!*

Cheers from the stands interrupted their conversations in intervals, but the girls did not mind. Seeing the smiling faces of the kids as they rounded the bases, some sliding into home plate, was worth the interruptions. As they took their seats on the bleachers once more, Katelyn asked, "So, this Stanley guy was shot on the beach? Our beach?"

Tori and Jillian both shrugged. "Mitch won't talk about an ongoing investigation," Tori explained, "so I don't know any more than what you read in the paper."

"What good is it to have my two best friends dating policemen, if you can't keep me up on all the info?" Katelyn huffed, only half joking.

"Well, I do know that Grant was in a pissy mood for a couple of days. It seems like the FBI hasn't been real forthcoming with their investigation."

Tori nodded grimly. "Mitch tried calling in some markers from his days in the FBI but wasn't getting anywhere. It seems the FBI and DEA don't always share all the info, especially when both are investigating."

"Well, at least Grant is happy with the kids here,"

Jillian added. "He's got a new one under his wing. See that little girl over by Ginny? Her name is Karly. He's been doing some investigating in the trailer park and met her mom. That's how he got them to come today."

"She's in my class," Jade said, smiling. "I'm glad he was able to get through to the mom. I haven't had much luck."

"You okay, Belle?" Jillian asked, noticing that Belle was more quiet than usual.

Nodding quickly, Belle's eyes stayed on the ball field, seemingly unaffected by the girls' conversation. Jillian did not want to embarrass her friend but wondered at her silence.

"This is all sweet," Katelyn said facetiously, throwing her hands up into the air, "but I still want to know about the dead man they found."

"Wow Katelyn, way to pick a gory topic to discuss," Tori said, wide-eyed, to which Katelyn initially looked contrite, but then just crossed her arms, expectantly.

"All we know is that he was the lawyer for the man caught carrying drugs through the Shore," Tori replied. "Mitch figured he was working for a drug gang or something like that."

"Yes, but why here? Why was he shot and dumped down here?" Katelyn prodded, lifting her long dark hair back from her neck before letting the weight of it drop down her back again.

Jillian sighed, knowing her best friend was like a dog with a bone when her interest was piqued. "I swear you should just go work for Gareth or open your own PI business!" she joked.

For once, Katelyn did not have a ready quip, instead sitting with her lips tightly pursed, her face turned away.

Before the conversation could continue, the game was over, and the crowd dispersed. As Jillian stayed to wait on Grant, she stared at the retreating backs of her friends, still wondering who might be right for Oliver.

21

Grant grinned at the sight of Jillian's scooter parked next to his house. Stepping into the entry foyer, he toed off his dirty shoes at the door. Not normally fastidious about his footwear on the old wooden floors, he was still wearing cleats from the game. He had driven Karly, Junior, and Bobby to their houses before heading home. The smells emanating from the kitchen drew him toward the back of the house, where he paused in the doorway at the sight of his mom and Jillian working side by side in the small room.

"What a view to behold!" he exclaimed, walking first to his mother and kissing her cheek before moving to Jillian and bending to capture her lips. "The two most beautiful women in the world right here in my kitchen."

His mother playfully slapped his arm, causing a giggle to erupt from Jillian. "You flatter just like your father," his mother accused with a grin.

"What can I say? I learned from the best," he boasted, leaning his tall frame over the two shorter women to peek down into the pot of bubbling chili on the stove. "Damn, that smells good."

"I got home, and your mom was here with the chili, so I asked her and your dad to stay for dinner," Jillian explained. "And there's so much, we also invited Tori, Mitch, and his parents to come too."

Marcia cried, "The more the merrier!"

Jillian noted the distressed look on Grant's face and leaned over to whisper, "Was that all right?"

Nodding, he sported a sheepish grin, his hand rubbing the back of his neck. "Yeah...just hope there's enough food, I'm hungry!"

Now it was Jillian's turn to roll her eyes as she shook her head. "Don't worry, there's plenty! In fact, your mom suggested I invite my parents over as well, since they just got back from their trip."

His eyes bugged out at the thought of being with Jillian's parents for the first time after he had caused their daughter so much heartache.

Taking pity on him, she leaned up and kissed his jaw, whispering, "It'll be okay. I promise."

"I think I just lost my appetite," he declared, nerves hitting his stomach.

She laughed as he poked his head back over the huge pot, eyeing it as though to ascertain how much chili was cooking. "Go shower and change before everyone comes. I promise it'll be enough!"

Twenty minutes later, he bounded down the stairs just as Mitch and Tori entered the front door, Tori's hands filled with a platter of brownies. Shaking Mitch's hand and kissing Tori on the cheek before she headed to the kitchen, he offered Mitch a beer. After retrieving two from the fridge, they walked toward the back deck where everyone had gathered.

Mitch's parents, Nancy and Ed Evans, as well as Marcia and Toby Wilder were already there, setting up the picnic table in Grant's small backyard. Jillian's parents, Claire and Steve Evans, newly back from their trip to New England, showed up a few minutes later. Claire had an apple pie in her hand, which she set quickly on the table before greeting her daughter. Seeing the two women together, it was easy to tell they were mother and daughter—thick blonde hair, blue eyes, trim bodies, and ready smiles. Plus, Claire was wearing a bright green sweater paired with sky-blue pants.

Steve walked over to Grant and clapped him on the shoulder. "Good to see you, son," he greeted.

Smiling to hide the fact that his stomach knotted at what her parents must think of him and Jillian together, Grant shook Steve's hand. Even though they decided to put it behind them, facing her parents brought a whole new tension when considering his behavior over the past year. "I know Jillian's glad to have you back in town." He held her dad's gaze and firm handshake.

Steve stared into Grant's eyes, taking his measure, before breaking into a smile. "We're glad you are back too."

Feeling as though he had passed a test, Grant

relaxed. "Need a beer?"

"Always!"

As they made their way outside, Grant watched as Steve fondly hugged Jillian and breathed another sigh of relief as he overheard her father say, "Glad to see you so happy, sweetheart."

The large gathering soon sat at the oversized picnic table in Grant's backyard, laughing and sharing. Jillian leaned over as the large bowls of chili were dished out and taunted, "See, I told you there would be enough!"

"I can't wait to see the shop," Claire said. "It sounds like the galleria is really taking off."

"Oh, mom, you must come tomorrow! The artists are fabulous, and I love being able to showcase the local work."

"I saw the article in the newspaper," Marcia added. "I think the pottery is beautiful. We'll have to meet the artist sometime."

Grant scowled at the thought of Jillian's mother, or his for that matter, meeting Oliver, but before he could retort, Steve asked about the recent drug problems that landed the small town in the news.

"Hell, boys, Claire and I've been vacationing for two months and while we're gone, it's like the Eastern Shore has become a damn French Connection!"

"Steve! Language!" Claire spouted, trying to shush her husband.

"Woman, there're no kids around until your daughter or nephew get busy," he retorted, causing both Mitch and Jillian to grimace in unison.

"Uncle Steve," Mitch said, "We're working on the drug case. We've made a few arrests so far. Some people are using the Eastern Shore to avoid the Washington, D.C. section of Highway 95, so we're working to keep us from being a stop on their run by keeping an eye on the kids and others who'd be likely to buy and deal."

"Well, it might be interesting for you to know that the stories of a man getting gunned down on the courthouse steps and now a body showing up on a local beach hit the national news. Hell, we were in a bed and breakfast on Cape Cod and heard about Baytown! You all ended up being on CNN!"

Steve shifted his gaze between Mitch and Grant, appearing to want to say more, but a grunt was all that left his mouth as Claire elbowed her husband in the stomach. Rubbing his abdomen, he turned to her and said, "I just want to know that these two have things in hand and are protecting my daughter!"

"Dad!" Jillian protested, her eyebrows dipping down as she pursed her mouth. "You need to—"

"Babe, it's okay," Grant assured her, wrapping his arm around her chest and pulling her back against his. Holding Steve's eyes, he said, "You're right, Steve. This is precious, and I'm doing everything I can to make sure Jillian and the whole town is safe. You can count on that."

"Well, then all right," Steve boomed, sending Grant a wink. "Now, where's the dessert?"

Hours later, Jillian curled into Grant's arms as they lay tangled in bed. Her hand played with his chest hair as her fingers traced the distinct muscles of his pecs, next to where her cheek rested over his heart. "Did you have a good time tonight? I know it was completely impromptu and unexpected."

His arms tightened in response as he shifted her slightly so that she was lying on top of him. "With what we just did, I'd think you had your answer," he joked, his hands pushing back the hair from her sweaty forehead.

"Well, sex to a man doesn't have to mean he did or didn't like something," she quipped, her grin meeting his.

"Oh, so you're an expert on men, now? His hand slid down her back, squeezing her delicious ass.

"Nope, just you."

Flipping over, he held her arms over her head as he nipped her kiss-swollen lips and nuzzled her neck. "I loved it, babe," he answered, lifting his head to gaze into her eyes, now seeing her smile reach their blue depths. "Coming home to you is a treat anytime. Coming home to a houseful of family and friends... perfect."

"My dad can kind of be...well, a bit strong," she added, biting her lips as she held his gaze.

"Steve? Don't worry about him," Grant assured. "He loves his town, he loves his family, and he's protective. I'd like to think I'll be the same when we have kids."

The words were out before he could pull them back in and heavy silence hung between them.

Grant's heart pounded, wondering what she thought of his implication. "Babe, I—"

"You want children?" she squeaked, her eyes wide. "With me?"

Chuckling, he rolled slightly to the side to ease his weight off her. "Yeah, Jillian. Now that I've finally accepted that you were the only one for me all along, I've got no intention of letting you go. I love you."

Her face beamed as her lips curved into the most beautiful smile. "I love you, too. But, then, you know that."

"I can never hear it enough," he confessed.

"So...um...kids?"

"Hell yeah, babe. I want it all with you. Marriage, kids, the house, the dog...everything." His smile became tight as he searched her face. "Is...well, is that what you want?"

"Grant, when I was twelve years old, I used to doodle your name in my school notebooks. By the time I was fourteen, I would scribble my name with your last name, just knowing I wanted to be Jillian Wilder."

"A lot's happened since then, babe," he said, his voice carrying a trace of sadness.

She reached up, cupping his cheek, feeling his stubble underneath her fingers. "Maybe we just needed to travel different paths for a while to end up on the same one again," she whispered, leaning up to plant a kiss on the corner of his mouth before her head plopped back to the mattress. "I love you, Grant. I always have and always will."

With a light heart, he claimed her mouth, exploring

every sweet crevice before claiming her body once more, long into the night.

22

_____

"It appears the FBI has made a connection between Stanley Martino and Juan Munoz, a known drug lord in the New York area. According to what Colt just told me, Juan has had Stanley on retainer for the past year, using him when necessary to try to work out deals." Mitch looked at his officers, before adding, "I've talked to Gareth, but the payments between Stanley and Juan were either cash or offshore, so that's why nothing turned up in his searches."

"Any idea why his body was dumped here instead of Baltimore?" Ginny asked.

"Gotta be because of that latest prick I chased down, who's now sitting in the same jail as his predecessor, Isaac," Grant growled, leaning back in his chair, his long legs stretched out.

"Or maybe a warning or threat to all of us to back off the investigations," Burt surmised.

"Fuck that," Grant and Mitch said in unison.

Sam stood to grab another cup of coffee from the

counter before sitting back down with a donut in his hand. "Look, I get how this all sucks with the drugs being run up and down our area, but other than an inconvenience, how does it involve our town?"

"My fear is that the meth lab found in the next county over will just move here. Meth is the poor man's cocaine," Mitch added.

Huffing, Burt commented, "And Lord knows, we've got the poor here."

Grant nodded as the group quieted for a speculative moment. Growing up, he never thought about North Heron County as the poorest county in Virginia—it was just home. His parents were firmly middle-class and, now that he thought about it, he never considered if his friends and classmates had money or not. Their school ball uniforms were old and worn but that never affected how many games they won. No one worried about what to wear to prom—they just wanted to show up with their favorite girl. His friends' parents had been farmers, shopkeepers, policemen, fishermen...*Hell, Callan's dad had been the janitor at the elementary school.* It just never mattered; but times have changed.

"Meth has replaced alcohol for some people," Ginny added, rubbing her forehead as she sighed. "So, there's a good chance it's here in our county."

Burt turned to Grant and asked, "Did you find out more about that guy in the trailer park?"

Shaking his head, he replied, "He hasn't been back home for a week and his stepmom didn't seem to know anything. I'm getting to know the little sister, but I've been reticent to ask her outright. I was hoping she would trust me enough to talk to me on her own."

"Word on the street, from some of the kids that hang out at the basketball court over at the Church of God, is that there's a big-time dealer making inroads into this area. Running, dealing, distributing," Sam said.

"Stanley's execution was definitely a warning," Mitch stated. "That'll make it harder for anyone to do any talking, for sure."

"You know, what sucks is that when we investigate the runners like Isaac, or even the crooked attorney's part of the drug trade, I sometimes forget how it can affect the ones right here. Like Karly, the little girl that gave us the tip about her stepbrother. The kids are the innocent ones that get caught up in this." Grant's frustration was palpable.

Pushing his chair back, Mitch nodded to his officers, adding, "Stay alert. I've got a feeling we're just touching the surface of what's coming through our city."

The group dispersed, Ginny and Sam heading out for patrol, Burt leaving to go home, and Grant sitting at a desk, firing up the computer.

Typing in Jermaine's dad's name, he wanted to see what he could find out about Hugh Hubbard. *His wife said he worked for the railroad...let's see if she's right.* A few minutes later, he discovered Hugh Hubbard did indeed work for the Canton Railroad Company. After an hour of searching, he found little else. *No arrests. No priors.*

Not even a traffic violation. Leaning back, he rubbed his chin, wondering what Gareth would ferret out.

With a wave toward Mildred, he drove to the Seafood Shack, buying a couple of take-out lunches before heading to Gareth's business. The PI welcomed him, glad to see the lunch boxes.

"Damn, man, just what I need!" Gareth greeted, hustling over to take the lunches from Grant. "You got something for me to check?"

Laughing, Grant ducked his head. "Yeah, sorry. I guess it looks like I'm bribing you with lunch."

"Hey, I'll never turn down food!" The two settled into chairs in Gareth's office. Once appreciative bites of fried clams and fries had been consumed, Gareth nodded toward Grant, saying, "Go ahead."

"I need to see what you can find out about a man here in town. He's not a suspect but his adult son, you remember I mentioned Jermaine Hubbard, may be involved in drugs and I want to check out the story his wife told me."

"Sure." Gareth quickly began searching, rattling off what he was able to find without too much digging. "Works for the Canton Railroad Company in Baltimore." Seeing Grant nod, he said, "Guess you knew that much."

"That and only that he has no criminal record."

"Okay," Gareth nodded. "Let's see what else comes up on an easy search. Credit is good. He's a union man and makes decent money. Basic checking and savings accounts and has a 401K retirement plan."

"He makes good money?" Grant asked, his eyebrows lifted in surprise.

"Yeah. For this area, it's good money," Gareth confirmed. "Why?" Looking back at his computer he said, "Oh, I get it. He lives in the trailer park. Hmmm."

"Nothing wrong with the park," Grant commented. "Lots of those places are real nice, but it seems like he could afford more...but, then, his wife did mention medical bills."

"Well, she worked part time as an aide at the nursing home but gets disability now due to a fall last winter that injured her back. Hugh also has an apartment in Baltimore...not a big one, but if he's paying twice on housing, that might be why they are renting a trailer."

"Yeah, maybe," Grant murmured. He sat quietly while Gareth worked.

"He's got a son from a former marriage...name's Jermaine—which you knew. He's eighteen. Didn't graduate from high school. His address is listed as the trailer park."

"He hasn't been there in a while. Can you dig up anything on him?"

After a few more minutes, Gareth shook his head. "Not much. No employment. No bank account. I'd say this looks pretty sketchy."

"The mom said he helped out with rent sometimes."

"That'd be hard to do with no employment. So, he's got to be getting money from somewhere."

Grant stood, wadding up his lunch trash and

tossing it into the trashcan. "Yeah, I was afraid of that." With a thanks and goodbye, he drove back to the station to report to Mitch, determined to do what he needed to do to keep Karly safe.

As the door to Finn's opened, the light and music spilled out onto the sidewalk. Inside, the bar full of townies, fishermen, and groups of friends crowded the old pub. Aiden and Brogan worked the bar, keeping the waitresses hopping as they took orders, while Katelyn served pitchers of beer to the gathering of Baytown Boys just back from another Legionnaire's meeting. Jillian and Tori arrived, heading to their men as the crowd parted for the two beautiful women. The local men appreciated the view, but ogling was kept to a minimum considering they were clearly walking toward policemen.

Grant looked up, a wide grin on his face seeing the orange T-shirt and yellow capris on Jillian. Her blonde hair, loose from its braid, hung in waves down her back. Standing, he welcomed her with open arms.

She walked straight into his embrace, loving the kiss he always placed on top of her head. Leaning back, she grinned in return, asking, "How was the meeting?"

"It was good, babe. We talked about the Auxiliary."

"Really?" she squealed, giving a little hop, bumping him on the chin. She heard a similar cheer from Tori and assumed Mitch must have given her the same good news. "We've got so many people who are interested in serving. Oh, Grant, it'll be so good for this county."

Letting go of his waist, she slid into the booth, scooting next to Zac, greeting him. Callan and two of his Coast Guard buddies were sitting across from her.

"Hey, girl," Zac said, leaning over to her. "I've got to make an inspection of the coffee shop and galleria this next week. I'm almost caught up on the fire inspections, but still need to get your section of Main Street."

"Aren't they supposed to be unannounced?"

Flashing his gorgeous smile, he shoulder-bumped her. "Some are, but with this one we just need to come in to test your sprinkler systems."

Just then, a woman Jillian did not recognize walked by, smiling at Zac. She winked and giggled before sashaying over to the bar. Zac stood up in the booth and, with a deft hop barely missing her head, made his way over the back, stalking after the woman while Jillian watched in awe. Turning back to the group, she shook her head. "How does he do that?"

"What?" Callan asked, his gaze following Zac as well. "Get the girl or hop over the back of the booth without knocking over drinks or kicking someone in the head?"

Laughing, Jillian said, "Both, I guess!"

"Practice...lots of practice," Callan answered. "It comes from having to hustle to put out the fires!"

Staring at Jason's arm resting on the table across from her, she bit her lip. He caught her staring and lifted his eyebrow.

"When will your shop open?" she asked. "The tattoo shop?"

"You interested in getting one?"

"Yes...something fun...something colorful," she confided.

Glancing down at her bright clothes, he chuckled. "I'd have never guessed." Seeing her seriousness, he said, "Hopefully soon. Hell, you can be my first customer if you want."

Clapping her hands in glee, Jason shared a glance with Grant.

"Don't mind her," Grant joked, "she's a goof!"

With a pretend glare shot his way, Grant grinned, shifting Jillian down the bench seat so that she was next to the wall. Pinned in by him, there was a small element of privacy, which he took advantage of with a kiss that bordered on the too-much-for-public kind. Not that Jillian was complaining as she melted into his arms.

Suddenly, they were jolted from the side as Katelyn sat down next to Grant. "I'm dead on my feet," she complained. Stretching her neck around, she complained, "Geez, Grant, let her up for air or y'all get a room!"

Laughing, he complied as he ended the kiss with a quick one on the end of Jillian's nose. Tori looked over at the girls and said, "Are you excited about the Auxiliary?"

Before Jillian could answer, Katelyn slapped her hand down on the table, causing those around her to jump. "Dammit boys, why don't you ever tell me anything?" she yelled at her brothers.

Brogan grunted but Aiden ducked his head. "Sorry, sis. I know you wanted to know, but we had to hustle back here to get behind the bar."

Katelyn turned to Mitch and said, "So, when can we get started?"

"I'll talk to Aunt Nancy and give her the info that I've got. Then we can call a meeting, kind of like we did when we got the American Legion started."

The three women grinned at each other, excited for a new challenge. Jillian felt Grant's fingers squeeze her shoulders slightly, and she turned her gaze up to his, her head cocked in an unspoken question.

Leaning down, his warm breath washed over her neck as he whispered, "Let's get outta here."

Beaming her reply, she nodded as they slipped out of the booth after Grant nudged Katelyn out of the way. Saying goodbye, Grant linked fingers with her, and they maneuvered through the crowd toward the door.

Hearing group laughter at the far end of the bar, Grant turned out of habit, to see who was there. Eyeing Jermaine Hubbard with several others, he quickly jerked his head toward Zac, who was flirting with the blonde at the bar. The unspoken communication between the men had Zac moving toward Jillian while Grant stepped back to the Baytown Boys still in the back.

Leaning into Aiden, he said, "Got some underage guys at the far end. Make sure to check their IDs."

Mitch stepped over, his attention on the group as well. "I'm taking Jillian home and then following them. I haven't been able to get a lock on where Jermaine is hanging out, and he hasn't been home in a week."

Brogan, listening, made his way back behind the bar, standing near the group, keeping his eyes concentrated on them. With a nod to the MacFarlane brothers, Grant walked back to the door, relieving Zac. Jillian looked up at him, her brows drawn together, but she did not question his actions.

"Thanks, man," Grant said, then grinned. "Better get back to your friend."

Zac spied the hook-up, leaning against the bar, a pout on her red lips. "No worries. I'll make it all better for her."

With a clap on the back, Zac sent Grant and Jillian out into the night. As soon as the light and music dropped off behind them with the closed door, Jillian turned to him. "What's up, Grant?"

Wrapping his arm around her he tucked her into his side as they walked toward his SUV. "I need to drop you off at home, babe, and then go back out for some surveillance."

Twisting her head up, she said, "I can get home by myself, honey. You can go do your cop thing."

Chuckling, he shook his head. "My cop thing, huh? Well, my cop thing can wait the few minutes it will take to get you home safely, and then I'll head back out."

Ten minutes later, after checking her house, they stood at the front door. Lifting to her toes, she threw her arms around his neck and kissed him soundly. He angled his head for maximum contact, delving his tongue deeply into her warm mouth.

Regretfully pulling back, he sighed as he kissed the top of her head. "I hate like hell to do this, but I've gotta go."

With a tight squeeze around his waist, she nodded her face against his chest. "I know. Be safe, honey," she whispered. "Come back to me."

"Always," he promised. "Always."

Grant called in his position as he followed the car Jermaine was in. Keeping his distance, he watched as they turned north on Highway 13 after leaving town. *So, he's not staying in town. Or at least, not hanging out here.*

There were no lights on the empty highway, making it harder for him to follow without being seen. He knew they had not been drinking in Finn's—Aiden and Brogan would have made sure of that-- but it did not mean they were clean. Having talked to some of the kids from the high school, he had a good idea that Jermaine and his friends were small time dealers.

He watched their vehicle turn west onto a smaller road about fifteen miles north of town. *Fuck, I can't follow too closely without them knowing.* Out of town, the county was not his jurisdiction anyway, so he noted the name of the road Jermaine turned down and waited a moment. Making the turn, he drove slowly down the road, scanning in the dark to see if he could make out their car. Passing a few farms, the lights out in the houses, he finally passed one with several cars outside and the windows lit brightly. Noting the address, he moved down the road until he was able to turn around before heading back home.

23

The dark night cast long shadows as Grant stood on Jillian's front porch instead of his own. He had almost arrived at his house when he checked his phone and read the text she had sent. **No matter what time – come to my house. I'm lonely without you!**

His heart twinged in his chest as he read the message and there was no doubt in his mind where he would go. They had shared house keys a few weeks ago, but this was the first time he would be joining her late at night, after a shift. With his hand on her front door-knob, he hesitated. Looking back over his shoulder, he glanced down her street, noting the row of neat houses. Jillian bought one of the older houses that had been refinished on a street just three blocks from the town beach, while he was renting a small house in town. The pleasant idea of coming to this house every day after work hit him—and made him smile.

Not a place to crash. Not a place to sleep off a wild

night spent partying. And certainly not a place to bring back a bar-hookup. But home. This house felt like home.

He had fought the idea of a home with Jillian for so long, but now that he had it, he relished the warm feeling in his chest. Julie had spoken of her home with her husband and child in such loving, happy terms. And now he understood—while her life may have been cut short, she had experienced the love that comes from living with someone you want to spend forever with.

Squinting his eyes tightly to ward off the sting of unfamiliar tears threatening, he knew he had found the same forever love. *Thank God Jillian gave me one more chance.*

Opening the door, he stepped through quietly, slipping off his shoes as soon as he entered. The foyer light was on as well as the hall light. Locking the door behind him, he turned when he heard the sound of soft footsteps coming down the stairs.

Jillian walked toward him, her sleepy eyes barely open and her blonde tresses wild about her head. An old blanket was wrapped about her body but as she stumbled toward him, her arms opened instinctively. Grant barely had time to throw his arms wide before she slammed into him, her blanket covered body plastered to the front of him as he enveloped her in his embrace. Tucking her head underneath his chin, he did not say anything for a moment, not sure if she was truly awake.

Finally, he whispered, "Baby?"

"Mmmm."

He smiled at her sleepy grunt and bent to scoop her up. At that motion, her eyes widened as she laid her head on his shoulder. Upstairs, he placed her back on the bed, settling her head on the pillow and pulling the covers up over her body. Kissing her forehead, he whispered, "I'll be right back," before moving into the bathroom. He was not sure she would even remember getting up; she slept so soundly, but he moved quietly, nonetheless. Within a few minutes, he slid underneath the covers craving the warmth only her body could provide. Wrapping his arms around her now sleeping form, he pulled her close. His mind wandered for a moment to the cases they were investigating, but then he forced them from his thoughts. *They'll still be there tomorrow, ready for me to tackle.*

Tucking her back to his front, he nuzzled her hair, the familiar scent of her shampoo teasing his senses as he allowed his body to relax. Home. This was home.

"All right, let's get started," Katelyn said loudly, followed by her famous whistle. The shrieking noise quieted the audience quickly.

The large gathering of women in the American Legion hall settled, all eyes on the women standing in the front. Jillian and her mother, Claire, along with Tori, Katelyn, and Nancy Evans stood, ready to hand out brochures on the American Legion Auxiliary.

Nancy spoke first, stepping to the microphone.

"Ladies, I'm going to read directly from the ALA website to explain our purpose for gathering here tonight. Then we'll start talking about what we can do." Clearing her throat, she began, "Founded in 1919, the American Legion Auxiliary is the world's largest women's patriotic service organization. The American Legion Auxiliary's mission is to support The American Legion and to honor the sacrifice of those who serve by enhancing the lives of our veterans, military, and their families, both at home and abroad."

Looking over the group, she continued, "Simply put, we are here to serve the needs of our veterans. Membership can be earned by being a mother, grandmother, sister, daughter, wife or any other direct descendent of an American Legion member or armed service member who has died in action. What we will do tonight is pass out information, decide if there is enough interest to move forward with a chapter here and, if so, nominate some of us to work on getting a chapter established."

The other women quickly began distributing the brochures while a pad of paper circulated about the room, collecting names, addresses, email addresses, and phone numbers. People began raising their hands with questions and the women at the front answered them as best as they could.

"What will we work on?"

"Is this just a women's club?"

"How often would we meet?"

Jillian pointed out the brochure on activities. "We

would volunteer and organize activities for youth, teens, active-duty military personnel, and veterans. I would encourage you to visit their website for information on what all we can participate in and how we can help."

"Will it take a lot of time? I work full time and—"

Corrine MacFarlane, Katelyn, Aiden, and Brogan's mom, stood up and looked over the crowd. "Ladies, some of you are here because of your grandparents, or husbands, and for many of us, our sons. Aiden and Brogan served, but as most mothers know...our children didn't come back the way they left...young and idealistic." Her eyes dropped to the woman sitting next to her, Tonya Bayles, and her voice softened as she reached down to grasp her hand. "And some of our Baytown Boys didn't return." Blinking back tears, she lifted her chin and continued. "So, before you pepper the ladies in the front with too many questions, I would encourage you to read the information to see if it's right for you."

Katelyn, smiling at her mother, added, "If you're interested already, then make sure to sign the paper making its way around the room."

Phyllis Banks, the mayor's wife stood and announced, "I'm in. My husband never served, but my father and grandfather did. I'd be proud to put my name on the list!"

Soon, other women, having read over the material quickly, began signing up as well. Jillian, Tori, and Katelyn all smiled at each other as the meeting came to a close. As the women slowly filed out of the meeting hall, Tonya walked over and silently hugged Katelyn. As her arms dropped back down to her side, she said, "Thank you, my dear. Philip would have been so proud."

Katelyn battled tears as she beheld the regal bearing of the woman she had once planned on having for a mother-in-law. Tonya smiled at the others but, before turning to leave, she moved back in to whisper in Katelyn's ear. "Philip loved you...but he would never want you to be alone. When you find someone else, do so knowing my son would want you to be happy. And so do I." With that, she slipped out of the room, leaving Katelyn staring in her wake.

Jillian swiftly moved to her best friend, sliding her arm around Katelyn's shoulders. "You okay, honey?"

Nodding, Katelyn dashed the tears from her eyes. "Fine. I'm fine." Sucking in a deep breath, she turned to the few leaders left and said, "Anyone want a beer before heading home? The Legionnaires go to Finn's after a meeting...don't see why we can't too."

With a laugh, the women headed into the evening toward the pub.

The dust from the road kicked up behind Jillian's car as she pulled into the driveway leading to Oliver's workshop. She had only been able to leave a message on his voice mail about dropping by but hoped he would be in the barn. Parking, she smiled as she climbed out of her vehicle. Taking in the farmland across the street and the woods behind his property, she smiled. Surrounded by the beauty of the Eastern Shore, she imagined it must be easy for an artist to find inspiration here. She still had not figured out which of her friends would be best suited for him but was determined to set him up soon.

Stepping inside, she called out, "Hello! Anyone here?"

Aubrey popped her head from around the corner, a smile on her pixie face. "Hi, Ms. Evans! Come on in."

"Call me Jillian, please," she responded, walking into the workroom. "Are you all alone?"

Aubrey nodded, wiping her hands on an old rag. "Yeah, Jonas has finished here, and Mike only comes occasionally. I really like it here so I'm hoping to stay for a while."

"I hope you do!" Jillian walked over to a shelf on the side of the wall and admired some of the finished pieces. "I still can't get over the colors...sunsets over water are what I think about when I see these vases and bowls."

"That's what Oliver is known for—the beautiful colors he gets from the different temperatures he heats the clay at." As Jillian looked back to her, Aubrey said, "I'm sorry he isn't here." She moved back to her wheel, adding, "Is there anything I can help you with?"

Opening her bag, Jillian replied, "Well, I have a check here for Oliver. I've been paid for the shipments to the galleries in California and Florida. There's another one in Virginia Beach that sent a payment as well. I have an itemized list and cut a check to Oliver, minus my commission."

She handed the envelope to Aubrey, who stood and motioned for Jillian to follow her. "Come on and we'll put it in his office. I'll be here until he gets back so I can make sure it stays safe."

The two women entered the small, messy office where Oliver worked. Opening the top desk drawer, Aubrey placed the check inside before closing it shut. Turning back around, she smiled and said, "Okay, safe and sound."

As they walked back through the workroom, Jillian said, "I assume Oliver pays you for the pieces that you create that are sent to the galleries? I was just told to pay him, so that's what I did."

"Oh, no worries," Aubrey said, sitting down at her wheel once more and lifting a measure of clay onto the wheel. "Right now, Oliver only sells his work to the galleries in other states. My work is still at the intern stage, so we keep mine local. He can work out the difference from the list."

Smiling, Jillian nodded. "Well, then, I'll be heading back to town. Please tell him I came by and make sure he finds the check." With a wave goodbye, she stepped out of the workshop, her sandals crunching down the driveway back to her car. Thinking of the cute art intern, she wondered if perhaps Oliver had a perfect date right under his nose. *Maybe a nudge in that direction would not be bad!*

The couple walked to the end of the town pier and watched the sun drop in the sky. The pier stretched out into the bay with the town beach on one side and the harbor bordering on the other. The fishermen had left for the day, leaving just a few people wandering along the wooden planks, ready to view the sunset.

Grant stood behind Jillian, his long arms stretched to the rail on either side of her, his front plastered to her back. She leaned her head against his chest and breathed in the salty air. They had talked about their day, his investigations, and her trip to the workshop.

"I'm proud of you, babe," he admitted. "You're really making a success of the Coffee Shop & Galleria."

Grinning, she said nothing as she appreciated the panorama in front of them. "Will you ever get tired of this view?" she asked. "I think I could see it every night and find it just as special each and every time."

"I always loved the sunsets here, but gotta admit that sharing them with you makes them even more memorable," he replied, kissing the top of her head. They continued to stand in silence for a few minutes watching the sky turn from various shades of blue to hues of pink and orange.

"I used to think about the sunsets...when I was in Afghanistan," Grant said, his voice barely above a whisper. "I'd watch them there and think about them here." Jillian said nothing, allowing his thoughts to flow freely. "I thought about you and wondered if you remembered."

The distant noise of families on the beach enjoying the sunset, along with the call of a few gulls, were the only sounds for a few minutes. The memory jolted Jillian from her happy place, sending her back in time.

I can't believe you leave for boot camp tomorrow," I cried into Grant's shirt as we stood on the pier watching the sun slowly disappear. "I'll just die without you; I know I will."

"Come on, baby," he said gently, lifting my chin with his fingers. "You've got to finish high school, and when I come home, you'll be old enough for us to get married."

Blinking back the tears, I stared up into his face. I loved the way his brown hair curled around his ears and the thought of the Army clipping it all off caused my tears to threaten once more. Swallowing deeply, I knew I had to be strong for him. Sniffing loudly, I said, "You better come back to me."

"I'll be with Mitch and Philip. We'll be fine. And they can be my groomsmen when we get married."

At that thought, a smile slipped onto my face, knowing he spoke of every dream I had ever had about him.

"Look!" he said suddenly, pointing out to the bay. "Just think of this. Every evening as the sun sets, I'll look at it from where I am and think of you standing here looking at it too."

It didn't matter that we would be on opposite sides of the world, in different time zones...I thought that was the most romantic thing he could have said to me. Taking a shuddering breath, I nodded, my eyes filling with tears again.

"Okay...we'll always look at the sunset together...no matter where we are."

"I remembered," Jillian finally said, her voice cracking. So many sunsets had come and gone since that night many years ago. *My God, was I ever that young and naïve?*

The wind off the bay blew her hair about her face where it escaped her braid, and she shivered slightly. Grant pulled her tighter, now wrapping his arms around her, providing more shelter.

"I talked to the counselor again the other day...I realized that I've made great strides in dealing with Julie's death, especially after talking to you, but that I hadn't really faced Philip's death yet."

Jillian twisted around in his arms, so her hands came up to rest on his chest, and her gaze sought his. "Did it help?"

His eyes roamed over her upturned face, and he lifted one of his hands to caress her cheek. "Yeah, it did." Sighing heavily, he gazed over her head to the ever-changing sky. "I didn't get to come home for the funeral. It was surreal and, even almost six years later, I find myself expecting him to meet us over at Mitch's for beer and crabs."

"I sometimes wonder if that's why Katelyn hasn't moved on," Jillian confessed. "I want her to be happy. I want her to find someone else, but," she shrugged slightly, "I don't know."

He dropped his eyes back to her, his brow furrowed. "Does she talk about him much?"

Shaking her head, she replied, "Not really, but I know she thinks of him. I know she still puts flowers on his gravesite, along with his parents."

Tucking her into his side, they began to walk back down the pier. "I'd like for her to have what we have... what Mitch and Tori have," she added.

"I think she will...eventually," Grant said. "Maybe when she least expects it."

24

The station parking lot was full as Grant pulled around back to park. Alighting from his vehicle, he nodded toward Chief Hannah Freeman as she drove up in her Easton Police cruiser. They entered together, greeted by Mildred, and walked into the already crowded conference room. Extra chairs had been placed around the table and against the wall. Colt was already there, plus the north county of Accawmacke's Sheriff, Liam Sullivan. The three visitors made themselves at home as Mildred bustled in with pastries and coffee, before heading back out to keep an eye on the reception.

Mitch began, "You all know that once a month, the heads of the local law enforcement agencies get together informally to discuss cases that involve each other, as well as ways we can support all of us on the Eastern Shore. Colt, Hannah, Liam, Wyatt, Dylan, and me got together yesterday and Colt, Hannah, and Liam wanted to meet with you all today."

Grant and the other officers nodded in acknowledgement. He knew Wyatt Newman and Dylan Hunt were the police chiefs of two towns on the northern end of the Eastern Shore, so assumed what was being discussed must be of particular interest to those officers in the southern tip.

Hannah began, "It's no secret that Easton's taken a big hit, literally and figuratively, making national news with a prisoner gunned down on the steps of the courthouse and the killer getting away."

She hid her anger well behind her consummate professionalism, but Grant noted the tic in her jaw as she spoke. "It's bad enough that our area is the new drug running highway, to avoid the D.C. area, but now they're setting up shops right here."

Her eyes cut over to Liam, handing the floor over to him.

The tall, lanky lawman rubbed his hand over his face before leaning in, placing his forearms on the table. "The meth lab we busted up was small. It produced some but wasn't a big contender. The FBI has informed me that they suspect meth is still being produced in this area and not just being transported through here. I've got my deputies, as well as Wyatt and Dylan's officers, with their ears to the ground, but there's no talk of another lab in my county."

"So that leaves mine," Colt provided, heaving a sigh.

"And your county surrounds our two towns," Mitch added with a head jerk toward Hannah.

"So, we're all in this together," Hannah agreed. She looked over at Mitch and his officers before saying, "Your town is bigger than mine. Honest to God, with

Easton having only a little over two hundred residents, I know each and every one of them. I don't think it's there."

"So, most likely we're looking at us?" Ginny asked. "Our town's bigger, with over a thousand residents, but I don't know of a crack house or a meth lab around."

Colt shook his head. "Fuckin' hell." He looked at Grant and said, "I took a look at the residence you followed, Jermaine Hubbard, too. Had no probable cause to search, but we've done several drive-bys. I don't think it's what we're looking for. Granted, it's got a couple of guys that are probably using, but not making. But my county is big and rural. There're a lot of places someone could hide what they're doing."

"I thought meth labs would have a lot of traffic...not necessarily easy to find, but with enough users and buyers going in and out," Sam queried.

"Not if it's a place that makes large quantities to send out...not to deal from the home." Mitch explained. "We were saying how it was the poor man's cocaine and how that fit our area, but meth has now replaced cocaine as the drug of choice in upscale nightclubs as well. So, there are labs now that mass produce to send out."

Burt huffed in frustration. "So, we could be looking at anywhere? But how do they get their raw materials?"

"Just when our government cracked down on Ephedrine, gangs started getting it from overseas labs," Liam replied.

Mitch added, "I've been studying this and reached back to some of my friends in the FBI. The major traffickers are operating from Mexico and are easily recruiting U.S. street gangs to carry and distribute both raw materials and the final product."

"Jesus, we need a fuckin' gang task force," Colt growled. "The other counties in Virginia have them, but on our shoestring budget, I'm doing the best I can."

A somber cloud settled over the group as they continued to brainstorm the investigation. Finally, Grant stood from the table. "Maybe it's time for me to have a conversation with Jermaine," he surmised, looking over toward Mitch for his opinion.

Nodding, Mitch added, "Take Burt with you when you do."

Pulling the cruiser up beside the new model, all black Charger parked outside the Hubbard house, Grant ran the license plates. *How the hell does a high school drop-out with no job buy a new car?* Suspecting the answer to that question, he and Burt stepped out of their vehicle.

Mrs. Hubbard answered the door again, her gaze shifting nervously. "Howdy, officers."

Grant noted her posture, observing how she stood in the doorway not inviting them inside. "Good morning, Mrs. Hubbard. I'd like to talk to Jermaine and notice his car is parked out front."

Fear flashed through her eyes as she licked her lips, nodding slowly. "He's...well, he's back in his old room, sleeping. Don't know when he got in last night...he's been gone for a couple of weeks."

"Can we come in? We just want to ask him some questions."

She hesitated, eyes darting between the two officers standing on her front stoop. Almost in resignation, she nodded, slowly stepping back, allowing Grant and Burt to enter. Once inside, Grant confirmed what he had suspected with his earlier visit—the trailer was clean and furnished nicely. He followed her directions, indicating Jermaine was in the second bedroom on the left and, with a sharp rap on the door, he and Burt entered.

Face down on the bed, Jermaine lay, passed out cold. Waking him with difficulty, the young man rolled over, his red eyes opening as his slack-jaw grin landed on them. Grant and Burt shared a look before Grant said, "Jermaine Hubbard? I'm Officer Wilder and this is Officer Tobber. We'd like to ask you a few questions."

"Sure, man," Jermaine slurred.

"Looks like you did some hard partying last night, son," Burt stated, his gaze darting around the room.

"Yeah, it was...um...just some buddies. You know how it is." Jermaine managed to sit up, leaning his back against the headboard, rubbing his hand over his face.

Grant stepped over to the dresser, noticing white powder and a few opened capsules, along with several empty beer bottles. "Looks like we can see how it is right here."

"Aw, man," Jermaine said. "You ain't got no cause to come up in here and bust my ass."

Grant and Burt recognized his lethargy, assuming, with the evidence in the room, Jermaine was crashing after his high.

"We're gonna have to take you in, Jermaine," Grant said, as Burt began collecting the evidence.

"Hell, naw," the younger man said, surging off the bed in a staggering attempt to throw a punch.

Quickly deflecting, Grant had him face down on the bed with his arms secured behind his back. "Let's not add assaulting an officer into the mix, okay?" Handcuffing him, Grant read him his rights as Burt placed the evidence in a bag.

"Fuck you, man. Dad's gonna shittin' kill me."

Walking out, Sheila eyed the trio, her lips pursed and a hard look in her eye. "Knew you were trouble," she said, staring at her stepson. "When you bragged about being eighteen and could do what you wanted, I told you that you'd better never bring nothin' in this house around my daughter." Her focus jumped to Grant, and she said, "I'll tell my husband, but I'm telling you all now, too. I don't want him back here around Karly."

"Ma'am, that's a family decision, but I think you're wise. He'll be in the county jail in Easton, if your husband wants to visit his son."

With a curt nod, Sheila opened the front door, watching as the officers escorted her stepson into the patrol vehicle.

"That was almost too easy," Burt commented as they drove back to the police station.

"He's a user, not just a runner or dealer. That makes him a risk to the organization that's moving this shit through the county." Sighing heavily, he added, "But knowing he was bringing drugs into the house, I'm glad to get him away from Karly."

Grant sat across from Jermaine, the jail's institutional, grey, metal table between them. The young man's eyes were clear today—and filled with fear.

"We've got you on possession and using. There was enough to also charge you with intent to distribute. But you've got to know the DA doesn't want just you. So, what can you tell us about where you got the meth?"

Jermaine's lips remained firmly pressed together, his fingers tightening as they lay clamped on the table, his only movement.

"That's a nice car you have registered, sitting in your dad's driveway. How'd you pay for it, considering you don't have a job or a bank account?"

Jermaine's eyes flickered. "My dad bought it for me. It was a gift."

"Was it now?" Grant said lazily, having already ascertained that the car was, in fact, purchased by Hugh Hubbard. "What nice thing did you do to make your dad buy you a car?"

"Can't a man buy his son a car?" Jermaine asked, his lips slightly curving.

"Sure, but usually it would be a reward for being a great son. Can't see that you've done too much to make him proud."

"He's plenty proud," the young man boasted, his

slight grin appearing more like a smirk the longer he stared down at his hands.

"Yeah, I just bet he's proud as punch to have a son sittin' in jail, twitching until he can get his next fix."

The smirk left Jermaine's face as he spouted, "Ain't got nothin' more to say to you, so don't waste my time."

"You talk big for someone who's facing time with the evidence in your possession. But," Grant said, scooting his chair backward, "I'll let you figure that out."

That afternoon, Grant walked back into the jail, meeting Chief Freeman as she walked toward him.

"The dad's been in talking to him. Jermaine's not giving up anything or anyone, but he's scared...just like the last guy you brought in."

"If they work for the same organization, then they're smart to be scared. Too bad they weren't scared before they got caught."

"The DA will go for no bail, even though this is his first offense, due to the situation. I think that's smart. He'll be safer here in jail anyway."

Nodding, Grant looked up as a burly man walked toward them, his physical resemblance to Jermaine making it obvious he was his father.

Stopping at Chief Freeman, Mr. Hubbard said, "He ain't talking, and that's what I've advised him to do."

"That's his right, sir," she said smoothly, "but when the DA speaks with him, she may offer a deal."

Mr. Hubbard's jaw tightened, and his scrutiny shifted away for a moment. "We'll see." With that, he turned and walked out the front door, leaving Grant and Hannah staring at his back.

Rubbing his chin, Grant wondered aloud, "Interesting. Curious that he wasn't demanding his kid be released...or protesting his innocence...or advising him to take a deal."

"What are you thinking?"

Jerking out of his musings, Grant said, "Oh, nothing in particular. Just...well, let me check on a few things, and I'll get back to you."

25

Jillian parked her scooter at the end of the gravel drive and walked to the front door of the small beach house. Sitting a few miles on the south side of town, the weather-beaten exterior gave evidence of a house that had withstood many years of the ever-present wind from the bay.

Knocking several times, she knew it would take more for the dweller to answer. "Lance? It's Jillian...and you know I won't just leave so you might as well open up!" A moment later, the front door opened, and she peered through the screen at the tall, dark-haired man.

"You always this much of a pain in the ass?"

Letting out a giggle, she nodded. "Yep, just ask my cousin, Mitch."

Shaking his head, Lance unlatched the screen and stepped onto the porch, not inviting her inside. "Just don't make this a habit."

"Look, I only came by to tell you that I need more of

your sea glass artwork. It's sold really well, and I'd like you to bring more."

Nodding, he said, "I'll have some pieces for you by the end of the week. I'm working on something new, but it takes a while."

Eyes sparkling, she beamed up at the quiet, ex-soldier friend of Mitch's. "I can't wait to see it!" Stepping forward, she placed her hand on his arm but removed it quickly as she watched him flinch. "Lance, I wish you'd let me pay you for the pieces."

"Materials come from the sea...don't cost me nothing but time, and I've got plenty of that," he replied.

"Okay, well, I'm doing what you said. I'm keeping track of the profits and then donating them to the American Legion.

Nodding sharply, he said, "Fine."

"Your work is really selling well and, if you want, I could give the profits to another organization as well... like...uh...maybe Semper Fi Fund or Wounded Warri —" His jaw tightened, and she caught the tic in his cheek. "Or not," she rushed.

Turning back to the front door, he said over his shoulder, "Is that it?"

Forcing a grin to ease the tension, she teased, "Yes, unless you want to invite me in for a cup of tea?"

A rare chuckle came from deep within his chest as he shook his head, disappearing back inside his house as he closed the front door.

Hopping back on her scooter, Jillian blew out a deep breath. Cursing her unintentional insensitivity, she drove back toward town wondering about the iconic recluse. *I wish I could find just the right woman for him, but I've still not found anyone right for Oliver.* Deciding she was a better shop owner than matchmaker, she putted down the gravel road.

"Girls' night!" Katelyn shouted, entering Jillian's house. Seeing Tori, Belle, and Jade already there, she grinned as she handed off the bottles of wine she brought from the pub.

"Come on back!" Jillian shouted from the kitchen, still plating the food she had prepared. With Mitch and Tori's wedding looming, the girls needed a night to plan, so they sent the men off to Finn's while they worked on details.

Avoiding the late season mosquitoes outside, the women piled into the living room. Katelyn and Tori ended up on the sofa, squishing Belle in between them. Jade took one of the chairs and Jillian plopped onto the floor, leaning back against the other chair. Setting her plate on the coffee table, she grabbed a pad of paper.

"So, what's on the agenda tonight?" she asked, looking over at Tori, who had just stuffed a cocktail shrimp in her mouth.

Trying to chew, Tori grunted instead. "Fwowa."

"Are you trying to say flowers?" Jillian laughed.

Swallowing, Tori blushed. "Yes, we need to decide on flowers."

"Baytown Floral usually does the weddings around

here, but I've heard there's a shop just outside of town in North Heron that does really gorgeous arrangements for weddings," Jillian said. "I used them for the Galleria event."

"I know the owner," Belle said. "She's the niece of one of my co-workers at the nursing home. She's really nice and I'm sure would love the business."

"Good. Write her name down on the list," Tori said. "We're going to have the ceremony at the Sunset Restaurant, and the reception will be there too. I honestly won't need many flowers for the ceremony, since the focus will be on the sunset behind us."

"Did you decide on food?" Katelyn asked.

Sucking in a deep breath, Tori shrugged. "There's no way I can afford a sit-down meal for everyone, so it'll just be a reception with finger food."

"I think that's fine!" Jade responded, her green eyes settling on her new friends. "So many people spend so much money on weddings, and half the time, they can't really afford it."

Giving a little shrug, Tori said, "The Sea Glass Inn is doing well, but I'm not rolling in dough, and I'm not going to ask Mitch's family to help; they've had a ton of medical bills with his dad's heart attack and recovery."

Katelyn snorted as she said, "And we know how much the police chief makes! Mitch really took a pay cut when he left the FBI to come be our chief!"

"I think simple weddings are the most beautiful," Belle declared, setting her plate down on the coffee table.

Jillian smiled at the dark-haired beauty, knowing

Belle had grown up in poverty and, even now, did not make much money as a nurses' aide. "I think you're absolutely right," she declared.

"Next," Katelyn announced, "bridesmaid dresses!" Turning toward Tori, she asked, "What hideous, obnoxious, poofy concoction have you decided on for us to wear?"

Belle gazed wide-eyed at the women as they burst into laughter. Seeing her discomfort, Jillian assured, "Don't worry, Belle, Tori's not insulted. We always used to joke that when we got married, we'd make each other wear awful dresses."

Smiling shyly, Belle said, "I can't imagine any bridesmaid dress would be ugly. You'd have to feel like a princess in a fancy dress."

"Hmph," Katelyn grunted. "Let's just prove you wrong." She pulled her iPad out of her bag and googled *ugly bridesmaid dresses.* The girls crowded around, hilarious laughter combined with snorts abounded, as they showed Belle just how ugly a fancy dress could be.

Holding her stomach, hurting after laughing so hard, Jillian asked, "Okay, we've seen what we don't want, but what have you decided on?"

Tori took the iPad and pulled up several pictures of what she had been thinking of. "I want the dresses to be pretty but not over-the-top." Oohs and ahhhs followed as the girls all viewed the dresses and voiced opinions.

Leaning back against the sofa cushions, Katelyn took in the empty plates and three empty wine bottles.

"Looks like a good planning session, girls. So what else is on the agenda?"

"When are you and Grant going to make it official?" Jade asked.

Startled while sipping her wine, Jillian coughed as she jerked her head away from the others to avoid spraying them. Catching her breath, only after Katelyn leaned forward to pound her on the back, she choked out, "Us? We just started dating not too long ago!"

"Yeah, but you were in love for years and years...just like Mitch and Tori," Belle said. "I remember you two in high school—"

"That was a long time ago," Jillian said. "I admit, he stays over a lot, but we're nowhere close to getting engaged."

"Oh," Belle sighed, and Jillian could have sworn the woman sounded despondent.

"Shouldn't waste time," Katelyn declared, and Jillian shot her a look, wondering when her friend was going to take her own advice.

"You know...I've been thinking about trying to set up Oliver with one of you," Jillian remarked, nonchalantly.

Katelyn rolled her eyes. "Not me and the mild-mannered artist!"

Jillian hated to admit Katelyn was right and shifted to survey the other two women. Belle's wide-eyed look of fear counted her out, so she turned toward Jade.

"Uhhh, I don't know about a blind date," Jade responded.

"Well, keep an open mind and let me know," Jillian said, draining the last of her wine.

"Who's ready to open another bottle?"

Hours later, the sound of heavy footsteps on the front porch carried over the music. As Grant entered, he shook his head chuckling at the sight of the five tipsy women, dancing and giggling in Jillian's living room. Glancing over his shoulder, he called out, "Glad y'all came. Looks like you're needed."

"Jesus, Tori," Mitch laughed, stalking over to his fiancé. "I thought you girls were wedding planning?"

"We did," she giggled, snuggling into his arms.

Brogan and Aiden followed, having come to take their sister home but instead finding Belle with a sloppy grin on her face sitting in a chair and Jade still dancing. "Looks like we've got driver duties tonight," Aiden called, reaching down to pluck Belle from her chair.

"We'll get Jade and Belle home safely," Brogan promised, as he guided both Jade and Katelyn out the door.

With goodbyes all around, Grant closed and locked the front door. Before he turned back, Jillian's arms snaked around his waist, plastering her front to his back.

"Mmmmmm, I'm glad you're home," she purred, her fingers undoing the buttons on his shirt.

Twisting in her arms, he turned around and chuckled at her smiling face. "Babe, how drunk are you?"

Pouting slightly, she said, "Not much. Why? Won't you do anything if I'm drunk?"

Chuckling, he shook his head. "Oh, I'll make love to you, sweetheart. I just want to know if you'll remember it in the morning."

Sucking in a quick gasp at his words, she promised, "I'll remember. I'll remember every moment."

Giving a rebel yell, he bent low and threw her over his shoulder, taking the stairs two at a time. She giggled as she bounced, glad she had not consumed more alcohol or she would be, quite possibly, throwing up behind him.

Tossing her on the bed, he toed off his boots while jerking his T-shirt over his head. While she pushed back her hair from her face to get a better look at his sexy muscles and washboard abs, he shucked off his pants and boxers in one swift movement.

"Wow," she stated, wide-eyed. "You're naked."

Bending over the bed, he crawled up her body until his face was right above hers. "You don't miss much, do you?" he joked, kissing her hard, plunging his tongue into her warmth. She opened up underneath him, barely noticing his hands on her sweater.

Pulling away from her, she mewled in discontent, her hands still grasping for his shoulders.

"You've got too many clothes on for what I have planned."

Grinning, she said, "Let's see if I can get undressed as fast as you did!"

Grabbing her sweater from him, she jerked it upward, only to have it catch on her necklace. Her entire head disappeared in the material as her arms waved above her head in a trapped dance.

Laughing, Grant snuck in and planted a wet kiss on her bare stomach.

"Aughh, I'm ticklish!" she screamed, trying to blindly wiggle away while still tangled in her clothing.

"Not so fast," he said, his hands moving to her waist. Unfastening her jeans, he slid them down her legs, kissing as he exposed the silky skin.

"Grant," she whined, "this is weird. I'm trapped up here and you're messing around down there!"

"Kind of like one of those romances you read where the guy ties the girl up, right?" he quipped. "You know, this could be better than my handcuffs."

"Grant! I can't breathe and my necklace is cutting into my ear! Get me out of this!"

Taking pity on her, he moved up to her head, managing to untangle the necklace and remove the shirt trapped on her chin. Kissing her red face, he smiled once more. "You are fuckin' adorable."

Huffing, she tried to pout, but his kisses continued down her body.

A stinging retort died in her throat as his mouth found her, and every other thought simply evaporated. She groaned as his lips moved lower still, her hands trying to pull him back.

"I'll be back, baby," he promised, his lips brushing over her ticklish tummy as she squirmed.

No longer able to reach his shoulders, she slid her fingers through his hair instead, dragging her nails lightly over his scalp. He took his time with her...

patient and deliberate, working her into a breathless, trembling puddle.

He paid close attention to every sound she made, every catch of her breath, reading her with quiet precision until he knew exactly when she was about to shatter. He gave her everything at once.

She cried his name as the wave broke over her, her whole body answering the call.

"God, you're beautiful," he mumbled as his mouth made its way back up to her lips, his body settled over hers.

Jillian was not sure she could move. Ever. At least not in this lifetime. Or maybe the next. The combination of alcohol and the sheer force of what he'd just done to her nearly knocked her out. Nearly. Until his lips found hers and she kissed him back with everything she had left.

With renewed vigor, she rolled, flipping him to his back and straddling his hips. "Mind if I take a ride, cowboy?"

Looking up at her, his hand spanning her waist, his voice caught in his throat. "How'd I ever get so lucky to have another shot at you?"

A sexy smile curved her lips as she leaned down, her hair draped around them like a curtain. Kissing him lightly, she said, "I gave you just one more chance."

With that, they came together slowly, her breath leaving her in a long, undone groan as she threw her head back.

She fell forward, bracing her hands on his shoulders, her long blonde hair falling around their faces like a curtain. She fought the urge to close her eyes, wanting to keep her gaze on his face as the tension between them built and tightened.

Boneless, she collapsed on top of him, hearing the breath leave his chest in a grunt. "Sorry," she breathed, unable to say any more.

They lay still, his arms now wrapped around her back and waist as he attempted to catch his breath. Sweaty, tangled, spent. *Just perfect,* he thought. When he was able to move again, he brushed her damp hair from her forehead, running his fingers through the strands, pulling it away from her neck.

Realizing she was incapable of moving, he smirked as he shifted her slightly to the side. Reaching down, he grabbed the covers, pulling them over their cooling bodies. Making sure to tuck them carefully around her, he pulled her in closely to his side, her head resting on his chest.

Jillian opened her eyes, the moonlight barely lighting the room but still allowing her to see his profile. Moving her fingers lightly over his chin and jaw, she smiled as he faced her. "I love you," she breathed.

"I love you, back, Jillian," he whispered, watching as her eyes closed in slumber. "Thank you for my chance," he said into the night, the beauty in his arms already sound asleep.

26

"Got a minute?" Grant asked Mitch, walking into his office.

Nodding toward a chair, he motioned for Grant to sit down. "Sure, what's up?"

"I've been following up on a hunch and figure it's time to bring it forward." Seeing Mitch nod, he continued, "Jermaine is too much of a kid and a greenhorn to be able to do anything on his own besides use drugs. If he's running or dealing, he's working for someone who's telling him what to do."

"Gangs use young kids all the time...a helluva lot younger than Jermaine," Mitch pointed out.

"I know and I'm not saying he's not involved. In fact, I think he's very much involved, but someone close by is helping. I've talked to him and he's not that smart."

"So, what's your hunch?"

Rubbing his hand over his jaw, he sucked in a deep breath before letting it out slowly. "I suspect his dad."

Eyebrows lifting, Mitch asked, "What've you found?"

Grant appreciated Mitch not questioning his line of investigation, instead showing immediate interest in the possibility. "Dad just bought Jermaine a new car—an expensive car. When I talked to Jermaine, he said something that struck me as odd. He said that his dad was plenty proud of him. Now, I checked, and dad paid nine grand down on the car—just staying below the amount of cash that would flag the CTR—and then, within two months, paid off the loan. He also keeps a separate bank account from his wife, which doesn't mean anything in and of itself, but some significant sums of money go in and out. While the trailer they live in is nice, it reflects the money he makes at the railroad in Baltimore, not the amounts he has going into this personal account. Hesitating for a second, he added, "And that brings me to my next line of thinking..."

Leaning forward, his forearms on the desk, Mitch said, "Baltimore. Our old friend Stanley also received frequent payments of nine grand into a personal account."

"Yep," Grant concurred. "Dad's right there on the main line of drug travel between New York and Florida, as well as Texas and California. He works for a railway. Could be an inside person who either receives or divvies out to runners for him to ship?"

Mitch nodded slowly and Grant watched his friend and Chief run through the possibilities. "You may be right. Good work, Grant. Now, what do you want to do about it?"

"I'd like to talk to Hugh...just to question him about his son's activities."

The two men shared a slow grin before Mitch said, "Bring him in."

Grant sat across from Hugh Hubbard in the interview room at the police station. When he approached Hugh at home on his day off, he immediately agreed to come to the station to talk about his son so that Karly was not in earshot. The burly man leaned back in his seat, eyes intent on the officer. "Before we get started, I'll say up front, I had no idea my boy had been using."

Grant said nothing, using silence to create tension. Most people liked to talk to fill up empty air, so Grant was not surprised when he continued on.

"He turned eighteen and hasn't been home too much, so I had no idea. And I'm gone most of the week anyway. My wife tells me he comes around some, but I didn't worry none. I figured he'd come home if he needed me."

"He doesn't have a job," Grant stated. "Nor a bank account. I would think it would be hard for him to make ends meet without coming to you for money."

Swallowing, Mr. Hubbard said, "He's got friends. He crashes at their places. You know what it's like to be young and not wantin' to hang out with your parents or kid sister."

"I wouldn't know, Mr. Hubbard. When I was eighteen, I joined the Army and was serving in

Afghanistan." Grant's voice, hard and steady, resounded in the room.

Once more silence filled the space as Grant tamped down his irritation. He was struck by the difference between himself and Jermaine at the same age. *Get it together! Don't get emotional!* Sucking in his breath, he continued. "So, he lives with friends, doesn't ask you for money, but you buy him a new car."

Hugh's lips tightened as his jaw ticked. "Figured he needed a car to get around. How's he gonna get a job if he's got no way to get there?"

"In talking to him the other day, it didn't seem like he's been looking too hard for employment. Does your wife know you bought him the car?"

"What's going on here?" Hugh growled, his fists clenching on the tabletop. "I thought we were gonna discuss my son's problems, not hound me? Should I get me a lawyer?"

Grant studied the angry man sitting in front of him, observing his defensive posture and threats. Mitch had already alerted the Baltimore office of the FBI as to their suspicions and Grant knew that both the FBI and DEA were already checking on Hugh's workplace.

"Having an attorney present is entirely your choice, Mr. Hubbard," Grant replied, keeping his face neutral and his voice steady. "Your son's charges include possession and intent to distribute, and in this climate, after recent events, he won't be offered bail. I'd like to help your son because I don't think he's a major player at all...but with his cooperation, he could get off easier."

He studied the play of emotions across Hugh's face as he wrestled with Grant's proposal.

"Don't know what to tell you," he finally said, shifting in the chair, causing the legs to squeak with his weight. "I bought him the car 'cause he hadn't caused us no problems even though he dropped out of school. I figured he worked some for cash and stayed with friends. He's young, but an adult, so it's not my place to watch over him. That's all I know and all I got to say. I'll be getting him a lawyer 'cause I figure that's the only way he'll have a chance in hell of getting any representation in court." With that, he scooted his chair back and stood. With a curt nod, he left the room, leaving Grant deep in thought.

A few minutes later, Ginny popped her head around the doorframe. "So, what'd you think?"

Looking up, Grant said, "He's lying. He knows what his son's been doing and he's running scared now. His wife's got no idea, and I want to make sure she and Karly are as protected as possible."

"I'm telling you, the boss isn't available," the rough voice on the other end of the phone growled.

Hugh wiped the sweat from his face as he sat in his car, cell phone pressed to his ear. "I need a lawyer for my boy. I've done whatever was asked of me, and now it's payback time." The silence on the phone had Hugh sweating more, realizing he took the wrong approach. "I'm sorry, I just mean that I need help."

"Yeah, well your fuckin' problem is just that—yours. You better get smart and cut the boy loose...and pray he doesn't drag your shit into his."

Hugh did not have a chance to beg before the call was disconnected. Sucking in a deep breath, he stared across the parking lot at the jail, trying to decide what to do. Looking at his watch, he only had a few hours before he needed to travel back for his workweek in Baltimore. With a last look back at the large, brick building holding his son, he started the car and pulled out of the parking lot, sweat still dripping off his face.

"We got a problem," Juan's underling, Miguel, said. "Our number one man at the railroad is a risk. His asshole son got caught using and had enough to be considered distributing."

Juan's dark eyes cut over to the man standing in front of him. He gave no indication of what he was thinking, but his gut clenched in anger.

"The kid was in the same fuckin' town that the other two runners were caught in...near where the lab was raided."

Juan's fist slammed down on the desk in front of him. "How is it that a shit-stain place like the Eastern Shore with nothin' but redneck cops have been able to wreck our trail? Fucking hell! Is there not one of them we can get on our payroll?"

Shaking his head, Miguel said, "They're tight down there boss."

Nothing was said for a moment as Juan pondered the situation. "Is the railroad compromised?"

"We don't know yet. So far, I don't think anyone's made a link with the railroad running and the man we have there. It'll be fine, unless his son talks."

"I don't like loose ends."

Miguel nodded as he stood, the silent order sounding between the two men. After he left the room, Juan picked up his phone, placing a call.

"There will be a slight delay in getting some product to you. Keep doing what you're doing, and someone will let you know when to expect more."

———————

The clouds kept the moonlight from penetrating the room where the sleeping couple lay, bathed in darkness, bodies entwined. Grant's phone vibrated, and he twisted around to see who was calling. *Mitch...fuck. Calls in the middle of the night are never good.*

Sliding his arm out from underneath Jillian, he sat on the edge of the bed. "Yeah?"

"Just got a call from a contact at the FBI in Baltimore. Hugh Hubbard's been found dead. Executed."

"Dammit!" Grant cursed, trying to keep his voice low, but he felt the bed shift and knew Jillian was awake.

"Hannah's put extra guards on Jermaine and Tyrone in the jail and called in the state police as well."

"So, was my hunch right? Was he involved?"

"Seems so. My contact couldn't tell me much but

said that they'd been watching the railroad workers for a while, knowing something was passing through. But it looks like Jermaine's arrest put his dad at risk, and we know these guys don't play around."

Rubbing his forehead, Grant said, "Who's telling Mrs. Hubbard?"

"The FBI will be coming in a few hours to talk to her and to search the house. You might want to be there for Karly."

"Got it," Grant said, disconnecting, tossing his phone to the nightstand again. He felt Jillian's arms snake around his waist as she laid her cheek on his back.

"That sounded like really bad news, sweetie," she said softly, her fingers lightly moving across his chest.

He placed his hands over hers, holding them against his heart for a moment. Sucking in a deep breath, he acknowledged, "Yeah, Karly's stepdad was killed."

"I assume it wasn't an accident?"

He shook his head slowly. "No. Seems he was into some of the same shit his son was, just higher up on the food chain in the organization."

"Will you be with Karly later?" After he nodded, she added, "Since Jade is her teacher, would you like me to call her and see if she can be there too? If I call early enough, they could get a substitute for her class."

Twisting his torso, he looped his arms around her shoulders, pulling her in tight. "That'd be great, babe. Thanks for thinking of it."

Lying back down, Grant knew sleep would not come, but he tucked Jillian back under the covers with him. The calm he felt as he listened to her breathe would be the only calm he knew for the coming day.

27

"What the fuck are you talking about?" Grant shouted, pounding his fist down on the table. A vein pulsated in his neck as he leaned forward, menace in his eyes.

"Chief Evans, you need to contain your officer," the agent in the requisite FBI dark suit ordered, his glower matching Grant's.

Mitch stood next to Grant, putting his hand on his shoulder in a show of solidarity, not censure. Without speaking, Sam, Burt, and Ginny moved behind them, placing the entire BPD on one side of the room, facing the two agents.

The female, Agent Hall, huffed, "This isn't helping. We're not here to arrest her, but she is a person of interest."

"What evidence do you have?" Mitch asked.

"If you will take a seat, we'll discuss this," she said, her voice brooking no refusal. The harsh scraping of chairs on the floors as the BPD took seats matched the angry current zinging through the room.

Agent Harden, his scowl still pointed at Grant, began, "We've been investigating Juan Munoz for over a year. He's one of the largest makers and distributors of meth in the United States, particularly from New York to Miami. We suspected he shifted some of his drug runs to come through this part of Virginia but, until recently, were not able to prove it. The meth lab in Accawmacke County and the arrests of Isaac and Tyrone have shifted our focus to this area."

"After we've done your work for you," grumbled Sam, who pinched his lips together after Mitch shot him a look.

Ignoring Sam, Agent Harden continued, "We also suspected Stanley Martino of being on his payroll but, unfortunately for him, he decided to run and his subsequent execution—again in this area—shifted our focus from the D.C. run to here."

Agent Hall added, "We, and the DEA, have also had our eye on the railways, knowing there were some employees working for Juan."

"So, why didn't you get them when you knew about them?" Grant bit out.

Mitch, a former FBI agent himself, answered for them, "Because you wanted Juan...not just the lower-level workers."

Oppressive silence hit the room, but barely cut through the anger filling the space.

"By waiting, you got a dead drug runner, a dead dirty lawyer, and now a dead railway worker. So, tell me, how's your plan going?" Grant queried, his voice as hard as his jaw which, considering the force of his clenched teeth, he wondered if it would crack.

Agent Harden shook his head in derision before settling his gaze on Mitch. "You were one of us...you know how this works."

"Yeah...I know...and I know I thought I left this fuckin' system behind when I got out."

Agent Hall cut in, "This isn't getting us anywhere. We need to move forward. And that involves Jillian Evans...and her transportation and shipment of drugs."

———

"Oliver? You here?" Jillian shouted into the entrance of the workshop. Looking behind her, she smiled at the two boys, barely able to contain their excitement. "Come on, guys. We'll go on in."

The trio walked inside the large room, and Bobby immediately ran over to one of the pottery wheels. Hesitantly, he reached out, dragging a finger over the surface, his eyes taking in the contraption. Twisting around, he said, "Do you think Mr. Dobson will let me make something sometime?"

"I'm pretty sure he was going to do that today," she replied, grinning as Oliver walked in from the back.

"Absolutely, boys," Oliver said, greeting them with fist-bumps. Turning his attention toward Jillian, he asked, "What about you? Are you in the mood to play with the clay?"

Laughing, she pointed down to her old jeans and T-shirt. "I came ready to make some pottery!"

"Well, let's get to it." Within a few minutes, he had each of them unwrapping plastic-wrapped clay and starting to use their own wheel after showing them the very basics. Allowing Jillian and Junior to manage on their own, he stood with Bobby, offering assistance.

"How much clay do you use?" Bobby asked, his small hands trying to shape the mound.

"A lot," Oliver answered. "I order big blocks at a time and keep them wrapped up until I need them so they don't dry out. Then I just use whatever is needed for the project that I'm working on. A big vase or bowl would take a lot more clay than a small cup."

Jillian loved the feel of the wet clay as it slithered through her fingers, but found the process to be harder than Oliver made it seem. She managed to get a lopsided vase finished and laughed as she saw Junior's creation.

Bobby's, with Oliver's assistance, was the best of all. "Now what do we do?" Bobby asked, his face as messy as his hands, with clay splatters where he had rubbed his nose.

"They have to dry, but I can show you what they'll look like later," Oliver offered. He ushered the group into the next room, explaining the glazing process before leading them to the side where three kilns stood. Two were quite large and the boys leaned in as Oliver opened the door. Reaching in, Oliver pulled out several bowls in blues and greens. "These were made yesterday and fired this morning. They've cooled now, so we can touch them."

"Can we make ours just like these?" Junior asked.

Jillian smiled affectionately, seeing his enthusiasm shining through his pre-teenage nonchalance. She replied, "We can certainly come back and work on these tomorrow, or whenever Mr. Dobson says we can."

Oliver said, "Boys, you can hang out here for a while. You can even work on another piece of clay if you like. I'm going to show Miss Jillian where to wash up and then she and I have some paperwork to look over."

Junior and Bobby needed no more encouragement and dashed back to the wheels, while Oliver led Jillian to a bathroom with a large utility sink along one wall. Scrubbing their hands and forearms, they quickly cleaned the clay residue off.

Wiping her hand on the proffered towel, she smiled up at him. "I want to thank you so much for letting them come today. This is such a treat for them."

He fidgeted for a moment before saying, "It's no problem for them to come." He studied his own hands for a moment before seeking her face. "I'm glad we can be friends...even if nothing else."

"Me too," she replied, her hand resting on his arm.

Sighing slightly, he said, "Let's head into the office and we'll take a look at some marketing ideas."

Smiling at the boys still in the workshop as they walked through, she followed Oliver into his crowded office.

Mildred knew she should not be eavesdropping, but the desire to hear why the FBI were in town to question Jillian was too strong. Hovering near the hall served the dual purpose of allowing her to keep an eye on the police department's reception area as well as listen in on the heated conversation. She heard one of the agents say, "This isn't getting us anywhere. We need to move forward. And that involves Jillian Evans...and her transportation and shipment of drugs." *Drugs? Shipping drugs?* Whirling from the doorway, she stepped quickly back to the front counter, her mind racing. With her hand clamped over her mouth and her breath coming in pants, she remembered Jillian taking boxes from the new potter, explaining that she sent them out and he paid her a handling commission.

Whirling around, she stepped toward the conference room, ready to defend Jillian, but halted, making a decision. *It might be illegal...it is illegal, but...* Her mind made up, she hurried over to her purse and grabbed her cell phone.

The afternoon sun sent slanted rays through the window in Oliver's office, highlighting the dust coating the furniture. Jillian stared at his profile as his head was bent over the catalogs of ceramics, working up price comparisons for the Galleria. Her phone vibrated and she dug around in her purse until her fingers touched the screen. Recognizing the caller, her eyebrows lifted in surprise. Standing, she said, "I've got to take this call. I'll just step outside."

Oliver looked up in time to nod as she slipped outside the room, before turning his attention back to the catalog.

"Mildred? What's wrong? Is it Grant?" Jillian's words tripped over each other in a rush as she hurried toward the door, in case she needed to make a quick exit.

"No, no," the whispered voice came back. "He's fine—"

"Why are you whispering? I can barely hear you."

"Shhh, quiet, Jillian and listen to me," Mildred demanded. "Where are you? At the shop?"

Stopping at the outside door, Jillian turned so that she could keep an eye on the boys as she replied, "No, I'm at Oliver Dobson's workshop with the two Montwood boys."

"Oh, Jesus, no!" cried Mildred. "You've got to get out of there and get somewhere safe before they come looking for you!"

Forehead scrunched in confusion, she repeated, "I have to get out of here? Get somewhere safe? Who's coming? What are you talking about?"

"FBI agents are here and they're looking for you!" came the harsh whisper.

Turning to face the wall, she whispered, "Why is the FBI looking for me? Mildred, you're not making sense."

"They say you've been shipping drugs and the only person I know you ship for is that potter—wait, I think they're coming out."

Her heart sinking into her stomach, Jillian repeated, "Drugs? There've been drugs in the boxes I've shipped? Oh, Jesus." The beginnings of panic hit her gut, and she wondered if her legs would hold her up. "Mildred—"

"I've got to go but get somewhere safe with those boys." With that, Mildred disconnected, leaving Jillian to whirl around, her eyes seeking the boys...who were no longer making any noise.

Grant stormed out of the conference room, his face red and jaw tight, with several others right behind him. As he started to move past the counter, Mildred's thin hand snaked out and grabbed his arm.

"Not now, Mildred. I've got—"

"Jillian's not at the shop." Gaining his attention, as well as the attention of the others filing out of the back, she straightened her back stiffly and added, "She's at Dobson's workshop with the Montwood boys."

Grant's eyes bugged out, furious that he forgot she was taking them there this afternoon. "Goddammit!" he cursed, whirling around to head outside.

Grant made it to the door just before Agent Hall demanded, "Let us handle this!"

Twisting around, Grant drilled them with his stare and growled, "Not a chance in hell. You've fucked this case up long enough!" With a nod toward Mitch, he ran into the parking lot. Burt got to the driver's side before he did, saying, "Ride shotgun. I'm driving." Not wasting time, Grant and Burt peeled out of the lot, followed closely by the others as Mitch called for backup from Colt and Hannah.

Mildred watched them leave, her lips pinched in worry, hoping she had done the right thing.

28

Jillian's heart pounded an erratic beat as she stared into the workshop. Aubrey was standing behind the boys, her eyes wide as her mouth gaped open. Bobby glanced between Jillian and his brother, whose eyes were glued to her.

With a darting glance toward the office, she rushed over toward the trio, whispering, "We've got to go!" Reaching Junior first, she bent to grab his hand. "Come on, guys, we've got to get out of here."

Aubrey had her hand on Bobby's shoulder as she said, "What's happening, Ms. Evans? Who was that on the phone?"

"Later!" Jillian hoarsely barked, her voice choked with fear. Turning, her heart jumped again as Oliver walked out of his office.

His eyes roamed over the group, his smile sliding from his face. "Are you leaving so soon?"

"Um...yes...I, that is we...need to go. I have to...get the boys home," she stammered, pushing Junior ever so slightly behind her as she stepped closer to Bobby and Aubrey, all the while not taking her eyes off Oliver.

Tipping his head to the side, he narrowed his eyes, "What's going on Jillian? Was it the phone call? Is something wrong?"

Jillian noted with dismay that he was positioned between her and the doorway. Sucking her lips in, she tried to remember if there was a back entrance where the kilns were placed.

Swallowing loudly, Jillian stepped another step closer to Bobby so that she could reach out to take his arm. Pulling him slightly, she intended to place both boys behind her, but he did not move. Quickly scanning his body, she noticed Aubrey's hand on his shoulder had tightened, her feet firmly rooted to the floor. Facing away from Oliver, she mouthed *Come on* to both of them. Instead of complying, Aubrey moved backwards, pulling Bobby with her. Eyeing the backroom doorway behind Aubrey, she prayed there was another exit.

"What's going on?" Oliver asked again, his eyes darting between the women, taking a step forward.

"Stop!" Jillian shouted, her palm up toward him. Chest heaving, she slid backwards again, trying to maneuver Junior closer to his brother and Aubrey. "I know, Oliver. And so do the police."

Brows drawn down, he halted, eyes narrowing. "What? Know what? What are you talking about?"

Not taking her eyes off him, she said, "The drugs in the shipments you have me send out." She felt lightheaded with adrenaline, her focus shifting sideways for a second to the backroom door Aubrey and Bobby were inching toward, their feet scuffling on the floor.

Oliver reared back, his eyes wide as his mouth opened and closed several times, no words coming forth. She continued to push Junior back, reaching behind her to grasp his hand. Hearing a noise from Bobby, she jerked her head around in time to see Aubrey pull his arm sharply. Before she could get Junior to them, Oliver advanced again.

"Jillian, I don't know what you're talking about. I swear, I don't. I...I..." his gaze moved from her face to Aubrey, his mouth falling open. "Oh, my God!" he cried out. "You?" Looking back at Jillian, his face pale, he said, "I didn't pack the boxes...she did all the packing."

Her braid whipped around as Jillian whirled to stare at the young woman, whose hand was now firmly clamped around Bobby's arm. "Wh...wh...you?" she gasped. She felt Junior's body vibrate as they noticed Bobby's chin quiver. Stepping closer, Jillian growled, "Let go of him!"

"You're not in a position to tell me what to do," Aubrey said, her voice low and controlled. Her free hand reached into the large purse hanging across her chest, slowly pulling out a small handgun. All eyes focused on the weapon in her hand, as a tear slid from Bobby's eye.

"Oh, Jesus, what have you done, Aubrey?" Oliver asked, "Why?"

Sucking in her lips, Aubrey continued to move into the doorway, Bobby's arm in her grasp as the gun remained pointed at Jillian. Her eyes slid to Oliver, and she shook her head slightly. "It's not personal. Honestly...it's just business."

"Business?" he shouted, his jaw tight with anger as his hands fisted at his side.

"I needed a way to ship—you provided it." Jerking her head toward Jillian, she added, "Her doing the actual shipping just made it better—it was the Galleria name on the boxes." Her mouth curved in a half-smile, as she said, "My supplier gave me a heads up that things were getting noticed down here, so I came in today to get rid of some stuff, before I take off. Honestly, I didn't know you all were going to be here today."

For a moment, only the sound of panting breaths was heard as Jillian tried to process the scene unfolding in front of her, Bobby's pale face staring at her. "Please," she begged, "let him go."

"Sorry, but I've thrown my shit into the kiln and the heat should soon take care of the evidence." Glancing down at Bobby, she said, "This little one here will be my insurance that you stay right where you are and don't move."

"No!" Jillian screamed along with Junior.

"I won't hurt him," Aubrey said, with a slight shake of her head, her eyes pleading for understanding. "I'll let him go as soon as I'm safely down the road."

"Take me, please. Take me instead!" Jillian implored.

"Sorry, but he'll be easier to control." With that, Aubrey jumped back through the doorway, pulling Bobby with her.

Driving slowly to keep the road dust to a minimum, Burt maneuvered the SUV to the end of the drive. Colt and several of his deputies followed behind, as well as the other BPD and the large, black FBI SUV. Alighting, Grant jogged over to Mitch's vehicle, wanting to rush toward Jillian but knew her safety would depend on following the plan. Before he could speak, Ginny ran over, binoculars in her hand. He took them, immediately catching Jillian's car parked outside the workshop near the large, open bay doors, next to Oliver's truck. A small camper was parked on the right side of the building, next to another open door.

Tossing the binoculars back to Ginny, he headed over to the group as they planned their tactical maneuvers. Unfortunately, Colt and Agent Hall appeared to be in a standoff.

"This is my fuckin' county," Colt stated, his voice hard and firm.

"We've got jurisdiction," Agent Hall argued back.

"Where's your fuckin' men? Huh? We've got this covered!" With that, Colt turned to Mitch and said, "Take your officers around toward the front—I've got mine near the back and side where the camper is."

"You can't just go storming in. If that trailer is a rolling meth lab, it could explode," Agent Hall said.

"All the more reason to get Jillian and the children out of there," Mitch growled, turning to Grant. "You okay?"

A curt nod was his answer, as he forced his mind

back to his military training, tamping down the fear curling in his stomach.

With plans quickly made, the group set out. Colt and several of his deputies circled around toward the back along with Hannah, who had just pulled up. The two FBI agents were on the phone to their field office, calling for backup.

Grant started to move forward, when Mitch halted him. Looking down at the hand on his arm, he lifted his eyes to his Chief.

"You gotta stay cool. I know...I know how this feels," Mitch stated.

Grant nodded curtly, acknowledging Mitch's own situation with Tori earlier in the summer. "I'm good."

The two of them moved toward the building, staying behind the vehicles parked out front. Covered by the others, Grant jogged to the side of the doorway, flattening against the outer wall. Hearing Ginny call over the radio that there was movement on the south side of the building, he inched toward the corner, watching as Mitch moved to the wide front door. He held his weapon, sucking in a deep breath, forcing his racing heart to slow.

As soon as Aubrey disappeared around the corner, Jillian and Junior both attempted to dash after her, only to be pushed aside by Oliver. Jillian stumbled into Junior as Oliver grunted, "Stay with him! I'll get her from the other side!" as he ran toward the door.

Righting herself, she heard raised voices sounding from the distance just before a shot rang out, causing her heart to skip a beat. Junior tried to lunge out of her arms, but she held firm.

An explosion sounded as a blast of heat shook the building's foundation, knocking Junior and Jillian down to the ground. She rolled over, trying to protect Junior with her body, as they both lay on the ground.

Grant's heart stopped as the building shook, the roar of an explosion sending heat through the open doorway as the glass windows shattered outward. *Jillian! God, no!*

Running around the corner, he took in Colt's deputies surrounding the trailer, Burt coming out with Bobby in his arms as the others rushed toward a body lying on the ground. His feet stumbled as he staggered forward, his eyes never leaving the bloodied body on the ground. As he got closer, he watched dazedly as one of the EMTs rolled her over...*Not Jillian!* Dropping to his knees, his breath left his body in a rush as he turned toward the flames coming from inside the workshop.

Staggering to his feet, he ran around to the front of the building, just as Mitch radioed for him to enter. Junior, his face covered in soot with debris scattered around, was attempting to stand as Mitch reached him. Jillian had scrambled up to run toward the back, unheeding the fire coming from the kiln room.

Jillian screamed as muscular arms banded around

her chest and waist, a familiar voice demanding, "Stop, I've got you, baby. We've got to get out of here."

Jerking back, her head hit his chin as the air rushed out of her lungs. "Grant—Bobby! She's got Bobby!"

"Burt's got him. He's safe." Grant's arms tightened for a second, assuring him that she was safe in his embrace, before he scooped her up and ran outside, following Mitch with Junior in a similar hold.

Once away from the burning workshop, the sound of sirens coming closer could be heard. The Baytown, Easton, and North Heron fire trucks were arriving, as well as the EMTs.

Dropping to the ground with Jillian still in his arms, Grant looked over just in time to see Junior dash over, throwing himself at the pair. Tears streamed down his dirty face as Grant assured him Bobby was all right. Inconsolable, Junior was startled as they saw Burt stalking their way with Bobby in his arms, setting the child down as soon as his eyes landed on Jillian.

Bobby raced toward his brother, slamming into all of them, his body shaking. The four huddled on the ground in a heap of arms, legs, hugs, and tears as the police, FBI, and EMTs all worked around them. Jillian wrapped her quivering arms around both boys with the feel of Grant protectively at her back. Gulping air, she twisted her head around, panting, "Oliver? I don't know where he went."

Grant looked up at Burt for an explanation, and he glanced at the boys before mouthing, "EMTs are with him."

Shifting her weight, Jillian transferred Bobby into

Grant's arms before pushing up to her feet. "I need to see him."

"Babe—" Grant started.

"He pushed me and Junior aside so he could get to Bobby first." Her words caught in her throat as she sucked in a sob.

"Wait," he ordered, his voice gentle. "Let me check first." Squeezing the boys, he said, "Guys, stay here with Jillian and Officer Tobber, okay? I need to check on someone."

Gaining the boy's nod, Grant stood and allowed Burt to kneel on the ground with them as he turned to Jillian. Squeezing her hand, he promised, "I'll be right back." With a kiss to her forehead, he jogged around to the side of the building, where a multitude of law enforcement had gathered around as the fire fighters sprayed the building.

Recognizing Zac on the floor next to Oliver, he made his way over, anxiety eating at his stomach. *This man tried to save Jillian and the boys.* Peering over the EMTs shoulders, he let out a whoosh of air, seeing Oliver alive and conscious, although his face was pinched in pain.

Zac nodded to the other EMTs and said, "He's ready for transport," then supervised as Oliver was lifted onto a gurney. Looking up at Grant, Zac said, "Minor burns and possibly a broken arm. Could've been a lot worse, but lucky for him, when the kiln exploded, he was still behind a wall."

As he was rolled toward the ambulance, Jillian watched in horror, but then Oliver gave her a wan smile. Rushing to his side, she cried, "Oh, my God, you're hurt!"

"He'll be fine," Zac assured. "He's stabilized and we're taking him to the hospital."

Grabbing Oliver's hand, she squeezed it, her voice hoarse as she whispered, "Thank you." As he was lifted into the ambulance her legs suddenly felt like jelly. As though he knew, Grant wrapped his arms around her, lending her his strength.

Clutching Grant's shirt in her hands, she whipped her head around as shouts were heard from inside the building. Heart pounding, she attempted to twist around to see what was happening but Grant's unyielding hold on her kept her in place. Afraid to speak, she sucked in her lips, swallowing deeply.

She watched in stunned silence as a body bag was brought around and loaded into another ambulance. Sheriff Colt and Mitch were behind the EMTs, as other deputies and police appeared from the sides of the building. A man and a woman, dressed in dark suits, stopped the group before moving on to the side of the trailer.

Grant, holding her weight, felt the change as her body tightened. "Easy, babe. She's gone."

Twisting around, her face a mask of fury, she bit out, "But she could have—"

"Babe, hang on right now...for the boys."

Her narrowed eyes widened, and she nodded jerkily, sucking in a breath. Opening her arms as the boys rushed over, they clung to her once more.

Grant gently pulled Junior away from Jillian's hold,

turning the young man toward him. "Listen, Junior. It's okay. You're safe...Bobby's safe...and...that woman can't hurt you anymore."

Nodding, Junior sucked in a shuddering breath, getting control of himself. He dashed the tears, and Grant pretended not to notice them. With a hand on the boy's shoulder, he squeezed lightly before adding, "You'll have a chance to tell us everything that happened, okay? But for now, just be happy that everyone's all right and know that I'm real proud of you."

Junior eked out a half-grin, his teeth starkly white against his sooty face. He looked up at Jillian, now standing by Grant again, before wrapping his thin arms around Bobby.

Zac and another EMT walked over to assess the boys and Jillian. Discovering nothing more than a few scratches, Zac shook his head. "Man, you guys were so lucky." Smiling down at Junior and Bobby, he grinned. "You'll have some cool stories to tell at school, won't you?"

"Zac!" Jillian started to protest but stopped as Grant gave a little warning squeeze.

"Watch 'em, babe," he whispered.

No longer tearful, Junior and Bobby grinned widely, first at Zac and then at each other. Sam walked over and said, "Boys, if you'll come with me, we're going to head back to the station. Your dad's coming in and, no doubt, Miss Mildred will have some donuts for you."

Jillian watched as the older officer walked off with Junior and Bobby, before whirling around to Grant.

"What the hell is going on?" she cried, finally letting her anger show.

Mitch appeared at the door of the workshop and headed toward the couple. Stopping at her, he lifted his hand to cup her face. "You okay, cuz?"

"Yes, but I don't understand," she began, but was quickly cut off as the noise of approaching vehicles roared up the gravel drive. FBI and DEA vehicles pulled all around them, accompanied by several large, unmarked panel vans. Agents in full HAZMAT suits poured from the vans and made their way around to the back of the building.

Staring in open-mouthed awe, Jillian leaned back against Grant's front once more, before he moved her toward the cruiser. "But..."

"We can't stay here," Mitch said, walking beside them. "It's an FBI crime scene now and, with the presence of meth, they have to decontaminate it."

"It was here?" Jillian screeched.

"She was using her trailer as a rolling meth lab," Mitch replied.

"She said she put evidence in the kiln to destroy it," Jillian remembered.

Grant and Mitch shared a look over Jillian's head. "Fuckin' idiot!" Grant growled. "That stuff is highly combustible." His arms hugged Jillian tighter against him, the adrenaline wearing off, the terror of what could have happened sinking in.

Reaching the cruiser, Mitch turned to Grant and ordered, "Get back to the station. We'll meet there and begin taking Jillian's statement. Sam's heading there now with the boys. I'm sending Burt and Ginny to your shop to process that scene as well. I've got no doubt the FBI will be crawling all over it soon."

"My shop?" she squeaked, her mind trying to play catch-up to the words she heard.

"Babe, you've got evidence in your shop, including bags of meth in any boxes ready for shipment. It's got to be processed and cleaned up."

Chest heaving, she felt the muscular band of his arm holding her against his front, as she struggled for composure. "But she could have—"

"She didn't."

"But she could have—"

"Babe, she didn't. She's gone, and you and the boys are safe."

Nodding slowly as his words penetrated, her body slumped against his, all the fight gone from her limbs. Grant scooped her up in his arms as she protested. "I can walk, you know," she said, but laid her head on his shoulder anyway, knowing, in truth, her legs still felt like jelly.

"Any chance I can get you in my arms, I'll take it," he smiled, stalking down the drive. As he set her in the passenger seat of her car and took the keys from her purse, he bent down to place a kiss on her lips.

Sliding behind the wheel, he turned toward her, relief flooding his mind.

29

Jillian sat alone on the beach, the moon shining over the bay. Digging a little hole in the sand, she set her travel mug of coffee in it before leaning back on her hands, closing her eyes as the breeze off the water floated over her. The past week had been a whirl. Giving her statement to Mitch, then getting grilled by the FBI agents. Having her shop and galleria searched and closed for several days. Her parents and the girls rushing over to check on her. Dealing with the mayor and town manager, both angry about the negative publicity surrounding her shop. And, finally, a visit to see Oliver in the hospital.

Oliver had smiled when she and Grant entered the hospital room, and she had rushed to his side. After assuring her he was fine, Oliver apologized for all the trouble.

"I had no idea what was happening," he said, his face flush with frustration. "I just wanted to create art.

If others could handle the sales, packing, and shipping...well, I thought it was perfect. Never in a million years would I have suspected Aubrey of something so... so...horrible!"

"I know," Jillian assured.

Oliver's eyes moved to Grant, and he asked, "What can you tell me? It's not like she was faking being an artist—her work was really good."

Grant stepped up to the bed next to Jillian and replied, "Not much more than what you've been told and that the investigation is still ongoing. I do know the FBI has been after a major drug dealer with a reach from New York, through Baltimore, down to Miami. They can't seem to get him but have been picking off his underlings. Aubrey's been involved with drugs for years...it appears that's how she paid for her art education. Being an artist allowed her to travel; the chance to ship drugs hidden in the pottery was just a convenient, added bonus. She used her small camper as a rolling meth lab. The Feds have been watching her for months, compiling evidence."

Oliver, visibly startled, his eyes blinking rapidly before he growled, "Then why the hell didn't they get her earlier?"

"Believe me, I've been asking the same thing," Jillian said, her lips tight with anger.

Grant tightened his grip around her shoulders, replying, "I know they wanted bigger fish than her... right now, I think the major players are still out there."

The trio was silent for a moment, each pondering how their lives had been altered.

"What will you do now?" she asked, knowing his workshop was closed. With a sly smile, she said, "I still have lots of friends for you to meet."

Chuckling, he shook his head. "Thanks, but I think I'll be heading back to New York. I've got an offer from an old buddy to work in his shop and gallery."

Squeezing his hand, Jillian leaned over to kiss his cheek. "I'll miss you, but I understand."

As she stepped back, Grant shook Oliver's hand, his thanks given in the gesture, but the words followed anyway. "You got there before I could. You've got my gratitude, man."

Oliver's gaze danced between the two as he smiled. "Take care of her, Grant."

Nodding, Grant returned his smile, before sliding his arm around Jillian's waist as they left the hospital.

And now, Jillian sat alone on the beach allowing the peaceful evening to soothe her soul after the harrowing week. Grant was on patrol tonight, but he would be coming back to her house when he was off duty. She smiled thinking of how he had spent every night at her house for the past week, falling asleep with his arms locked around her saying she kept all nightmares away. In fact, just this morning, they decided for him to move into her house and give up his smaller rental.

The gentle surf swept up on the beach and she wondered what sea glass was being deposited on the sand. *Maybe tomorrow I'll ask Katelyn and Tori to go sea glass hunting with me.* But for now, she was satisfied to allow her thoughts to drift along with the tide.

A soft footstep was heard and stopped right behind

her. Dropping her head back even further, she grinned, viewing Grant upside down, kneeling. With his hands on her shoulders, he sat in the sand, his long legs caging her body between them. His chest pressed against her back, and she felt his crotch nestle against her ass as his muscular arms encircled her from behind, wrapping across her chest.

"Hey," she whispered, laying her head back on his shoulder.

"Hey, yourself," his breath washed against her neck.

"I thought you were on patrol?" She felt his chuckle against her back, resonating inside her chest.

"I am. I got a tip that there was someone drinking coffee on the city beach late tonight. Thought I'd better check it out...the mayor doesn't want any vagrants here at night."

"No, can't have that, can we?" she joked. "So, when you find this trespasser, what will you do? Arrest them? Throw them in jail?"

His fingers traced a path up and down her arms, firing her blood, causing it to warm. "I might have to take them into custody. Maybe handcuffs will be needed. Definitely I'll need to pat them down."

Giggling at the visual, while simultaneously turned on at the idea of Grant using his handcuffs on her, she twisted her head slightly, placing a soft kiss on his jaw.

The two sat quietly for a few minutes, joining in the peace of the ocean, the endless sky and the moonlight bathing them both.

"What are you thinking, babe?" Grant asked. "I know you come here when you need to think."

Heaving a tiny huff, she replied, "You sound like my mother."

"Babe."

The one word tickled against her ear, sounding both like an order and a plea. Grinning, she said, "I just needed to be out here, where my thoughts can be as free as the wind." Twisting slightly again, she viewed his profile in the moonlight, suddenly blinking back the moisture gathering in her eyes. "I used to come out here when I was thinking about you and wondering what had happened that made you not want me."

"Babe," he sighed, this time the word more of an apology.

"It's okay though," she whispered, her hands clutching his forearms. "I love my coffee shop and galleria, and I was just thinking that being by myself gave me the push to do things on my own. I needed to find out what I was good at and interested in, and then go for it."

"And now?"

"Now I have that...and you. It's the best of both worlds."

"I'm sorry it took me so long to get help," he confessed. "Somehow, when the Army offers counseling help, you're so into being an indestructible soldier that needing help is the furthest thing from your mind. And when you get home, you think the nightmares will eventually go away." Her fingers gripped tighter as his arms flexed around her. "I'm one lucky man, you gave me one more chance."

"I'll always take a chance on you, Grant." She shivered as his lips landed on hers, stealing away her thoughts as she melted into his embrace.

Moving his lips over hers, memorizing each soft touch, he took the kiss deeper. His tongue slipped inside, teasing hers as the taste of cinnamon from her coffee filled his senses. Pulling back slightly, he nibbled at the corner of her mouth, her warm, panting breaths tickling his lips.

Finally parting, they shared a sigh of contentment. Lifting his hand, he brushed back a few breeze-blown strands of hair from her face, leaving his hand cupping her cheek. Stroking her silken skin with his thumb, his eyes devoured her face. "I love you, Jillian," he vowed, lightly kissing her lips once more.

Her smile beamed, warming his heart as she replied, "I love you back."

Leaning against his chest again, silence slid over them as the bay continued to wash up on the shore. She felt one of his arms unwind from her body as he reached behind him. Twisting her head, she knit her brows as he handed her an old notebook. Recognizing it as one from many years ago, she looked up at him in question.

"I asked your mom if she still had any of your old school stuff and she found this for me."

"But why?" Her eyes dropped from his to the faded blue notebook in his hand.

"I wanted to see if what you said was true," he replied. His hands shook slightly as he opened up the pages, finding Jillian Evans Wilder written in schoolgirl cursive all over the edges.

"Oh, my God, I had no idea mom kept any of these!" she exclaimed, feeling the heat of blush rushing to her face. Lifting her gaze back to his, she said, "Why on earth did you want this?"

Sucking in a deep, shuddering breath, Grant answered, "Because I wanted to know if you'd like to permanently make this your name."

Jillian sat unmoving for a few long seconds, her mind unable to catch up to his words as she opened and closed her mouth a few times without saying anything. Just as Grant was about to speak again, she jerked in his arms as she whirled around. Kneeling, facing him, she grabbed his face in her hands, crying, "You want me to take your name? Seriously?"

Chuckling nervously, he replied, "Yeah, babe. That's what happens when two people get married." Dropping his smile, he added, "Unless you want to keep Evans, that's fine, if you—"

"No, no," she whispered, pressing her lips to his. "I do want you...and your name...always."

Their lips met, tasting and tangling, sealing their vows of forever. As tears slid over her cheeks, he wiped them with his thumbs, not ending the kiss until they were both breathless. A cool breeze blew from the bay, and she shivered.

His arms tightened again, offering his warmth. "I need to get you home, sweetheart," he said regretfully, desiring nothing more than to stay on the beach kissing. "You good now?"

Grinning, she nodded. "Yeah, I'm ready." She waited as he stood and offered her hand for him to pull her up.

Walking, arms around each other, they made their way back to their house as the bay continued to wash against the shore behind them, depositing shards of smooth glass upon the sand.

30

ONE MONTH LATER

"Our Chapter has been approved, and I am holding, in my hands, our charter!" Jillian announced to the large gathering of women and smiled as the thunderous applause erupted. "As your temporary chairman, we will begin our duties. We will need to adopt the temporary Unit Constitution, which you've all had a chance to read. Nominations for officers will come next and then we'll determine the dues per member."

As Jillian continued the meeting, Katelyn and Tori circled the group, passing out work papers and more information. Nancy and Claire Evans walked around, answering questions as the women filled out their forms for membership.

Jillian stood at the front, scanning the eclectic community, remembering what Grant had said about the American Legion being filled with so many different veterans. Jillian observed old and young, wives, widows, mothers, daughters, sisters...so many touched by the lives of the veterans they loved.

Sucking in a deep breath, she stepped down from the stage and walked among the women, collecting their membership applications.

As she returned to the microphone, she spoke again. "Ladies, we have an opportunity to make such a difference in our community and the lives of veterans and their families throughout the Eastern Shore. I do have a job for all of you at this time: I want to establish our Cavalcade of Memories. This is where we will gather and chronicle our history through photographs, documents, and personal mementos. So, as you go about your daily life over the next few weeks, see what you can come up with to honor those we love who have served."

Claire moved beside her daughter and wrapped her arm around Jillian. "We have lots of work to do, but I, for one, am excited about our new Chapter." Once more, enthusiastic applause rang out in the hall.

With the closing prayer, the official meeting ended, and the women slowly made their way out of the basement hall as excited chatter continued. Finally, Jillian, Katelyn, and Tori locked the door behind them and stood on the sidewalk in the cool night air. Wordless grins passed between them as they flung their arms around each other.

"We're doing it," Katelyn whispered. "We're finally doing it."

Jillian pulled back from the other two and said, "Let's go celebrate at Finn's."

Katelyn shook her head, saying, "You two go on. I've got something I need to do tonight. I'll see y'all tomorrow." With no other explanation, she headed to her car, leaving Jillian and Tori staring after her in curiosity.

Arm in arm the two walked the few blocks to Finn's, knowing Mitch and Grant would be waiting there for them. Sure enough, as soon as they walked into the bar, Mitch and Grant turned in unison from their bar stools and grinned. Tori rushed to Mitch as he was getting down, but Grant was already halfway to Jillian before she made it to him.

His long arms encircled her as he pulled her close, kissing the top of her head. "How was it?" he murmured into her hair.

Leaning her head back so she could see his face, she rushed, "It was wonderful. Just like you said it would be."

Grant peered into her eyes, an unmistakable twinkle aimed right at him. "You want to stick around here or head for home?" He would gladly stay if she wanted but hoped she was ready to leave.

Giggling, she squeezed his waist and said, "I'm always ready to go home with you. Got anything special planned?"

Grinning, he was about to reply when Aiden called out, "Where's Katelyn?"

Shifting so she could answer around Grant's tall body, she answered, "She said she had something to take care of."

"Hmph, she should have known we would need her here," Brogan grumbled, as Gareth slapped his beer mug down on the bar, sloshing some liquid over the rim. As Jillian turned from the bar to slide under

Grant's arm, she noticed Gareth tossing a few bills on the bar and nodding his wordless goodbyes to the group, before he headed out.

Her attention swung back to Grant as he tucked her in closely and whispered, "Let's take a chance no one will miss us and get out of here."

With a smile, she looked up at him and winked. "I'll always take a chance with you."

One Year Later

Grant stood at the end of the Sunset View Marina, looking out over the white chairs filled with friends and family facing him. Mitch, Zac, Aiden, Brogan, and Callan stood beside him as he winked toward Junior and Bobby, seated behind his parents. His gaze jumped to the long aisle as he watched Tori, Katelyn, Jade, Belle, and Rose walk toward the front, moving to his right and lining up opposite the men. The music changed and his breath caught in his throat.

Here she comes.

Escorted by her dad, Jillian walked slowly, in time to the music, toward the front. The weather cooperated, offering only a slight breeze to ruffle her long, ivory dress as she moved. Seeing Grant waiting for her, she was unable to hide her smile, fighting the urge to run to him. Around her neck lay the necklace he had given her as an engagement gift—a delicate silver chain with a glistening piece of green sea glass nestled in the silver filigree.

For a second, Grant got a flash of the little blonde girl he had known since they were both tiny, running on the beach with their friends. With a quick shake of his head, he focused back on the woman walking toward him, ready to give him her hand and her heart.

As Steve handed Jillian over to him, Grant linked his fingers with hers, drawing her nearer. Facing each other, the setting sun behind them, they pledged their love. With cheers from their friends, he bent to kiss her upturned face, claiming his wife.

Don't miss Katelyn and Gareth in
Clues of the Heart

ALSO BY MARYANN JORDAN

Don't miss other Maryann Jordan books!

Baytown Boys (small town, military romantic suspense)

Coming Home

Just One More Chance

Clues of the Heart

Finding Peace

Picking Up the Pieces

Sunset Flames

Waiting for Sunrise

Hear My Heart

Guarding Your Heart

Sweet Rose

Our Time

Count On Me

Shielding You

To Love Someone

Sea Glass Hearts

Protecting Her Heart

Sunset Kiss

Baytown Heroes - A Baytown Boys subseries

A Hero's Chance

Finding a Hero

A Hero for Her

Needing A Hero

Hopeful Hero

Always a Hero

In the Arms of Hero

Holding Out for a Hero

Heart of a a Hero

Hidden Hero

More Than a Hero

Falling For a Hero

Baytown Legacies - A Baytown Next Generation Series

Jack's Legacy

Trevor's Legacy

Jeremy's Legacy

For all of Miss Ethel's boys:

Heroes at Heart (Military Romance)

Zander

Rafe

Cael

Jaxon

Jayden

Asher

Zeke

Cas

Holiday for a Hero (Miss Ethel's love story)

Lighthouse Security Investigations

Mace

Rank

Walker

Drew

Blake

Tate

Levi

Clay

Cobb

Bray

Josh

Knox

Lighthouse Security Investigations West Coast

Carson

Leo

Rick

Hop

Dolby

Bennett

Poole

Adam

Jeb

Chris's story: Home Port (an LSI West Coast crossover novel)

Ian's story: Thinking of Home (LSIWC crossover novel)

Oliver's story: Time for Home (LSIWC crossover novel)

Lighthouse Security Investigations Montana

Logan

Sisco

Landon

Devlin

Home for Justice (LSIMT crossover novel) Tyler's story

Todd

Casper

Bert

Hope City (romantic suspense series co-developed with Kris Michaels

Brock book 1

Sean book 2

Carter book 3

Brody book 4

Kyle book 5

Ryker book 6

Rory book 7

Killian book 8

Torin book 9

Blayze book 10

Griffin book 11

Saints Protection & Investigations

(an elite group, assigned to the cases no one else wants...or can solve)

Serial Love

Healing Love

Revealing Love

Seeing Love

Honor Love

Sacrifice Love

Protecting Love

Remember Love

Discover Love

Surviving Love

Celebrating Love

Searching Love

Follow the exciting spin-off series:

Alvarez Security (military romantic suspense)

Gabe

Tony

Vinny

Jobe

SEALs

SEAL Together (Silver SEAL)

Undercover Groom (Hot SEAL)

Also for a Hope City Crossover Novel / Hot SEAL...

A Forever Dad

Long Road Home

Military Romantic Suspense

Home to Stay (a Lighthouse Security Investigation crossover novel)

Home Port (an LSI West Coast crossover novel)

Thinking of Home (LSIWC crossover novel)

Time for Home (LSIWC crossover novel)

Home for Justice (LSIMT crossover novel)

Meadowlark Creek Mystery

June's First Murder

A Pumpkin Patch Murder

Letters From Home (military romance)

Class of Love

Freedom of Love

Bond of Love

The Love's Series (detectives)

Love's Taming

Love's Tempting

Love's Trusting

The Fairfield Series (small town detectives)

Emma's Home

Laurie's Time

Carol's Image

Fireworks Over Fairfield

Please take the time to leave a review of this book. Feel free to contact me, especially if you enjoyed my book. I love to hear from readers!

Facebook

Email

Website